LIVING IN CEMETERIES

"Does friendship/love or ghostly determinism rule the day? The spirits are alive on Cape Cod in Corey Farrenkopf's *Living in Cemeteries*. A strange, beguiling, ghostly romp that reads as though Wes Anderson novelized Peter Jackson's *The Frighteners*. I'm here for it." —Paul Tremblay, the nationally best-selling author of *The Cabin at the End of the World* and *A Head Full of Ghosts*

"Imaginative and totally engrossing, *Living in Cemeteries* is a compelling debut from a truly unique and inventive voice. A curious tale about morality and atonement, this book invokes the charming familiarity of Neil Gaiman's fantasy novels as well as the macabre eeriness of Nathan Ballingrud's horror-specific work." —Eric LaRocca, author of *Things Have Gotten Worse Since We Last Spoke*

"With echoes of Karen Russell and Ray Bradbury, Farrenkopf paints a world in which one can come to know the manner of their death, the how and why, all of it, but asks if the pursuit of such knowledge is the best use of our dwindling time. Reading this made me want to live more in the present, and was a reminder that we have neither the past nor the future, but only the current inhale...exhale."—Scott J. Moses, author of *Our Own Unique Affliction*

"A deeply human novel. At its heart, *Living in Cemeteries* is a story about the care we owe to each other, whether living and dead. The best speculative fiction holds a mirror up to our society and our values, and Farrenkopf understands that perfectly." —A.C. Wise, author of *The Ghost Sequences*

"A horrifying and thought-provoking premise presented with humor and heart. A contemporary Lincoln in the Bardo taking place in a world different from our own in one crucial way. How would people behave if they knew their descendents would be punished for their sins? How would you live if you knew what was coming for you and when?" —Sarah Pinsker, Hugo and Nebula-winning author of *Lost Places* and *A Song For A New Day*

"In Corey Farrenkopf's *Living in Cemeteries*, fine writing and a macabre imagination combine to tell a wholly original love story of life in death." —Jeffrey Ford, author of *Ahab's Return* and *Big Dark Hole*.

"Farrenkopf has powers of conjuration on par with David Mitchell, Neil Gaiman, and Clive Barker. But *Living in Cemeteries* is much much more than its magic tricks. Farrenkopf grounds the supernatural with real emotion in a beautifully tactile world." —Daniel Hornsby, author of *Sucker: a Novel*

"With supernatural strangeness and an abundance of heart, Farrenkopf beautifully captures how our obsession with death—both loved ones' and our own—can stop us from truly living." —Eric Raglin, author of *Extinction Hymns*

"A lush confrontation with grief, *Living in Cemeteries* grounds the uncanny in the everyday. Farrenkopf knows our sweat drips through this world into the next, our very existence just a permeable reality." —Andrew F. Sullivan, author of *The Marigold*

"The writing seethes and smolders; darkly vibrant and alluring as an epic contemporary fantasy should be. Farrenkopf is set to wow a few people with *Living in Cemeteries*." Laird Barron, author of *Not a Speck of Light (Stories)*

"Corey Farrenkopf's *Living in Cemeteries* perfectly captures that uneasy feeling of life on the precipice of "What comes next?" Through a wonderfully, and at times gruesomely, literalized exploration of how the sins and obligations of the past claw at us from beyond the grave even as an uncertain future beckons, vengeful Spirits aren't the only things haunting Farrenkopf's debut novel—there's genuine hope and beauty out there, too." —Gordon B. White, Bram Stoker Award finalist and author of *Gordon B. White is Creating Haunting Weird Horror(s)*

"How Corey Farrenkopf managed to write a novel that's simultaneously bighearted, wise, unnerving, and a wildly hallucinatory exploration of grief and love, I have no idea. But he did it with *Living in Cemeteries*, and it's fantastic." —Keith Rosson, author of *Fever House*

"*Living in Cemeteries* is a horror love story, a haunting tale that followed this reader into the dark. In the tradition of Peter S. Beagle and

Neil Gaiman, Corey Farrenkopf deserves his own place on any list of great graveyard fiction. I loved it!" —M. Rickert, author of *The Shipbuilder of Bellfairie*

"In *Living in Cemeteries*, Farrenkopf takes reality, deftly shakes up its bottle, and adds one fantastical element that changes the whole formula. An enticing and ultimately compassionate debut that uses death as a means to think through the myriad possibilities of life. —Brian Evenson, author of *The Glassy, Burning Floor of Hell*

"An assured, haunting debut full of prose that bristles and pops, *Living in Cemeteries* cements Corey Farrenkopf's status as one of the horror genre's most promising and original voices." —Andy Davidson, author of *The Hollow Kind*

"*Living in Cemeteries* conjures a death-haunted version of our world where vengeful spirits lurk and the dead speak. Farrenkopf writes with humor and heart, and like all good speculative fiction this vision reflects our own reality with plenty to say about how we grieve but also how we love and live." —Lincoln Michel, author of *The Body Scout*

"How would we live if we knew when we will die? In this unique and tender debut novel, Corey Farrenkopf explores how our lives impact those we leave behind, giving us a sharp lens into his characters' emotions as they cope with the vengeful spirits that stalk them. Living in Cemeteries unearths our dearest wishes, our sharpest anxieties, and our deepest fears of death." —Michael Wehunt, author of *Greener Pastures* and *The Inconsolables*

For Richard + Diane!
I hope you enjoy your time in the Cemeteries!

COREY FARRENKOPF

LIVING IN CEMETERIES

JOURNALSTONE
YOUR LINK TO ARTIST TALENT

Copyright 2024 © Corey Farrenkopf

All rights reserved. No part of this book may be used or reproduced by any means, graphic, electronic, or mechanical, including photocopying, recording, taping or by any information storage retrieval system without the written permission of the publisher except in the case of brief quotations embodied in critical articles and reviews.

This is a work of fiction. All of the characters, names, incidents, organizations, and dialogue in this novel are either the products of the author's imagination or are used fictitiously.

The views expressed in this work are solely those of the authors and do not necessarily reflect the views of the publisher, and the publisher hereby disclaims any responsibility for them.

ISBN: 978-1-68510-119-0 (sc)
ISBN: 978-1-68510-120-6 (ebook)
Library of Congress Catalog Number: 2024930450

First printing edition: April 19, 2024
Printed by JournalStone Publishing in the United States of America.
Cover Artwork: Mikio Murakami
Edited by Sean Leonard
Proofreading, Cover Layout, & Interior Layout by Scarlett R. Algee
Author photo by Gabrielle Griffis

JournalStone Publishing
3205 Sassafras Trail
Carbondale, Illinois 62901

JournalStone books may be ordered through booksellers or by contacting:
or
JournalStone | www.journalstone.com

For Gabrielle, with love.

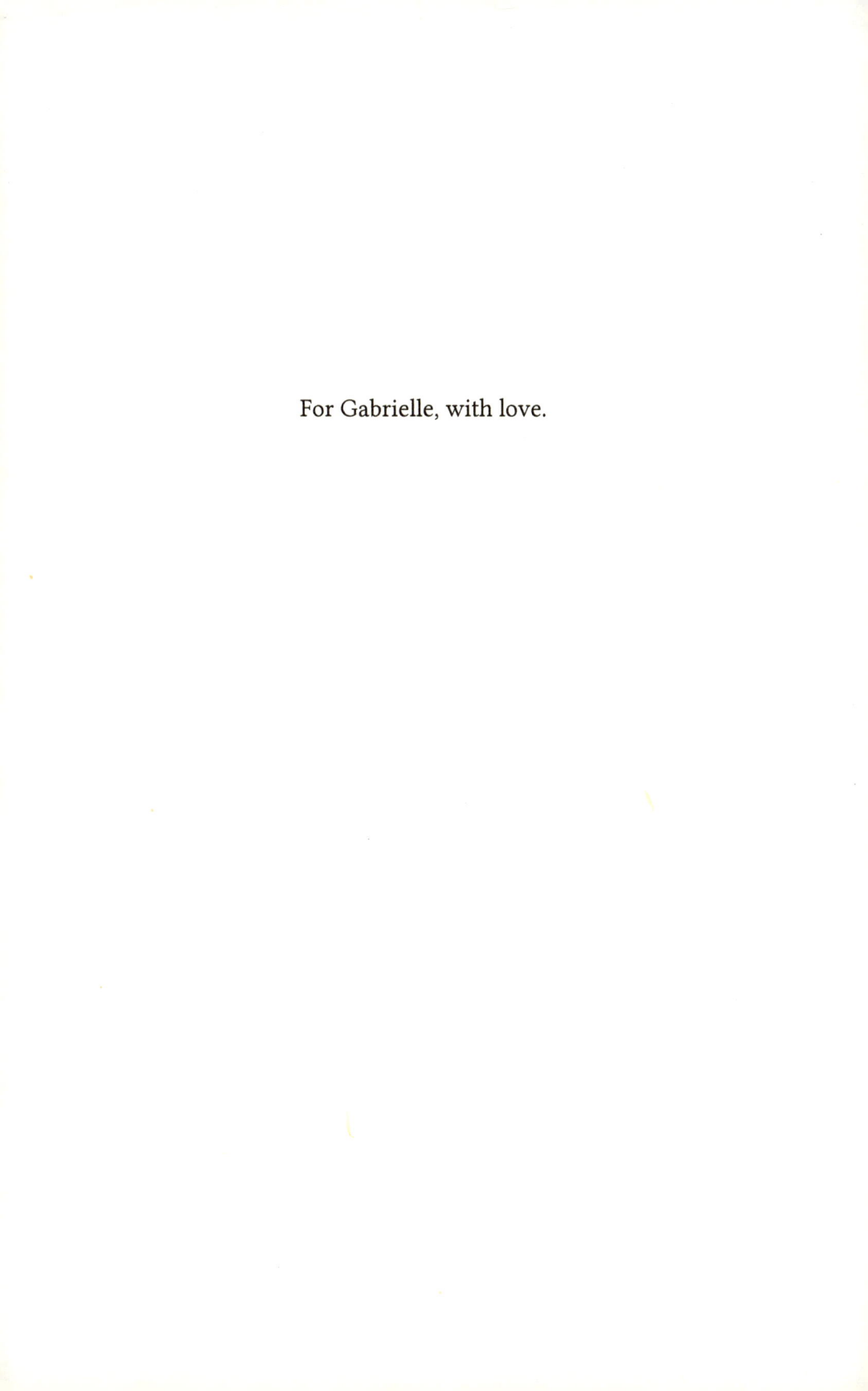

LIVING IN CEMETERIES

CHAPTER 1

Up close, the bull's musculature was grotesque. Bulging spheres of taut tissue pushed against black hide, a darkened sheen rippling between the valleys and foothills of its back. The party had been peaceful: plastic chairs arranged around the lawn, Clint's family discussing life's minutia, sangria Solo cups in hand. Then the beast upended an abandoned picnic table. The crack of splintering wood sent partygoers scrambling up oak trunks. I dodged a shower of hot dog buns and condiments, sprinting for higher ground.

A flood of bodies swarmed around me. I hurried out of the beast's path as the creature's hooves trampled the weeded stretch of lawn, clover and milk thistle shorn at the roots. The guacamole I originally searched for now coated the surrounding vegetation.

I knew the bull hadn't come for me, but that didn't slow my heartbeat and coursing adrenaline. My mother had worked tirelessly erecting an accurate model of our family's genealogy. Each fractal supported a picture, a date, an occupation, a scant biography, and a list of uncertain deaths and their less-certain recipients. Any possibility of the bull rallying in my direction was out of the question. None of my uncles ever held the matador's red cape. The family tree never dropped a cattle farmer from its branches. I was in the clear.

The Spirits' lank hands spurred the creature on. Whips cracked with every lunging stride. Each ethereal face was hidden by a mask of bone, chipped and fractured around the edges. Their calcified features were expressionless, no remorse for the life they had come to claim. Their black bodies moved as if composed of a solid ebony mist.

The Spirits looked different to each person. Some saw buzzard beaks, elk antlers, fanged jawlines. After my history class sophomore year, they wore the long, curved beaks of plague doctors, as if flying from one bubonic household to the next, setting my stomach roiling.

The tallest of the gaunt doctors cocked a spindly arm overhead, dangling a whip. The bull nosed about, swinging its great head from side to side as Clint's family dispersed into the trees. A sudden lash, and the beast's hooves pivoted, realigning its trajectory. The whip's frayed popper scored a second strike against the bull's hide, causing it to rear back, exposing its thickly muscled chest. With a final resonant crack, the bull came to a stop, looming over Clint.

I ran toward him, fighting the flow of partygoers fleeing in the opposite direction. The relief I felt at my own safety crumbled as I watched my best friend cower in the beast's shadow. Until that moment I'd assumed they'd come for one of his cousins, maybe the cellphone-obsessed Virginian sexting his girlfriend or the budding poet. There must have been a hundred and fifty people scattered around. The odds should have been in Clint's favor. But there was the bull, Clint, and nothing in between. My feet couldn't move fast enough. I needed to get to him.

Clint held a whiffle ball bat like a fencing foil, the last line of defense in a futile war.

The bull charged, head lowered, horns level with the groin of Clint's Levi's. He parried the blow to the side; the yellow plastic bat shredded as the bull passed. The move was impressive. His dead uncle's crimson cape wasn't needed, nor the *picadores* with their sharp-tipped *varas*. I searched desperately for anything he might use to fend off the attack: steak knives, broken bottles, the spear-like tiki torches encircling the yard. Nothing was within reach.

The bull skidded through the loose dirt and grass, tearing up gardenias and hyacinths, unearthing horizontal tracks of mud from beneath the lawn's crust. Another lunge, and the bull's horns caught Clint's laces, causing him to stumble into a flowerbed. Clint sprawled on his side, the crooked necks of lilies in his lap.

The Spirits' whips whirled the air into a symphony of percussive cracks. Clint rose, sprinting toward an oak whose low-lying limbs were within reach. The bull followed, head lowered, matching him step for step. I grasped a foldable lawn chair and tossed it into the creature's path only to have it trampled beneath the bull's hooves.

Panting, out of breath, everything grew quiet, the bull a foot away from my best friend. Then there was the sudden intake of breath from the party, the exhale of steam from the beast's nostrils, my own ragged scream rising out of the momentary quiet. Clint stumbled as he neared the tree. Then the horn plunged through his chest, tearing apart the fabric of his t-shirt, along with muscle and bone. The white keratin tip appeared on the other side of his body in a sudden burst of blood. He only had three more feet until the tree's gnarled base. In a heap of shredded cloth and gore, Clint collapsed to the lawn, limbs sprawling.

I sprinted to my friend's body.

The Spirits had begun to skulk away, passing through the crowd without looking at anyone. As the last Spirit filtered through, a single bone mask turned in my direction. The vacant space where its eye should have been met my own, the endless dark of a starless sky spread out before me. I froze, unable to blink, to turn back toward my friend and his final breaths, the beat of my heart climbing my throat.

After a moment, the Spirit shook its head, shrugging its narrow shoulders before walking on, trailing the procession. Then they disappeared into the forest, pushing vines and saplings from their path.

The bull grazed on a patch of clover in the corner of the yard by the split-rail fencing.

A single nightshade vine pushed up through the ruined garden, purple flower in sudden bloom, as I made it to Clint's side, dropping to my knees, pulling his body toward mine.

"Buddy..." I choked.

"Really ruined the party, didn't I, Dave?" he asked, attempting a smile.

"You couldn't have helped it. You didn't know."

"I should have gone to Spain. I would have seen it coming, avoided this." His voice was weak. Blood spurted from his chest. The stream of twenty-five years covered my hands.

The whole cookout formed a ring around us, Clint reclining in my arms as I tried to stop the bleeding.

Everyone knew what the long dead matador had done during life. Praise from Spanish crowds was lost on the Spirits. Clint's death: their critique on murder for spectacle. Someone had to answer for the man's fame and flaws, the deaths of so many animals.

Clint's parents held back amid aunts and cousins. His mother tugged at his father's hand, attempting to grip something solid, something concrete. His father remained stoic, shaking off her worried grasp.

"Europe seemed like a waste. I thought it would be one of them," Clint said, swinging a shaking finger toward his cousins. He laughed, then brushed off my hand, laying back into the grass. "I had more important things to do. My plants..."

His sentence was cut short by a gout of blood burbling between his lips.

An aunt tossed me a green water-resistant pillow from the hammock. I gently propped his head up. The bull wasn't coming back to sweep through the crowd a second time. Tension drifted from the air. Athletic relatives descended from trees. Some cousins slipped away to straighten overturned furniture or return to half-emptied pitchers of sangria. Their lack of concern brought a flush of anger to my face, but there was little I could do. I couldn't abandon Clint.

"I could have talked to him for you," I said, dabbing at the wet gore obscuring his face, my t-shirt growing slick with blood.

I passed his uncle's graveyard on a study abroad trip. I saw the tomb from outside the gate, topped with a smoothed marble sculpture of a bull, three spears protruding from its back.

"He wouldn't have spoken to you. Selfish guy didn't talk to anyone who visited," Clint said.

"Forget I mentioned it. Can I get you anything? A drink? More pillows?"

"No, just get them to come closer," he said, gesturing to the relatives who meandered about the yard, seemingly oblivious to the scene before them. "I want to talk for a little longer."

I yelled for everyone to gather. They left plastic chairs where they lay, hotdogs still plastered to patio bricks.

They lined up single file for a final word.

"Get on his good side while you can," I heard an uncle whisper to a younger cousin. It wasn't the time or place tell them to screw themselves, otherwise I would have.

Clint's relatives clasped his hands, kissed his cheek, and wished him well. Some brought up old memories, recollecting long dead laughs. I couldn't conjure the emotion to join in.

His mother and father came last. She wrapped an arm around the back of his head, cradling his final thoughts close to her chest. Blood speckled her Hawaiian-print blouse. His blood ceased to gush, his veins all but dried up. His father's eyes were tearless, fixed on the distant tree line where the bull had begun to tear a path through the underbrush. He refused to speak.

The man had always been removed. I knew it was a way to put distance between himself and unwanted emotions. When the Spirits found a child before they found the parents, language lost its utility.

Clint let out a last dry cough and was gone, eyes staring blankly at the soft sky.

I began to sob, kneeling beside him, ignoring his father's insistence there was nothing I could do.

***

Out of respect, Clint's family called off the rest of the reunion. The burgers were left charred black on the grill. The scent of burnt hot dogs mingled with coppery blood in my nostrils, the faintest taste of the fluid left on my lips, mixed with the salt of shed tears.

Turning to walk to my Volvo parked along the street, Clint's father grasped my shoulder and began to discuss burial plans. *What's the going price on gravestones? Plots? How much notice does your boss need?*

As Clint's father spoke, a flock of family members coalesced nearby. Fake conversations and exaggerated hand gestures did little to cover the fact they were eavesdropping.

"It's a little soon," I said, trying to keep a polite tone.

"It's got to be done. The sooner he's in the ground, the sooner we can talk to him," he replied. "Some of the family's sticking around for the week. It will save them the trip back."

A murmur of agreement swept through the gathering. Clint's uncles and aunts nodded at the economical decision.

Then there were the specifics I had no desire to discuss so soon after my friend's death.

Clint's father wanted him buried in the presently empty family plot just beyond the ninth hole of the public golf course. I never understood why the town built a putting green next to a historic graveyard. Ghosts watched strangers drive for birdies, chip shanked balls from behind headstones. It seemed insensitive and sacrilegious. As an alternative, I mentioned the open plots in Island Pond Cemetery, another graveyard I took care of, hoping his father would see fit to bury Clint near his long-dead girlfriend, Carla. The man wouldn't hear of it. He had never approved of their relationship.

Regardless of his decision, I'd oversee the burial.

An uncle slapped me on the back. An aunt handed me a piece of chocolate cream pie wrapped in tinfoil. The poet scribbled down a few lines in his notebook, tore them out, and extended them as a gift. I crumpled them into my blood-soaked pocket to be destroyed later by our washing machine. Clint's body lay on the grass over the poet's shoulder, alone, propped up by hammock pillows.

I left before anyone carried him inside.

CHAPTER 2

Clint was number six from our high school's graduating class of seventy-six. A relatively low number of deaths, considering the seven years that stretched between then and now.

That night, I was unable to sleep, sweat soaking my sheets, eyes refusing to close.

I cycled through endless reels of memories as the early hours of morning appeared on the clock, juxtaposing images of the bull with bar rooms on Friday nights, the bloody hole in his chest with soccer jerseys on middle school athletic fields.

My girlfriend, Jessica, mumbled in her sleep beside me. Her blonde hair fanned out over our pillows. She hadn't cut it in years. Her face was calm, eyes fluttering behind closed lids. She was beautiful without makeup. Her lips parted as she breathed. I tried to catch her words, but they slipped past my ears, leaving me to wander old memories and new fears alone at two a.m. I thought I heard her say Clint's name, but I also thought I heard her mention an albatross and jelly donuts. Coherence wasn't the right word to describe dream logic.

I placed a hand on her lower abdomen, feeling the raised lines of old stretch marks pulled tight over new muscle. She rolled to the side in unconscious avoidance of my touch. I should have told her earlier how I felt, how my worry morphed into anxiety, causing erratic thoughts to multiply and take root.

I couldn't believe my best friend was dead. From pre-school in an old clapboard church to the graduation podium, our seats were never far apart, our lives connected with every fiber. Clint had become a phantom limb, an appendage hacked away, yet still felt.

I remembered the day my father sat us down. He saw it as his place to educate us on the ways of the world, of the Spirits. We sat in my living room on a gray couch upholstered with faded paisley print, a stack of comics between us. My father leaned forward on a stool he dragged from the kitchen. He was blunt. *After you're eighteen, you're free game. Four more years and you'll always be looking over your* shoulders. *You'll see Spirits everywhere, in empty windows, mirror reflections. Just a glimpse, but they're never really there...until they are.* He made a quick glance over his shoulder and laughed. Neither of us joined him. His humor was rarely humorous in classic dad fashion, but I missed those days when he still felt inclined to joke at all.

He explained how it worked, how each of us at birth was linked by the Spirits to one of our ancestors, how we'd suffer for their wrongdoings and misdeeds. It was the death awaiting all but a select few descended from metaphoric saints. *If Uncle Jimmy did something bad, and I mean real bad, they'll be here sooner rather than later dragging a casket to your feet.*

It was the clarification of a ghost story we'd heard in gym class locker rooms. Only one or two of our friends had seen it happen. Someone watched their mother drawn and quartered in their back yard, the remnants of a colonial judge's unjust scales. They described the masks, the spines of bone. They didn't know who the Spirits were or why they were taking their mother away. We were left to speculate over games of dodgeball and capture the flag, wondering if a pack of boars would trample our teacher before the bell rang.

My father never intended on scaring us into docility. Just to inform. He did it with the same tone he used on his patients at the medical center. Simple. Clear. Occasionally gruff.

Lying in bed, Jessica's toenails kicked at my shins. Five puffed ridges rose as I ran my fingers over the spot, trying to alleviate the burning sensation. No blood, just warmth. She was never a sound sleeper. Childhood bullies hurled taunts at her in dreams. She jotted them down in a journal kept in our bedside table. She showed me the entries once a week, the two of us analyzing Freudian concepts and correlations, only agreeing on the fact that teenagers were often jerks.

Knowing her restless movements were just beginning for the night, I slipped from bed, retrieving my pants from a heap on the floor. I moved quietly down the hall, not wanting to wake her. Outside, the night air was cool on my bare chest, a slight breeze brushing through nearby pines. The moon was full, illuminating the brick path stretching from our backdoor to the greenhouse at the edge of the woods. It wound through a field of saplings I'd grown from seed, hawthorn and crabapple, dogwood and cedar that only reached my knee. Spring had come early, pulling fresh growth and new buds from soil and stem.

The polyethylene sheeting stretching over the greenhouse's curved ribs rattled in the wind. Its translucent skin shone in the moonlight, allowing a fogged glance at the crowded space within. At the door, I jammed my key into the lock, listening to the tumblers role free. Clint had insisted on the added security.

The scent of fresh turned earth and organic pesticide met my nose as I closed the door. Two long tables hammered together from pallets ran the length of either wall. Nightshade blossomed along their ledges, grouped by different strains. Purple petals hung swollen on thin necks sprouting from ceramic pots. In the far corner stood a cluster possessing the smallest berries. Others produced flowers of varying hues running the spectrum from light lavender to an almost red wine. Several crept higher than their neighbors, their stalks supported by wooden shafts sunk into soil. Their rampant growth gave me more pleasure than most things in life, knowing I had a hand in their germination.

I left the grow lamps mute, not wanting to disrupt their circadian rhythm. The glow from the moon was bright enough to move through the dark.

Dragging a stool from beneath the table, I positioned it before the corner cluster and leaned in. The scent of unripe tomatoes hovered around the berries. The belladonna's purple flowers had begun to fade to a pale lavender, white markings bisecting each petal. The moon emphasized the discoloration, the unusual quality of its existence. I touched the foliage with my fingertips, feeling the thin familiar meat of the plant's skin. Then I slouched back on my stool, thinking.

Clint heard rumors of his far-removed uncle and his career in bullfighting. There were the thousand bulls he put down, the posters and pamphlets that cluttered the streets of Barcelona for nearly a decade. Clint's mom showed me one when we were in high school. It was old and tattered, yellowed from its sun-blotched travels. The guy looked like Clint with his furrowed eyebrows, aquiline nose, and widow's peak. The mustache didn't fit. Only subtle differences kept the images from overlapping. If physical similarities were any indication of connection, Clint would have known about the bull, but tracing the Spirit's trajectory wasn't easy.

Lineage was tricky: it unwound in a maze-like pattern the Spirits followed to everyone's doorstep. Grandfather, aunt, cousin, attach a great or two onto that, maybe a twice removed and it gets complicated. Forget it if you were adopted.

No one knows unless they visit the graves. Thinking back on early cemetery visits, my mind wandered to Carla, Clint's first, and last, girlfriend. When we spoke to the ghosts, some were straightforward, others offered up riddles. The well-versed considered themselves poets, butchering lines from Keats and Eliot, attempting to uphold an image. Carla's great aunt fell into the same category.

The woman's bloated ghost would only speak if Carla brought her a pack of hand-rolled cigarettes and a collection of Baudelaire's poetry. Her vast, translucent folds of flesh quivered beneath a threadbare nightgown as she made her demands, the three of us cowering with every exclamation. A constant precipitation dripped from her matted hair. Clint held Carla's hand throughout the whole thing.

Even when the leather-bound book was placed on her aunt's headstone, the woman refused to tell it straight. She offered up a poorly constructed rhyme instead:

In early life I started just right.
Worked all day, slept through the night.
My husband was kind, my children I didn't mind.
Until I could no longer refrain
And with each little drop, the water did plop.
Through bucket and pipe,
Their lives no longer ripe.
As I plucked from the vine,
Their lives unwoven from mine.
All was silenced by rain.

Thinking about those lines sent a shiver down my spine.

Carla never deciphered the riddle, not for lack of trying. The Spirits found her lounging in her family's jacuzzi, snow falling around the edge of the tub, early for November. Carla's great aunt had drowned her children in a cast-iron bathtub before they reached the age of ten. Schizophrenia. She thought the children weren't her own, that they were duplicates placed in their beds by the Spirits to trick her, to catch her being an incompetent mother, changeling-like in their construction. Clint read about it in a psychiatric evaluation uncovered a month too late. It's self-explanatory what the white masks did once they placed their hands on Carla's shoulders. She was the first in our class.

Clint was heartbroken. He wept, swore, couldn't eat. He lost twenty pounds. His once round cheeks became skeletal, eyes sunken. He spent two months at Providence Behavioral Health Hospital. I visited him twice a week, always finding him sitting in an empty white room, staring out the window overlooking the water. I tried to convince him to come home, but he stared blankly ahead, as if he were peering over an infinite abyss, destined to be forever alone. When he emerged, he refused to date, saying the only woman he would ever love was dead and buried.

Carla's death sparked Clint's obsession. He had been reading English mythology when the Spirits found her. He became fixated on deadly nightshade. It was legend whoever crossbred the poison out of belladonna could resurrect the dead.

Scores of natural philosophers had attempted it. All fell short.

But then, in the early nineteenth century, a grief-stricken father attempted to hybridize the bloom that would bring his dead son back to life. At first, cross pollination failed. The man was unable to produce the petals possessing the markings of a human tooth. White roots stretching down purple petals were the only indication of the specimen's fleeting venom. In order to complete the process, the man was forced to ingest the berries his plants produced. It was the Spirits' way of challenging those who attempted the feat, proving themselves selfless in the pursuit to reinstate life.

After years of failure, the man devoured the berries after a manic episode, subsequently planting the purple flower over his son's crypt when death hadn't crept down his throat. The boy clawed his way through the soil, looking the same as he did on the day he died.

That motivated Clint to study botany in college, a desire we'd shared since youth. Carla's death led to the construction of our greenhouse in the seclusion of my back yard. Clint spent three years amid the rootstocks of the belladonna. When the bull's horns tore a path through Clint's torso, we were molecules away from producing the desired breed. The images of teeth had begun to emerge as dark purple dimmed.

On a rainy night at the bar, Clint spoke excitedly about eventually planting one of the blossoms above Carla's grave, confident he was ready. He was going to eat the berries, risking delirium and death to bring her back. Not that dying really mattered to Clint at that point.

I lifted a cluster of berries dangling from a stalk. Eating two from a normal nightshade would be fatal. But those berries, so small and inconsequential in size, could hold fewer toxins than the others. The blooms were more vibrant than ever, white teeth puncturing the otherwise uniform purple hue.

If Clint was right, someone would have to eat the berries to fulfill the legend. I had a sick feeling it would be me.

Two weeks before, I purchased an engagement ring. The shade of the gem mimicked that of Jessica's eyes. I carried it around in my pocket, kept in a thin manila envelope. It was a simple gold band with a singular blue sapphire fixed at its center. I fingered it through the fabric of my pants, tracing its circumference.

Before Clint's death, I'd been sure about proposing, but now things weren't so simple. My doubt had nothing to do with our love, the closeness I felt to her. No, I couldn't leave Jessica widowed in her twenties if my death waited just around the corner. I needed to know how I'd go before I bent the knee. It wouldn't be fair otherwise. If we were going to start a family, raise the son or daughter we'd always dreamed of, I'd need certainty, some promise I wouldn't be abandoning her in my much-too-early grave.

Adding nightshade to the conversation didn't help.

***

I left the greenhouse, locking the door at my back. Then I returned to the apartment, no more drowsy than when I left. In the hallway, before turning into our bedroom, I paused at a portrait of my father hanging on the wall. He was smiling in a yellow polo shirt, his glasses halfway down the bridge of his nose, a folder of medical records spread across his writing desk.

Mom said we had the same eyes, dark, barely a trace of pupil. Our hair was an identical unruly brown tangle, our heights matched just above five-nine. He was much paler though. My days beneath the summer sun tanned my skin, making the vine-torn scars crisscrossing my forearms stand stark against the darker background. It was hard to be a landscaper and escape unmarked.

My father would be gone two years that month. So that made it three since we last spoke. Seven since the divorce. Even in the grave he refused conversation despite the fact I needed to know what retribution might await me. He'd been a selfish, hermetic jerk the last years of his life. Nothing like the man I'd grown up with. He used to take me on long nature walks, explaining how to identify medicinal herbs in neighboring forests. He'd even call out from work if he knew a specific flower was in bloom nearby.

I missed the previous iteration of my father.

I left him to hang there in his frozen frame, mute as ever. With a silent touch, I twisted the bedroom doorknob, careful not to wake Jessica. Standing on the threshold, I looked at her and thought about how I wanted to live the rest of my life by her side, how I'd be a better father to our children than my father had been to me. But how much life I had left was a mystery.

To figure it out, I'd visit relatives I'd neglected to call upon, all those I'd avoided for fear of harsh predictions and unwanted deaths. I couldn't put it off any longer. I needed clarity, some concrete sense my life wasn't eroding like a collapsing dune.

Getting into bed, I draped an arm around Jessica's shoulder, drawing her to my chest. I wanted her close, skin on skin, the measured beat of her heart hammering against mine.

CHAPTER 3

When I pulled into work the next morning, I was greeted by the cough of our excavator waking into life. The black Bobcat emblem was all but worn away from the yellow frame. Rust crept around the driver's cage and peeled off the gearbox in rigid yellow snowflakes. Some days the pistons wouldn't fire, but I didn't have to jump the battery that morning, and that was all that mattered.

Mark let me drive the machine across the graveyard to Clint's plot, but insisted he dig the hole. Mark had worked for the cemetery department for twenty-five years. Visitors could mention a name and he'd know exactly where the stone lay. *Hull, just beneath the cherry tree in row three.* We never consulted the maps tacked to the work shed walls. Mark sent mourners over hill and dale with an outstretched finger and a suggestion. They always found the stone.

He called the shots. I never questioned seniority.

The caterpillar treads fumbled over the grounds of Mount Pleasant. Harwich graveyards were nothing like military cemeteries. The headstones weren't flush with the ground and the roads weren't arranged like New York City blocks. Mt. Pleasant had the rolling green hills advertised in burial brochures, oaks and pines for plenty of shade, angel statues perched atop graves. They were beautiful for families to look at, but when I had to run a lawn mower over a sixty degree incline, I started to see the impracticality of the aesthetic.

I passed smaller stones as I neared the Chase mausoleum at the cemetery's center. The crypt rivaled the height of surrounding maples. It had the rough shape of a cottage one would find along the shore – that is, if cottages supported column-lined porches made of marble. It was the grandest structure in the entire cemetery. A stained-glass window of a kneeling woman adorned the rear wall.

Its inhabitants, Captain Chase and his wife, stood out front, translucent hands waving as I passed. A young girl dressed in black sat on the front step, weaving a wreath of black-eyed Susan's. She was probably visiting her distant uncle and aunt in hopes of illuminating her own demise.

I didn't have time to stop and say hi as I did most mornings, so I waved back and drove on.

***

Mourners wouldn't arrive before noon. We had five hours to get the grave arranged. Trees would be pruned to Seussical twists, weeds plucked from surrounding graves, dandelions snipped at the stem.

"Sorry about your buddy," Mark said, as I parked the Bobcat next to the gravesite.

"Thanks. I'm... Well, sorry if I'm spacey today." I swung the door forward, descended ladder rungs, and landed atop Clint's burial plot.

"Completely understandable considering the circumstances."

Mark's six or so feet of muscle and beer belly engulfed me in an awkward hug. His arms were rigid as they wrapped around my back. I could smell the sour sweat from his reversed baseball cap, his auburn hair already slick from the humidity.

"Flag out the boundaries and make sure you get the measurements right. I don't want to dig into another vault," Mark said after he released me, retrieving a clutch of yellow flags from his back pocket. Then he climbed the ladder and took my place in the driver's seat.

I strung the length of measuring tape between two abutting gravestones.

A pallid Mrs. Jones offered up advice as I planted the yellow flags along the boundary of her plot. "It looks too wide," she said, her translucent finger pointing toward the perimeter of her property line.

"It'll be fine," Mark replied. "Dave's using the measuring tape this time."

"Yeah, two-and-a-half feet by eight feet. Right, we're all set," I replied, snapping the metallic film back into the canister.

"I heard you say that last week," Mrs. Jones muttered.

"She's got you there," Mark said.

The last burial site I flagged was off by a foot. Mark dug the bucket through the vault of an existing grave, spilling old brick into freshly upturned dirt. That's the problem with older sites. Wooden coffins were placed in brick boxes a foot or two beneath the earth. With the slate top eroded by rain, the brittle covering was hewn in two. The ribcage was visible inside the rotted box stuffed with the dead's paraphernalia: a decaying black dress, tarnished rosary beads, gold jewelry. Mrs. Ellis, the owner of said rib-cage, shrieked as if I had walked in on her changing into her nighty. Bones to the dead were like exposed genitals to the living.

She wouldn't stop screaming until I replaced the last brick of her vault two hours later.

Mark tore the bucket through the loose earth. Fist-sized stones tumbled from the pyramidal heap of dirt beginning to form by the grave. I chiseled my shovel around the edges, unable to keep up with the hydraulic arm. All I could manage was to keep the edges crisp and straight. It wasn't important in the scheme of things, but I needed to feel like I was playing a part in sculpting my friend's new home.

Mrs. Jones had taken to pacing around her plot, hands woven behind her back.

With a final scoop, Mark moved the bucket away, waving me on for a final perimeter check. I ran my measuring tape around the edge of the hole once again. It was off by a centimeter. Not enough to mention. I gave Mark a thumbs-up and he began to back away.

Mrs. Jones shook her head, pointing toward the measuring tape in my hand, her translucent form looming over me. "I saw that," she said.

I shrugged. We weren't going to fret over so little.

***

Two hours later, the funeral procession crept down the street.

The slow churn of loose rocks against pavement came from the end of the row. The hearse climbed a slight rise in the road, the rest of the procession trailed behind. I straightened, brushing dirt from my t-shirt. They were within earshot. Mrs. Jones was silent, having slunk back to sit on her gravestone, no longer decrying border discrepancies.

Greeting mourners was the most difficult part of my job. There were only so many ways I could say, *I'm sorry for your loss, they're in a better place now.* The English language never seemed adequate to express my feelings of sorrow and condolence. Even though Clint hadn't been close to his family, they deserved authentic emotion as much as anyone did.

"Thanks so much, Dave," Clint's mother said as she approached the edge of the grave where I stood.

I hugged her and shook Clint's father's hand. "I'm going to miss him," I replied, voice cracking.

Mourning attire morphed into a Rorschach blot across the grass, black suits drifting in uniform swirls. The crowd swelled as the line of cars emptied.

Tears bloomed across my work shirt. There was only so long I could hold them back. Most of Clint's relatives seemed unmoved by the burial, maybe a little anxious with their tapping fingers and shifting eyes, but nothing more. They checked cell phones. Young cousins played finger-gun games. Fathers discussed baseball scores as they dabbed perspiration from their brows.

I wiped at tears, anger swelling in my chest at their mounting disrespect.

A priest in a sweat-soaked cassock led an *Our Father* as we lowered the casket into the grave. The whine of ropes and pulleys added to the slow tempo of the prayer as the fibers slid against the mahogany box. I should have greased the bearings before the ceremony. The others followed in prayer, forgetting that heaven was just a plot of land and a tombstone. I never believed the eulogies about the rapture, Jesus stepping down from the clouds to separate ghosts from graves.

With a soft thud, the casket reached the ground. Mark untied the ropes, coiling arm-length stretches as he drew them from the darkened hole.

"Now, folks," the priest said, "while these two men fill the grave, there will be sandwiches and refreshments served in the next row. Please join me while we wait for Clint's arrival."

Two fold-up tables stood between the headstones, heavily laden with ham and roast beef sandwiches. Fluorescent bottles of soda, cookies in plastic wrappers, and a chocolate birthday cake with Clint's death date scrawled in blue icing sat on the adjacent table. The Rorschach slid over the grass and enveloped the space. The fizz of carbonation and children crying for corner pieces filled the air.

Only Clint's parents remained as Mark and I spread dirt over the casket. We never used the excavator to replace the soil. It was disrespectful to the family.

"How long before he arrives?" Clint's mother asked.

"As soon as we put our shovels down," I replied.

"I hope he knows what he's going to say," Clint's father said.

"He'll think of something," I replied, beginning to worry about what he would say to me.

"I worry about his anxiety. I'd hate for his first day of death to be stressful," his mother added.

"I'd hate for him to let these people down," his father said.

"Give it a rest, Henry. The boy's gone through a lot," Clint's mother scoffed.

I appreciated her sentiment. Most relatives' concerns were solely centered on themselves when ghosts arrived. I heard it in the way they spoke. It was rare to hear the living worry over the deads' well-being. Most talked to them as if they were crystal balls, not the last remaining threads of a human life.

Rolled sod was the last thing we laid down. The piles of neatly arranged grass fit together like puzzle-pieces. We jammed each section in place, recarpeting the freshly dug grave.

With the last edge tamped down, Clint's translucent head peered above our work. Two hands accompanied his apparition, gripping the ground as if it were the ledge of a swimming pool. He dragged himself up, arms shaking under the strain, severing the ties between body and soul.

He looked lost, eyes squinting into my face then over to his mother's. His rower's shoulders were hunched, stooped from the confines of his crypt. Death hadn't mussed his hair, every strand combed back in a slick wave. He moved to brush dirt off his loose jeans and flannel shirt, but found none. His body was no longer influenced by the physical world. The dead were always buried in whatever clothes their families believed would be most comfortable in the afterlife. Some chose suits for a refined look. Others sported sweatpants and their favorite football jersey. I was glad Clint's parents decided on the middle ground.

The heavy-heeled clatter of dress shoes resounded off the pavement dividing Clint's row from the next. The amorphous inkblot had dropped their sandwiches and swelled in a rolling mass of black cotton. They pushed me aside. A hefty cousin led the stampede, yelling, "Me first!" as his shadow towered over my deceased friend.

A chorus of questions resounded. Their mouths couldn't be restrained. Young and old bombarded Clint with demands. The priest scrambled about, arms raised above the throng, trying to reinstate order. He was ignored, lost along with the rest. Elbows and palms jostled him until he was pushed out among the neighboring headstones.

"Any more bulls?"

"Did you have a drug problem? I hate needles."

"Tell me you didn't steal cousin Tommy's insulin pump when you were a kid."

"Did you ever cheat? How many times? Girls? Guys? Were venereal diseases involved?"

"Prostitution?"

"Extortion?"

"Murder?"

The crowd was an inquisitive hydra. When Clint's voice cut away one question, two more rose in its place.

Clint's head swung in one direction, then the other, spitting out answers as fast as his mouth could form syllables. His angular jaw jutted, straining under the declarations, as his once orderly hair fell over his face. Eyes bulging, arms outstretched, he attempted to step back, to put distance between his family and himself.

They swallowed him.

I waded in, trying to separate the bodies, grabbing some by their shoulders and shoving them away. I caught an elbow to the ribs, then an uppercut from a rather irate uncle, knocking me out of the fray. From the ground, I watched Clint's arms and legs pass through their solid forms, appearing through backs, flailing through necks and foreheads. He couldn't find his footing among the heap of bodies. Panic lined his face as it appeared from beneath the surface, the last breath of a drowning man.

Then the sputter of an engine belched and churned. Each relative devoured their own voice as the excavator's claw climbed above their heads. The teeth lining the rim of the bucket tore a momentary silence in the crowd.

"The Spirits!" a whalish man in the center of the throng called over the engine's din. Each cousin and aunt scrambled against the flow of the crowd, climbing over bodies hand and foot. They pushed smaller nephews to the ground in an effort to escape, surely adding another mark next to their names in the Spirits' book.

I stood a short distance off. I could see Mark reclining in the driver's seat, hands yanking controls. He smirked as he followed one particular person with the mechanism, making them think it was their time, before picking another target.

An elderly aunt eventually noticed my coworker's tangibility and alerted the crowd. The raging whirlpool quit turning, swirling eyes stared up at the machine's cockpit.

"Are you guys going to listen to the priest or what?" Mark called through the open door.

The crowd searched each other in a dull stupor, finding grass stains about their cuffs, hair-dos off kilter, dress hems torn. They muttered in animal tones. *Who started... Who did?* They searched for one culprit among the many to saddle with blame.

Then the priest emerged and climbed the dirt-encrusted tread of the excavator. "Custom dictates you form an orderly line. One question per person. We must respect tradition," the priest called, cupping his hands around his mouth.

I walked next to Clint's headstone where he sat reclined with his wrists against the block of granite, chest heaving in air his lungs no longer swallowed. "The line starts here," I called, marking the point with the base of my shoe.

Clint's relatives shuffled into place, all except his parents, who would never be accountable for his mistakes. They stood on the outskirts of the gathering, listening to what their son had to stay. Clint was looking at me. Our eyes met, or as much of a meeting as could be possible when one of the recipients was transparent.

"You ready, buddy?" I asked.

"Not really much of a choice, right?" Clint replied.

"You don't have to talk if you don't feel like it. They can wait, come back later. I'm more than happy to make them leave if that's what you want."

"That's low. I'm not going to be one of those ghosts. They're here. I'll say what I can."

"That's kind of you. Are you going to be straight with them?"

"As straight as I can be. I can't figure out how to word it right, not yet anyway."

I nodded. That's how it should be. Right to the point, no frills, no purple prose about the beauty of death. Would it be thirty years? Seventy? And how? Train, plane, automobile? Flood or fire? The jaws of an alligator on a family trip down the Nile thanks to a gold-hungry uncle and his obsession with famous explorers?

"Tell Jim to come here," Clint said, pointing at the pudgy cousin still at the front of the line. "I want to get some rest."

The line trotted by. No pushing or prodding. Everyone got one question and one curt reply. Clint didn't rhyme, disregarding poetry, unlike so many other ghosts who wandered the cemetery. I didn't know if I could handle another Shakespearean sonnet from one of my residents.

Clint's answers narrowed the prospective pool from fifty down to seventeen: They would be blonde. The brunettes and redheads drifted to their cars, loosening ties and slipping off high heels. Those who could pull their Audis and Hondas from the procession did so. Other ghosts cursed careless drivers as they pulled away, nearly scratching the polished faces of their headstones.

The remaining seventeen relatives were sweating through their shirts, the air tinged with sour body odor and fragrant perfumes. They fidgeted and rehearsed their questions under their breath.

"Will it be soon?" was the common question.

"It should be far off, but I'm not sure," Clint replied. "Not yet anyway, but really, my end was worse than what's coming your way."

"Can you give us a little more? Just a bit?" an uncle asked from the front.

"Dogs. Stay away from strays. That's all I can say," Clint answered.

"Ending on a rhyme, a little cliché," I whispered to my friend.

He shrugged, laughing.

No one ever gave final answers on the first go. Ghosts had to do something to ensure company would visit, even if it was only for a little while. The crowd was aware of this. Common practice. Some pulled out planners or cell phones on the way to their car, looking for the next free Saturday, an unhampered Thursday.

Clint's mom and dad were the last to go. His mother leaned in toward his outline and attempted to wrap an arm around his insubstantial form. The motion was awkward. She stumbled through him, coughing as if she inhaled a cloud of cigarette smoke.

His father gestured an uncharacteristic peace sign instead of repeating his wife's misstep. Clint mimicked the gesture with a smile that wasn't returned. They said their goodbyes without asking questions about their impending deaths. It's never the son who's responsible for the father's demise. Then they took to their maroon Jeep, the last vehicle standing between the stones.

"So, do you know who they're coming for?" I asked.

"Of course I do. It's the first thing I realized when I came back. This unfocused Polaroid of how it's going to happen. That's what it looks like," Clint replied.

"Are you going to tell me?"

"Nope. Got to leave some loose ends to keep you coming back to talk."

"I'd come anyway."

"I know."

"So?"

"Still not going to tell you."

Mark tapped me on the shoulder. I jumped. I hadn't heard him approach.

"I'm going to punch out. It's my turn to make dinner for the kids," he said.

"No worries," I replied.

Mark had a fifteen-year-old daughter and a one-year-old son. He was great at mapping graves, but other forms of planning weren't his strong suit.

Mark nodded to Clint. "Good job today," he said and walked away.

A moment of silence passed until Mark was out of earshot.

"I need you to finish it," Clint said, turning to me.

"What?" I asked.

"The nightshade."

"You know I don't know enough to manage without you," I replied, stomach dropping into my shoes. Trees were my specialty, not nightshades and forced pollination.

"Just because I've ended up here," he said, pointing to the cemetery plot beneath his feet, "doesn't mean I've failed. I can walk you through it, every step. We can still bring her back."

I took a deep breath, looking past Clint to the rest of the cemetery and the ghosts slouching through their days. My thoughts wandered to when Clint was in the hospital, his obsession with the flower's ability to resurrect the dead all consuming. I always believed when anyone focused on one thing alone, they lost sight of life as it continued on around them. I had hoped Clint would give up his obsession in death.

"But what's the point?" I said. "You'll still be dead. Shouldn't I bring you back? That way you can breed another one or something."

"No, I can't wait. Carla wasn't meant to die."

"Clint, I don't know any other way to say this, but what if it's just a myth, what if nothing happens?"

He shook his head, as if he couldn't fathom the words I was saying. He bent down and ran his hands through the blades of grass like they were petals of nightshade, testing their weight, examining their coloration.

"It's not a myth. I need you to do this, for me," Clint said, looking up from the ground.

I couldn't deny my best friend's dying wish. If it was Jessica buried beneath the ground, I'd ask the same thing. Death should never stand in the way of love.

"Fine, I'll do it," I replied after a hesitation, unable to tell him where my thoughts went. Instead of the flowers, I pictured Jessica standing over my grave, an early death brought on by toxic shock, delirium rolling my eyes back into my skull, carrion beetles swarming at the first scent of rot.

I had things I needed to live for, my own love being exhibit number one. I felt guilty, selfish that I couldn't put my friend's concerns before my own, but I only got one life. I didn't need to end it in choked contortions on the floor.

Clint nodded and extended his hand before realizing the physical connection no longer existed.

"Can you do something for me in the meantime?" I asked, hoping his desire would wane without reaching the toxic climax. He'd come to his senses eventually.

"Not sure there's much I can do around here," Clint said, gazing about the cramped cemetery.

"There is. Could you talk to my dad?"

My father's simple, square-cut headstone stood in a gully three rows over. A patch of clover crept up the base of the monument. I had to weed-whack the encroaching greenery.

Clint didn't answer, his face screwed into a frown.

"You know, after I leave for the night," I added.

Cemetery inhabitants congregated during the evening, leaning over each other's stones, recollecting the memories time had left them. Some flirted to pass the hours, others played games describing senses they lacked. I had seen the camaraderie while driving by at night, heard their corny pickup lines while working overtime. *I can see right through your shirt, baby, any chance I could get you to come back to my crypt?* They were more lethargic during the day, loafing around as if buried by dreams, eyes half-lidded, heads inclined toward the sun.

"You know he wasn't my biggest fan," Clint said.

Clint had walked in on my mother changing one day after we went to the beach. We were in third grade. Saw everything, her purple bikini already hanging from the shower curtain rod. He said he knocked on the bathroom door, but, to my father, that was speculative.

"He's got to be over it by now," I said.

"Hopefully," Clint sighed. "I'll try. No guarantees. I don't even know what dead people talk about. The weather? The outrageous price of coffins?"

"Whatever works for you. I'll take care of the nightshade. You work on my dad."

"Fine, but you try first. Maybe you won't need me."

"Doubtful."

"Do it."

And I did. I walked to his stone, called him by name, *Dad, Dad... David?* I offered up whatever small talk I could, bits and pieces of my day, but I was just talking to a rock. His body refused to rise from the soil.

Remember that time you taught me about death cap mushrooms?

Remember how it took you weeks to explain the way moss growth works as a compass?

Not even nostalgia pulled him through the earth.

I knelt down at the stone's base, knees covered in clovers that dampened my jeans. I leaned my head against the cold marble, muttering further pleas as I ran my fingers over the name carved before me. *David Lawrence Gallagher, III.* No pearly face appeared. No intangible hands reached to comfort my shoulder as they had when I was young, no matter how much I craved the connection.

Birds sang, frogs croaked in trees, but my father remained silent.

CHAPTER 4

A week later, as I stepped through the front door, the scent of cumin and garlic hit me. Beneath was a barbecue twang, smoky, beans and caramelized onion. The aroma of rising bread mingled in a hot breath bathing the hall. For a second my stomach longed for Jessica's cooking, until I placed the familiar aroma. It was the traditional stew and the leavened Spirit bread we ate on April twenty-seventh – Day of the Departed, her favorite holiday – a way to coax luck from unvisited ghosts, a plea for their honesty.

I hadn't noticed the sprigs of synthetic nightshade hanging from the kitchen archway, or the papier-mache bone masks suspended from light fixtures. The bouquet of dead flowers on the hall table, roses and gardenias, lacked scent. I never understood how the florist managed it, camouflaging the rot. I couldn't find the answer in any of my botanical encyclopedias.

Jessica draped purple garlands around my windowsill garden, looping thin ribbons over my prized bonsaied maple and the thorny white skin of the *Pachypodium*. My tray of black-cherry and mulberry seedlings were left untouched. Their sprouts were little more than a finger length in height, fragile in their infancy. I was thankful she left them unadorned. They were part of the next crop I hoped to plant around the cemetery, their edible berries providing food for flocks of native birds.

My thoughts went to the nightshade in the greenhouse. The successive generations Clint had crossbred to produce desired traits. If I had gone to college as planned, I would have studied botany or forestry. I'd always been fascinated by the variation within tree species, the splicing and graphing of trunks, peach and pear growing alongside one another. I wanted to reforest the Cape and surrounding areas devastated by logging booms in the 1800s. The meager pitch pine forests supported only a fraction of the life their ancestors did. Most of America's forests weren't what they were supposed to be.

Instead of pursuing the degree, I stayed on Cape, planting oaks and elms in small batches, while I remained by Jessica's side. She hated the thought of being too far from home, too far from the sea. Accruing the student loan debt most of our friends were now buried under also wasn't very tempting. Thanks to the pro bono jobs my father did, there was very little inheritance attached to his will. Money was always a constant worry.

If I had to choose between plants and Jessica, I would always choose the latter. Hugging a tree was never as rewarding, but I managed to balance the two.

In the kitchen, Jessica hummed festive songs that would live on as earworms for days.

"Dammit," I muttered.

In the living room, Lenny, our roommate, laughed. He knew I dreaded the holiday. He didn't care for it much himself, but he never objected to a free meal. I unlaced my work boots, patted straggling grass clippings from my pant cuffs, and walked into the next room, tiptoeing past the kitchen to avoid Jessica's attention.

Lenny sat on a fold-up wooden chair before his easel. A portrait of a woman fleeing a pack of frothing hounds was balanced on the stand. The woman's red hair blew behind her in a streaming tangle. She neared the end of an alleyway, spray paint signatures and grease dumpsters filtering past. A Spirit's mask peered through a second-story window. It was Lenny's trademark.

He paid rent by painting portraits of people's last moments.

They would come to him and describe their forthcoming deaths and an estimation of years stretching between. He'd add wrinkles and receding hairlines to adjust for the passage of time. Sometimes they sat before him to pose, others he had to draw from memory or a snapshot. The woman's candid smile was taped to the easel's upper corner.

"Who's she?" I asked.

Lenny hesitated, paintbrush hovering over the canvas. Even seated, he was tall. Six-four, six-five, I couldn't say exactly. I studied the back of his head: black hair, short along the sides, top grown ragged in a stylish cut. Very artsy. His thin muscles twinged beneath the skin of his forearms as he held his position, paint smattered across his florescent striped tank-top.

"Casey," he replied, dabbing white over the points of bared teeth.

"Did she make an appointment, or is this one of your pro bono jobs?"

Lenny occasionally worked for free. Not as an act of charity. No. Just girls he met at bars and bus stops with thin waists and well-sculpted features. I supposed it helped them as much as it did anyone coming to grips with their own mortality.

"Appointment, but she could have talked me down in price," Lenny replied.

"How much is this one going for?" I asked, sitting on the couch behind him.

"A little over five grand. Part of it's the size. The rest falls on the dogs. She was specific about the different breeds. Way more detail than I'm used to."

German shepherds, black Labs, corgis, greyhounds, and Australian sheep dogs made up the mass of fur and fang. Each looked hyper real. Lenny's high price was worth it for the frills alone.

I wondered what Casey's ancestors could have done to draw such a crowd. Animal abuse was a common lure for the Spirits.

"And she thinks this will help?" I asked.

"Yeah. She's definitely not searching for some glamorous scene to put above the mantel. She's not the narcissistic type."

Some of his patrons came to him to preserve a legacy, to boast about historic lineages connecting them to the dead. Often rich white men, they would brag to Lenny about a Civil War general who they had to answer for, timber barons responible for clear-cutting old growth forests translating into a shortened life expectancy. They were disgusting, gloating over the corruption and violence of their ancestors.

The money was the same either way, but Lenny preferred to help those in need of psychological relief, not an ego boost. He had a tender heart under his calculated artistic persona. It had taken him two years to relax after learning his own fate. He wanted to help others achieve the same peace...and occasionally get laid. Very multifaceted.

Lenny finished shading Casey's face before defining the edge of the Spirit's mask. Watching him paint made me want to do the same, but I quit art lessons in third grade, my attempts to capture the dragons of my imagination never satisfying on paper. My green thumb was the only real artistic expression I felt confident in.

Lenny rounded out the curve of Casey's chest with a flourish of the wrist, another sign linking her to his preferred clientele.

Jessica walked into the room. "I didn't hear you come in, Dave," she said, leaning in to kiss my hair. She wore spandex running pants over her toned thighs, a fluorescent pink jersey with the name of a recent 5K scrawled across her chest. She must have started baking after she returned from the gym, her long blonde hair pulled back in a fountainous ponytail. She paused to look at Lenny's portrait, lips hovering above my scalp. "Will we be meeting this one, or just hear her at night on the other side of your wall?"

Lenny's freebees often ended in such fashion, yet Jessica held out hope Lenny would find the joys of monogamy. If not for his future relatives, then for her unstable sleep patterns.

"Who's to say?" Lenny replied. "Depends on what she thinks of the painting, what sort of emotion it brings her."

"Probably fear," Jessica replied.

"To you, maybe. But for her it might be comforting. It's the whole transposition from nightmare to reality. No longer in her head. Tangible. Something that can be forgotten if she just looks away or covers it with a sheet."

"That's deep," I said.

"Yeah, it's part of my sales pitch. I stand by it though. This shit helps," he said, pointing his paintbrush toward the pack of dogs.

"That's nice and everything, but I could use a little help, if you two could spare a moment," Jessica replied, moving back to the kitchen. Lenny promised he'd be done in thirty minutes. I had no excuse. So I changed into less-dingy attire and waded into the kitchen's thick barbecue haze.

A steel pot boiled on the stovetop, brown liquid burbling, expelling plumes of the delicious odor. Through the oven's window peered the outline of a Spirit's mask formed in an aluminum bread pan, golden brown skin, facial details hidden within the mold.

Traditionally, the Spirit bread pans were sculpted by familial elders, replicating the Spirits they saw devouring their kin. My great-great-great-great-grandfather modeled it after a contorted Greek theatre mask, the mouth stretched to grotesque proportions. I was glad he didn't replicate the plague doctors I saw in my dreams. I'd have no appetite otherwise.

The table was bare besides an embroidered black cloth Jessica's mother gave us: old-timey depictions of pilgrims running through sparse woods to escape hordes of Spirits were printed along the border. It added a nice air to the evening, a pleasant reminder of the night's purpose. A single red candle burned at the center of the table, wax dripping like blood, pooling around its silver base.

"How'd your day go?" Jessica asked as I set the table.

"Fine. Clint's still having trouble adjusting to everything. But other than that, nothing out of the ordinary," I replied, folding napkins into triangles.

"He'll be alright. At least he has you there to help. Think about what it would be like if he had to do it alone."

"The other ghosts help a bit."

"But they're not you. None of them have been friends with him for more than a week or two. It's different. He trusts you."

"True. Hopefully that helps. How'd your day go?"

"Alright. I left the office early to get things started here," she said. Jessica worked at a non-profit focused on helping women on the Cape get adequate employment and educational opportunities. She ran resume workshops and meet-and-greet events at the community college, edited cover letters, and developed fundraising strategies. She had a Bible-thick file of job postings everywhere from Provincetown to Bourne. It sounded like a lot of paperwork, but the outcome was worth it, she said.

"Well, you're doing an awesome job," I replied.

"I'm not going to burn it again," Jessica said, pointing toward the bread browning in the oven.

The previous year, Jessica overcooked the dough. Charred black. It bothered her, all those hours of preparation spoiled by a miscalculation of temperature and time. Several hand-written lists lay among the glass vials of spice on the counter, each detail of the meal labeled and annotated. It's how she dealt with most things. Calm, prepared, a series of steps for when the mind wandered.

As I read over her shoulder, she backed up from the stove, rubbing her butt against me in a seductive salsa step. Looking over her shoulder, one hand stirring the pot, she smiled and sambaed back toward the counter. A warmth spread through my chest, desire thick in my veins. It had been a long day and I craved her touch. If Lenny wasn't in the other room, I might have untied that apron on the spot.

Some things were worth burning bread over.

***

The flashing timer on the stove ticked down. Twenty minutes left. I poured three glasses of orange wine, a strainer held at the bottle's mouth to catch citrus rinds as they swam through the neck.

"Did you talk to your father today?" Jessica asked, sprinkling a mixture of basil, cilantro, and dried chipotle into the soup.

"I tried, but he still isn't very receptive," I replied.

It was tradition to talk to at least one deceased family member before the festivities, preferably the one most in need of coaxing. I, of course, had met with the same result as always. Silence.

"I'll make you a plate of leftovers to bring him tomorrow. Your mom said he loved the bread. We can save some for him," Jessica said.

"He might be offended..."

"No, he'll understand what you mean. It's a compliment, naturally."

"Hopefully," I replied. Since Clint's death, my nerves prickled whenever I thought about my own fate. I told myself what would come would come, but seeing my friend skewered on the horns of a bull shredded something inside me. I'd bring Dad a slice of bread if it would calm my dreams, alleviate the images of my own crucifixion, drowning deaths, and gas chamber asphyxiations.

"This is going to be the year," Jessica said.

"Of my death," I said, more deadpan than I intended.

"Do you think I'd be excited about that? No, you're going to figure out how it's going to happen." Jessica always twisted my morose humor into something palatable.

"I've been meaning to talk to you about that," I said.

"Yes?" she asked, stirring the soup.

"I want to get married."

Jessica stopped stirring and turned to me, a sheepish look in her eye. "Are you proposing to me now?" she asked, a slight curl to her lip as she looked over my gym shorts and ratty band t-shirt. Definitely not her idea of THE romantic moment.

Luckily, the ring was still in my dresser drawer, tucked beneath a sea of socks.

"No. After I find out how I'm going to die. I need to know first. I'm not going to leave you widowed before you're twenty-seven."

I had been planning it for months, even before I picked out the ring, my knee bent in the soft sands of Lighthouse Beach, the tower's glowing light shifting over the dunes as I asked for her hand. I'd signal Lenny, who waited in the parking lot, car stereo turned to full volume, ready to crank Jessica's favorite love songs. I wanted the moment to be perfect, but it could never be unless I had my own guarantees of longevity. I had the ring. All I needed were the answers.

"You know I don't care how long we have together, as long as we're ha..." Her voice trailed off.

The timer over the stove flashed zero and a chime went off.

"Figures he wouldn't help," Jessica said as she opened the oven, stoking the baked bread scent. "Can you get Lenny, please? Tell him the food's ready. We can figure everything else out later."

As she ferried the bread from the oven, I moved into the next room to find Lenny dabbing his brushes in a cup of water, squeezing paint from the bristles. Casey was complete. The look of terror on her face absolute.

Lenny looked up at my approaching footsteps. "Do you think I should give it to her for free?" he asked as I stepped closer to examine the final details. "She was pretty shaken up when we spoke. A few too many glances over the shoulder, if you know what I mean."

"Do you have enough for rent this month?" I asked.

"I have enough for the next five. What do you think, I'm living month to month off this stuff?"

"Great. Just give it to her then. You'll definitely get a date out of it."

"I'd get a date either way."

I laughed, knowing he was right. "Dinner's ready. Do me a favor, don't mention Casey or anything. Jessica's still a little angry about the other night."

"I got it, man, no worries," Lenny replied.

Sunday night Lenny slept with a girl named Doris who used to make fun of Jessica in high school. Mostly weight-related barbs, standard fare for the age group. Unfortunately, Doris stuck around for breakfast. Jessica loathed sitting across from her old rival over eggs and bacon, smiling, still flushed from a night of supposedly athletic sex. Somehow the conversation strayed to once familiar territory: Doris inquiring after Jessica's "recently shed muffin-top." Lenny didn't even laugh at her joke. *Exercise*, Jessica said. *Thanks for bringing that up. Real classy.*

The rest of the breakfast was spent in silence.

When we entered the dining room, the Spirit's head stared up at us from the table, hollow eyes unblinking, mouth gaping, golden crust replicating bone. We took our seats on either side of the loaf. Jessica sat at the head of the table. She didn't look at Lenny when he sat down, only smiled over at me and raised her hands toward the ceiling, palms up. Lenny followed suit, sticking his tongue out the corner of his mouth and going a little cross-eyed for dramatic effect. Jessica didn't notice. Hers were closed, as they were supposed to be. I joined them, raising my hands, weaving my fingers with Jessica's, who in turn wove hers through Lenny's. Then she led us through the prayer:

Another year has come, and answers still elude. To all the noble dead, we offer gratitude. Among us sits one so wary, nervous of what the Spirits will carry. And to you we offer this meal, this feast, in hopes that you see fit to share, at least, the littlest hint or biggest reveal, to help David understand all that's been concealed.

Then Lenny began to saw away at the Spirit bread with a serrated knife. He carved a piece from the chin, the moist bread cleaving easily. He deposited it on the empty plate at the far end of the table, the symbolic seat of our ancestors, or the Spirits. I could never remember which. To finish the ceremony, I poured a final glass of wine for our non-existent guest and thanked them for coming.

There was a moment of silence while Jessica doled out delicacies, dicing bread, ladling bowls of cumin and sour cream scented stew.

As we ate, I couldn't shake the image of Clint and the bull. That was the first Day of the Departed I actually wanted to believe prayers and offerings were anything more than superstition.

"So, who are you painting now?" Jessica asked, looking up from her dish.

"Just this woman I met at the last art fair. Can't remember her name. I'm trying to put more distance between my clientele and myself. I keep getting too attached. Too affected by their stories," Lenny replied, looking at me for affirmation. I nodded subtly. Sometimes Lenny wasn't as douchey as Jessica made him out to be.

"Cool," she replied. "I'm glad you're taking it more seriously."

"Yeah. It's better for my health. Anyway, I've been thinking, now that I've actually established myself somewhat and I'm running an honest business, how about you let me paint your portrait?" Lenny asked.

Jessica choked on the wine she sipped, a harsh cough, then a hurried hand to block the stream of liquid trickling down her chin.

One thing to know about Lenny: he had addiction problems, women being top of the list, painting a close second. Some part of him always wanted to know, wanted to capture that last moment. It was voyeuristic, a little perverse, always wanting more, never satiated. He dabbled in drugs, mostly to impress women or stay up all night finishing paintings.

He'd been complaining for three months about Jessica's refusal to let him paint her death, no matter how benign it truly was. He only knew half the story, which killed him. She hesitated, tongue probing her lower lip, forehead scrunched in thought. Lenny's smile grew in anticipation.

"No," she said. "I'm not comfortable with it. You've got plenty of other portraits to paint. Just let it go, please."

"But you're my white whale. Metaphorically speaking, of course," Lenny replied.

Jessica's pale complexion reddened. She never read *Moby Dick*, completely missing the allusion. When we were in high school, she was a bit heavy set. Doris, Lenny's snarky overnight guest, had a particular affinity for pointing it out in gym locker rooms or when she struggled to make it around the track field. After high school she started CrossFit, flinging kettlebells, doing burpees, box jumps for hours, all the things most people liked to avoid.

Pounds slumped away like a snake shedding skin. Memories did not.

"I'm sure he didn't mean it like that," I said, placing a hand on Jessica's.

She flinched, but regained her composure, breathing deep.

"I know he didn't. Just don't paint it, okay?" she said.

"Scout's honor," Lenny replied, prodding his shoulder with three fingers. A look of struggle marred his face. He knew a bit about her death, but not the whole story. Few people did. Part of me wished I could believe him, but I knew how things worked. He'd grow obsessed, fall into a manic state, fueled by Adderall, and paint a rendition based on scraps of information he'd compiled. There would be yelling, maybe a few swings taken, many a threat, and Jessica wouldn't talk to me for days, as if I had painted the portrait, not Lenny.

But at the moment, that wasn't the case. We were eating dinner peacefully, albeit a dinner focused on my death, but peaceful nonetheless. They were civil.

Stay in the moment, I repeated to myself. The bread was growing cold and I hadn't touched my soup.

***

After a while, I lost touch with the meal, with Lenny and Jessica. Their conversation fell away. My eyes darted to the empty chair, the sacrificial bread on the plate. For a moment, a Spirit's white mask appeared, long beakish nose dipping toward the bread. A shadowy black, bone-crusted hand tapped atop the silverware, hollow eyes staring directly at me. It picked up the knife, dicing a thin morsel from the bread, golden flesh impaled on its fork. The Spirit raised the offering to its hidden mouth.

I screamed and dropped my fork, which rattled on the ceramic. I jerked my head as if falling from a dream. The Spirit was gone, Lenny and Jessica's conversation halted by my echoing fear.

"Who'd you see?" Lenny asked, eyes wide.

"Did you see your father? Was it Uncle Thom? Who?"

I couldn't speak, breath coming in gasping heaves.

They both knew myths of relatives appearing in the vacant seat, promises they made over a well-cooked meal. People reported seeing grandparents, cousins, and great-uncles who swore peaceful deaths or violent ends.

None of the tales ever mentioned the Spirits sitting in on the festivities, so I hesitated as my heartbeat slowed.

"Clint," I replied after a moment. "It was Clint."

"But he can't help you with this," Jessica said.

"I know. I think he just wanted to be with us for a few seconds. That's all."

Lenny looked across the table, eyebrow raised. He could always tell when I was lying. "Glad it was something pleasant," he said, before resuming his self-inflicted engorgement on a third helping of stew.

CHAPTER 5

It pained me to watch Clint struggle through his first few days of death. But it was also hilarious. Ghosts, in the beginning of their afterlife, cling to the habits of the living. Rather than float from graves, they claw at the earth each morning, as if trying to drag themselves above ground. I watched Clint's arms flail through the lawn, the only appendages visible, the rest stuck somewhere in between. It reminded me of a child struggling to stay afloat during swimming lessons. He smiled nervously after remembering the limitations no longer placed on his body.

I stood by the side of Clint's grave, staring off in the direction of my father's. I had placed the plate of dissected Spirit bread at the foot of his stone like Jessica wanted. The man didn't even utter a thank you from beneath the ground. A single crow dropped from a nearby elm to pick at the offering. At least someone would enjoy it.

"That's where I'll be buried," I said, pointing to the empty plots next to my father's stone. He had planned ahead, purchasing a family plot in case I desired to spend the afterlife trapped beside him, along with my future progeny.

"At least you'll be close. I'm sure we'll figure out how to pass the time," Clint said, seated, hovering an inch above his headstone.

Ghosts were apathetic creatures. Rarely productive or self-motivated. More likely to mope about their plots than explore their cemeteries, the limits to their world. Take Mr. Brooks, for example. The man never wandered out of sight from his stone, having little interest in a world he could no longer sensually experience.

"There's only so many times you can play charades before you hate your partner," I replied.

"Be optimistic."

"I'll be optimistic when Dad tells me about my death, or any relative for that matter. There's not many left to ask."

"I thought you didn't care," Clint said, toying his voice up into a mockery of my own.

"At some point that was true," I replied. "But things are different. I want to get married, and..." I shrugged.

Clint slid from the headstone, awkwardly tripping through the air. He attempted to pat me on the back, but his hand passed through my chest, sending a cold wind through my veins. For the dead, the restrictions of touch were the hardest to shake.

"Didn't mean to do that," he said, straightening up.

"I know. You'll get used to it," I replied. "They all did." I waved toward the field of souls. Some lay supine on the ground, staring at cloud movement above. Others stood stock still, a windless cornfield of ghosts, watching golfers on the nearby putting green. Occasionally you'd see someone stroll down the roads dividing one strip of graves from another, circling the Chase mausoleum, walking laps to kill time.

"How long does it take?" Clint asked.

"A month or two."

"Well, it could be worse. Now, tell me about the flowers."

"They seem like they're almost ready," I replied, describing the hue of the petals, the white markings running down their lengths. In some ways, they resembled human teeth, in another they were just abstract lines, which made me nervous. I watered the plants morning and night, pruning away yellowing leaves, making sure nutrients flowed freely to the purple blooms.

"And you've kept the greenhouse sealed?"

I nodded, having patched creases in the polyethylene sheeting where the structure's ribs bent and pressed outward. "All taken care of," I replied.

"Good, 'cause when you eat the berries...you know." He drew his finger across his throat, tongue lolling out of his mouth.

I mimed the hallucinatory demise I would meet, stumbling, clutching at his stone as I waved off the flock of ravenous buzzards that had come for my eyes.

Clint laughed.

"Maybe there's another way to test it," I replied.

"No. The myth says you have to ingest the fruit. There's no other way." His confidence was unnerving, like the rants of roadside preachers promising the coming end of days. He looked right in my face and told me I would live when everyone else before had died.

My humor faded, replaced by a dull discomfort, a tinge of anxiety. I pretended to laugh, but I could feel the throb welling in my chest, the warm prickle in my veins.

Thankfully, I had time. The berries wouldn't ripen for another couple months, plenty of time for Clint to change his mind and release me from my promise.

"Yeah, yeah. We'll figure it out," I replied. "I've got to get going though. Mark needs me to collect the old wreaths and bouquets. It's that time of the month."

"Do what you got to do," Clint replied, moving back to his headstone, probably to ponder the clouds and think about his departed Carla.

It was a shame Clint's father didn't bury him next to her. He believed Carla persuaded Clint to study botany at UMass Amherst, throwing away the practical career he had envisioned for his son.

The man never let it go.

I didn't actually have to collect the flower wreaths that day. I was growing anxious around Clint and didn't want to lose my composure. I needed to figure some way of appeasing my friend without killing myself in the process. Lying wasn't an option. It wasn't how I did things.

Before I made it too far, I looked over my shoulder toward my father's grave. The crow continued to tear apart the hunk of bread, my father nowhere to be seen.

CHAPTER 6

"What were the chances they knew each other?" Lenny asked, shirtless, reclining on our cracked leather sofa. A blue crystal on a leather strap hung between his collar bones.

He was in the middle of one of his stories. Another of his innumerable sex partners that slipped in and out our front door. He had picked up a Bulgarian woman at a rave a month prior. I never saw her; sitcom reruns silenced her footsteps across the carpet. Later, I heard her voice through the wall dividing our rooms.

We had this unwritten rule in our apartment: *Thou shalt play music or run thy fan on high whenever thou makest love.*

The sounds of synth and bass beats had flared up, but died immediately as the power drained from his stereo. The Bulgarian woman liked to make love undisturbed; Lenny's usual mix of melodies, Celine Dion, Jazz trumpets, Meatloaf, all silent. In bed, sitcoms behind us, Jessica and I learned of the new girl's loose grasp on his name. I had no idea who Mikhail was.

"I get this text last night from Becky. It's a picture of her and that Bulgarian chick throwing back margaritas at Sam Diego's," Lenny said.

Becky was another girl he picked up from the rave, same basement, different night. She dripped neon paint across our carpet and left a bouquet of hair extensions entangled in our shower drain. I was surprised that he was surprised they knew each other. It seemed logical, unless my image of the basement's dimensions were vastly askew.

"And what did they say after the picture?" Jessica asked. She sat on the red armchair her father picked up at a flea market. It was faded from years of sun and the hours of scrubbing we put it through when we learned of its origin. It stood strategically across the room from the sofa, the greatest distance between Lenny and herself. She had always loathed his stories, but had grown even less fond as of late, Rachel's departure fresh in her mind.

"Dance sometime? We could use a third for Taco Tuesday," Lenny replied, leaning over to show me the text.

"They weren't mad?" Jessica asked.

"They knew we weren't going to date. Just sex. We're upfront about it," Lenny replied.

"They're being sarcastic. Don't be surprised when their brothers show up with baseball bats," Jessica said.

"Nope. Not going to happen. We're getting those margaritas. I'll remember the fan this time," Lenny said, looking over at me, grinning, his well-manicured beard expanding over his high cheekbones.

"That's all we ask, buddy," I said, looking away from Jessica.

She ground her teeth when Lenny pushed her buttons. I could hear her molars shearing a fine mist of enamel from across the room.

There wasn't any point asking him to hold back the details anymore. I tried. *Save them for when it's just us, man.* He was incapable. It wasn't his style; free speech in the house, let the stories of sexual deviance abound. I couldn't imagine what his book looked like in the Spirits' hands, all those instances of drunken debauchery, no condom, no concern.

There was one thing I did know: from the look on his face, there was no way he was going to turn on the fan.

***

I don't remember where or when I made Lenny's acquaintance, just that he'd been present in my life for years. In barrooms and concert halls, smoking weed in public bathrooms, drinking beer on the beach with Clint and me. We had nothing in common except our love of books. Two floor-to-ceiling bookcases towered over our television set, crammed with novels and botanical texts. There were even some yellowing holographically bound *Goosebumps* serials thrown in there. At twenty-six, Lenny liked nothing better than a good choose-your-own-adventure story set in his grandfather's haunted basement. He had a thing for basements.

Lenny knew he had five years left. He went clubbing a minimum of four nights a week, spraying on Armani cologne like deer pheromone. He would stop at Embargo – the most expensive bar in town – buy one fifteen dollar gin and tonic, and attempt to convince women he was an investment banker. When that didn't work, he hopped between bars in Hyannis, grinding against strangers in dancehalls and seedy bars. Knowing his time was short, he grasped every moment he had.

Lenny heard his fate from his cousin's ghost. Five more years until a salute of shotgun shells emptied into his chest, gun smoke clouding the Spirits' silhouettes. Bedroom traffic had been at an all-time high since.

"Probably not going to dodge that one," he said, joking over Thai food. No one ever eluded the Spirits. It was going to happen, his existence collapsed into the single point of a bullet. He wasn't going to have kids, at least not intentionally. Why worry about ramifications?

***

Jessica didn't want to hear further details about Taco Tuesday, so she slipped off the chair and headed to our room. The lock clicked into place, making up for her wordless departure.

"You know, if you were single I'd invite you to come," Lenny said once the fan in my room began to spin.

"Even if I was single, I wouldn't want your scraps, buddy," I replied, an involuntary twinge pinching my spine.

He laughed, then caught himself. "Screw you."

"I didn't mean it like that," I said.

"Better not have. I was just trying to share the wealth," Lenny said.

"Well, at least the intention was there," I sighed.

"Sounds like you're going to have a good night," he said, thumbing toward my bedroom.

"She always sleeps with it on."

"Don't give up hope, young one. There's still time to find a new girl. Your finger is ringless," he said, grabbing my wrist, inspecting the digits beneath the overhead lights. "I've got fifteen numbers in my phone ready for you whenever."

It bothered me when he referred to his lady-friends without names, replacing them with numbers or body parts. I tried to explain it to him, the disrespect, the misogyny, but the idea never took root. It seemed more like he was describing a trophy room rather than lovers. Breasts on plaques. Legs in glass cabinets.

I couldn't bring myself to tell him I was going to propose to Jessica once I learned about my death. He wouldn't be supportive.

"Now go get some," Lenny said, slapping my butt as I rose from the couch. He said something similar every night. By the way Lenny spoke, it felt like he had a drive-in screen situated in his head, a looming white billboard on which my life played out, my days edited down until only sex scenes remained. I was unsure if he realized other things went on besides vigorous, sweat-soaked sex inside a bedroom.

I wished him goodnight, the uncomfortable twinge in my spine returning.

It was hard to relegate the two Lennys: the one who painted portraits to ease pain, the other who broke hearts on a regular basis. The two rarely aligned.

I fiddled with the door handle. The lock mechanism popped. It had been broken for months. The slightest jiggle and anyone had free access. I told the landlord, but he never showed up.

***

Jessica sat on our full size mattress, legs crossed. She wore a pair of blue sweatpants with the letters CCCC, an abbreviation for Cape Cod Community College, stretching down her right leg. It's where she got her associate's degree. A Japanese manga lay open in her lap, something about an alchemist and a suit of sentient armor. Her blonde hair was tied in a bun, slouching off strands from beneath the elastic. Her nipples were visible beneath the thin fabric of her maroon t-shirt.

I was horny.

"He needs to move out," she said as I relocked the door.

And then I wasn't.

"You know we can't afford the rent if he isn't around," I replied, pulling off my jeans and fishing a pair of gym shorts from beneath the bed. The oscillating fan's cold breath swept across my back.

"We'll find someone else. Those stories. How are you two even friends?"

"Hey, I'm tired of them just as much as you are."

"Then why's he still here? It's degrading and I'm not even the one having sex with him. How do you think those other women feel?"

"Well, he keeps getting invited back..."

"Honestly? Think about Rachel. You saw what happened to her."

Rachel was one of Jessica's best friends and coincidentally the closest thing Lenny had had to a legitimate girlfriend. Jessica thought Rachel could change Lenny, make him into an honest man. She was tall and pale, brown eyes that bordered on black. They were unsettling, as if an unnamable longing lay beneath their surface. She was under the impression they were exclusive, that the other six or seven girls he was juggling didn't exist, despite Jessica's warnings. Months went by. The names of the other girls changed; hers was the only one that stayed the same.

At the beginning of their relationship she had a clean bill of health; then, one Pap smear later, a positive STD test, possible infertility, and the risk of ovarian cancer even though the disease was curable. *He must have had it before...a late diagnosis. No, no. Where else would he have gotten it?* She denied everything, stopped talking to Jessica even though they slept one room apart most nights. She grew louder during their lovemaking, more frantic, wild. I heard her cry early in the morning as Lenny's snores filtered through the wall.

When she found another woman's toe ring on Lenny's nightstand I thought I was going to go deaf. She wailed as if she wanted to rupture a lung. I dropped off a grocery bag filled with her stuff: tubes of eyeliner, tank tops, the leather pants she wore dancing. She didn't look at me as I handed her the bag. Her eyes turned past my shoulder as if some figure was waving from the road, as if she expected Lenny to be there. To apologize. To take her back.

"You can't argue that," Jessica said. "He ruined her life. Probably all their lives."

She shook her head, unfolded her legs, and climbed into bed, her back to me.

"I know I can't," I replied, the beginnings of an apology forming around the lump in my throat.

"Then don't," she said, reaching over and turning her lamp off.

I removed my shirt in darkness, then peeled my side of the sheets away. I wrapped an arm around her chest, attempting to pull her close. Spooning usually made her relax, the muscles in her back loosening against my chest, but her body remained rigid, refusing to fit into the concave lines I formed with my own.

She swatted my hand and grumbled indecipherable syllables into her pillow.

When we first started living together, Jessica refused to sleep without my arm tucked around her hips. Later, I'd wake with the patterns of her waist bands etched into my forearms. I hated the numb, tingling sensation that crept up my fingers, but I ignored the discomfort for the sake of closeness.

"Good night," I said.

"Good night," she replied through the feathers of her pillow. "I love you."

"I love you too," I whispered.

A copy of Shirley Jackson's collected stories sat on my nightstand. A book light was clamped to the lip of our carved wooden headboard, angled away from Jessica's side of the mattress. I flicked it on to reread "The Lottery."

I wished I had been going to bed drenched in a wash of sweat from our bodies, salt crystallizing on my moistened lips, the smell of sex permeating the air. I would fall into dreams about our life together, places I'd never seen, events I might never live to view.

"You need to talk to him," Jessica mumbled, not as asleep as I believed her to be.

"I'll figure something out," I replied without looking up from my page.

I had drawn the marked slip of paper and would have to hold up my end of the bargain.

CHAPTER 7

I never saw them on plots constructed after 1950. The ankle-high graves clustered around family stones with surnames like Whitcomb and Bearse. The Bradfords had three. Four over at Bassett. They were bland looking, scraps leftover from parent stones, pieces deemed unusable by quarrymen.

When I pushed aside the tall grass and weeds, bringing the stones' upturned faces into view, the only engraving I found was the word *Baby*. The shrunken stones lacked other markings. Too young for proper names, dates, the *Lost at Sea* or smallpox that claimed their relatives. They shared the green and gray lichen of neighbors, but little else.

I ran them over with my mower more times than I'd like to admit, getting my deck hung up, blades whirring, shards of granite and powdery smoke coughing out of the belts and filters, as a chorus of ghosts yelled at me for my lack of caution. My first year working in the cemeteries, I had to replace two. With high grass, they became overshadowed, obscured like a child's toy in an abandoned lot.

I didn't have to dig down far to reset them. Only six inches or so for the base, nothing compared to replacing one for their parents.

Infant ghosts never climbed from their shoebox caskets. Only their parents could tell their stories as they hunched over the small stones: the miscarriages and labored deaths, bubonic lice and poisonous mushrooms growing near the woods, the same species my father warned about during our educational nature walks. Their parents would tell me about names they'd considered, what he or she looked like with eyes born closed. It was better not to linger by their sides, to watch as they fished in the dirt, trying to lay their hands on what remained of their deceased child. I never knew what they might drag to the surface.

***

Mondays were mowing days.

Mark rarely forgot to remind me about the infant stones. But he didn't that day as he had the hundred before. I rode around on my forty-eight; that's how we referred to our mowers: the numbers corresponding with the width of the mowing deck, carving low lines through the grass. My hands were sore from operating the brakes all morning. I listened to old punk songs through noise-canceling headphones to drown out the engine. I'd go deaf otherwise.

As I circled Clint's plot, he lunged at me from behind his headstone. It was his new thing after finally getting his sea legs. Thanks to movies of men in sheets howling from unexpected shadows, he wanted to play the part. When I didn't react, he stepped aside as my mower skimmed the face of his headstone, spraying grass clippings through his chest. He raised his arms as if to shield his eyes from the projectiles, but they passed right through.

"Lunch today?" he mouthed, inaudible under The Flatliners' guttural vocals.

I locked my emergency brake and stepped off the sulky's rear wheels that dragged behind the mower's deck like a small chariot.

"Yup. I'll be back around twelve," I said, taking off my headphones.

"Can you take it a little wider next time?" he asked, pointing to the edge I snipped by the front of his stone. "I can't help thinking about that whaler's grave you split in two."

"Hey, that was my first week. I won't hit it. The grass looks better this way. You've got to buzz it down," I reassured him.

"You talk like you're a barber."

"There's not much difference between trimming around ears and trimming around stones."

"Except you can crack a stone in half. My dad paid a lot of money for this," Clint said, attempting to place his hand on top of the grave.

"And barbers can lop off ears. You can't grow those back, and we can always reset a stone."

"I'd prefer to keep it intact if you don't mind."

"I do. You'll get used to the closeness," I replied, stepping back on my mower and continuing onward.

Mark plodded along a different stretch of grass, passing stones on either side. He looped around the mausoleum. The Chases' black-clad relative lounged on the marble porch, talking to the captain. She'd been hanging around a lot recently. Not exactly how I would have wanted to spend my teenage years, but who was I to judge? Mark veered off when he realized she was there, avoiding showering her with clippings.

He didn't ride his mower as I did, always insisting on working with the sulky up. He needed to get his exercise. Beers took up residence around his waist faster than he could evict them. I remembered seeing a folded pile of work t-shirts stacked on his desk between towers of paper and Dunkin Donuts cups. From a large to an XL. He'd be walking for the rest of the summer unless he could pull his old shirts out of the closet again.

Lenny's stories circled the stones with me. So did Jessica's pillow demands. I didn't want to disappoint her, yet I didn't want to cast off one of my few living friends, even if he was deeply flawed. There was still the possibility he might change. His absence would instill a calm in the apartment we had never known, but I didn't know if I wanted placidity every moment.

Maybe Jessica would forget what she said the night before. Maybe not.

***

At twelve, I silenced my mower and draped my protective gear over the handlebars. I grabbed my yellow lunch box from the tool shed: peanut-butter and jelly on a plain bagel. An overripe banana made everything within the zippered plastic smell fermented.

"Lenny stories?" Clint asked as I approached.

I spread the contents of my lunch across Clint's stone and recollected the tale of Taco Tuesday.

"I'm surprised he didn't get slapped," Clint said as I finished.

"He somehow avoids it, even though he clearly deserves it. I swear it's pheromones," I replied.

"I wouldn't doubt that."

"Just for a heads up," I began, trying to sound nonchalant. "I'm going up to Maine tomorrow to visit my dad's family burial ground, so I won't be around for a bit. I have a few uncles I need to speak to."

Since Clint's death, I knew I'd have to visit them. The small cemetery on the corner of my family's old apple orchard was just over the New Hampshire border. I hadn't visited the gnarled trees and strawberry fields since I was ten, back when my father would play dodge-apple with fallen fruit while my mother warned about hornets and unknown allergies. That was before he had too much going on at his office to take the highways north.

The family plot contained thirty-five graves, consisting of four generations of farmers with nearly the same names. My father was named after his father. My uncle was named after his uncle. The only way to know one David Lawrence Gallagher apart from the next was the dates on the stones and the amount of gray moss sprouting from their corners.

I watched as Clint narrowed his eyes. Then came the question I knew he would ask. "But what about the nightshade? Who's going to water them?"

"I asked Lenny to do it."

A look of revulsion crossed Clint's face. Then his features sagged, like a child whose family vacation was canceled.

"I ran him through everything," I said in a hurry. "I showed him exactly how much water to use, how to turn the grow lamps on if it's cloudy. Nightshade's hardy, it'll do fine. Lenny knows this is serious."

"Lenny doesn't understand serious. He brought a bunch of sex toys as an offering last week. We're not even related. We can't leave this to him," Clint said, gesturing to the base of his headstone. On the grass was a pile of plastic penises and vaginas-in-a-can. I had meant to move them a few days prior, but couldn't stop laughing when I rode by on my mower.

"What about his paintings?" I asked, stifling a chuckle.

"He does those to get laid."

"They help some people. But really, he's not going to mess this up."

Clint shook his head. "You can't go."

"I'm sorry, but you can't make that decision for me. If I don't travel, I'll never learn how I die."

"I know," Clint said, slouching his shoulders, "I just worry about things like this. I thought my anxiety would go away once I was dead, but nope." His voice dwindled to a whisper.

It hurt to see the way Clint's body sagged in on itself. He usually stood over me, posture stiffened from years of crew practice rowing on the Connecticut River. At that moment, it seemed like his spine couldn't support his weight any longer, that I had pulled a vertebrae free and he would topple over. If I didn't go to the cemetery, I'd be letting Jessica down. If I stayed, the inverse would be true. As much as it pained me to injure my friend, I needed to do it.

"I didn't want to worry you, I couldn't just disappear for a week without an explanation. You know that."

"No, you're right," Clint said, straightening up. "I don't want you to end up like me, caught unaware. Just make sure Lenny understands his role in all of this."

"I will," I promised. "I wouldn't leave otherwise."

Clint nodded. "I tried to speak to your father the other day."

"And how'd that go?" I asked, glad for the conversation shift.

"He sank back into the grass as soon as I started talking," Clint said, which was the usual response. My father only peered above ground once the living left, spoke little, and avoided eye contact.

"It might not even be him," Clint said, attempting a smile. "You've still got plenty of other family to talk to."

"Yeah, I know," I replied. "Maybe I'll learn something in Maine."

"I hope you do," Clint said.

At that, I moved to pick up my lunch box and banana peel from his stone. We shared our customary goodbye, an open air high five that never connected, and I began my stroll back to the tool shed. There was a part of me that didn't want to leave Clint alone, like a father dropping his son off at daycare for the first time. I worried about him, fretting over possible regressions.

The last few years of his life had been unstable, if not neurotic. Shadows of the months he spent at the mental hospital bled through. Some nights I found him sleeping in our greenhouse. Other days, when Mark and I mowed Island Pond Cemetery, I'd find him curled around Carla's grave, still asleep in the early morning sun, his clothing soaked from dew. I didn't want him to feel that way anymore.

There was already so much sadness in the grave.

***

I washed my hands with orange-scented Gojo in the shed's drop sink. Five minutes remained in my workday. Clots of dirt and grass swirled down the drain. When I was younger, I hadn't imagined I would end up in a tool shed huffing exhaust fumes and fertilizer. Studying wildflowers in Norway or monitoring redwood growth on preserved land was more like it. Occasionally, my mind roamed to those far flung forests, those classrooms held in greenhouse heat.

But Jessica couldn't bring herself to leave the Cape. She really made a difference with her job and couldn't stand living away from the sea. She was a thirteenth generation Cape Codder. It was in her blood. Half the names on the headstones I mowed around were branches on her family tree.

I made the most of my botanical yearnings, pruning yews and maples around grave plots, ensuring the best growth possible. I'd been petitioning the town for years to expand our cemetery budget so I could plant more mature trees between the graves, not solely relying on the slight saplings I grew in our back yard. It made no sense to deforest numerous acres just to plant bodies in the ground. Acres of grass equaled sterile spaces. I wrote to local papers about trees being carbon sinks, the effect second growth forests could have on global warming, but the vote never went my way, despite the hours I spent championing it at town hall.

It was disheartening, but I still had my trays of seedlings back home. It was a small gesture, but when they were tall enough and hardened off, they'd be ready for planting, regardless of taxpayer support.

CHAPTER 8

Jessica caught me wedging our mattress into the folded backseat of my Volvo. The plush pillow top curved up around the edges, space tight, not exactly accommodating the dimensions of the bed. Lenny helped me drag it into the driveway while she showered. I wanted to surprise her.

When we first started dating in high school, we would cram my old twin mattress through the hatchback and drive to Nickerson State Park for the weekend. It's where we slept when we drove cross country, starry nights through curved windows as we lay in Yosemite, mist speckling the glass in a parking lot neighboring Niagara. We lost our virginity in Nauset's sand dunes, the Volvo's protective canopy hiding our naive movements.

The car's headrests fought me as I elbowed the bed into place.

"So that's where it went," Jessica said, her hair twirled in a pink towel, a thick strand plastered to the edge of her cheek. She always looked her best after a workout, slender and toned, her make-up stripped off in the bathroom sink. I couldn't help staring down at her pale legs and the short blue athletic shorts she wore.

"You like it?" I asked, giving the pillow-top a final nudge. "Figured we could use a little nostalgia."

"I love it."

"Are you all packed?"

"Mostly, I've just got a few more things to get together."

Jessica stood in silence, doing calf-raises, twin muscles flexing along her thin legs as she extended her toes. She'd fallen into the habit of doing such exercises when contemplating matters. She stared over my shoulder to where our neighbor Jerry's house stood. He ran a junk shop off the premises, which I never understood the legality of. Acre upon acre of upturned lawn mowers covered the property. Their blades were rusting, gears frozen with corrosion. Next to these were kayaks and canoes in varying states of repair: patched hulls, fiberglass holes mottling their green and red skin. The collection of random artifacts was astounding, hard to ignore whenever we were outside.

"It's supposed to be warm," I said, dragging her attention back. "Real humid."

"I'll take that into account. Make sure you've got the GPS this time," she said before walking into the house.

I wasn't good with maps, compasses, or any navigation device for that matter. Without the automated voice directing each turn, we'd end up in Portland, Oregon, rather than Portland, Maine.

The farm had belonged to our family for decades. Holstein cows and hay threshers moved across the hill below our twenty-seven room farmhouse. Loans had accumulated and the mortgage lay forgotten in the drawer of my grandfather's writing desk. He used to write poems while looking out from the third-story window over sloping fields. Since Dad died, my last living uncles refused to even slit open the envelopes the bills arrived in. The farm was foreclosed. Some apple conglomerate with ties to a supermarket franchise snatched up the acreage. I could buy a bushel at Stop and Shop and see the old farmhouse emblazoned across a stiff paper bag.

It was never the same as eating them fresh off the tree.

***

I tacked a to-do list to the inside of the greenhouse door, along with a detailed watering schedule. I noted how the building must remain sealed to prevent pollinators with tinted yellow legs from slipping in. I outlined where the extra key hung above the sink. Knowing Lenny, he'd lose the first. I had a third clipped to my key ring. I told myself it would be fine, but my fingers wandered to the key, ensuring myself it was still there.

Rain knocked on the polyethylene sheeting over my head. I moved down the length of nightshade-laden tables, stopping at the end where the variation possessing the shrunken berries resided. Our crossbred belladonna's purple flowers grew more distinct with each passing day. The white markings looked undeniably tooth-like. The skin on the berries was stretched taut. They seemed like they would burst if I lay a finger on them, but as I cradled the cluster, the casing held, light in my hand. The thought of eating them seemed less daunting considering the changes that occurred over the past month.

I withdrew a Q-tip from a sealed jar on the table. Across the room, I ran the cotton swab against the dusted stamen of another variation with the lightest petals until the white tinged yellow. Then I ran the fresh pollen over the stigma protruding from the center of the purple flowers. Clint said we didn't need to transfer any more pollen, that the process should be underway on its own, but I figured it couldn't hurt.

As I dipped the Q-tip inside the flower one last time, the yelling began. Jessica's voice jolted beneath the back door and tore its way through the greenhouse. I had never heard her seethe like that. From the cut up sentences and dull rebuttal of Lenny's voice, I knew he said the wrong thing once again. Another portrait request? Maybe. Only sharp, mangled words met my ears.

Bra.
Inconsiderate.
Whore.
House.
Gone.

Nope. It wasn't about the portrait.

I sealed the Q-tips away, then locked the door in a hurry, sprinting to the house, dodging puddles forming over the brick path between the knee-high forest of saplings. Lenny was standing at the kitchen table, an assortment of colorful bras stacked in an interlocking tower, padded cups dipping into one another. He must have had thirty of them.

"I was just seeing if you wanted any of these. I heard you two talking out there. I would have picked one out for you, but didn't know your size. You'd look good in this red one," Lenny said, slipping the bra out from the middle of the stack.

"You're disgusting. I'm not taking anything from your lost and found," Jessica replied, white knuckles clenched around the back of a dining room chair, shoulders heaving beneath her spaghetti straps.

"They're not lost. I know who most of these belonged to. See, Stephanie," Lenny said, holding up a black bra with lime green polka-dots. "And this was Jill." A plain white garment rose from the heap.

As he wrenched a third bra free from the dismembered tower, Jessica stopped him by sweeping the accumulated lingerie from the table.

"I'm not wearing one of your trophies," she said.

"I don't hang them on my walls."

"You're sick."

"Hey. It's not like I made a joke about your small tits or anything. Take it easy. I was just trying to help you pack."

Jessica frowned, blurted an incoherent syllable, and ducked into our bedroom, where she continued to scream. The howl grew muffled, sheetrock stifling the flow of words. Across the table, Lenny's smile said many things, none of them pleasant.

"Why'd you do that?" I asked.

"Thought it would be funny," he replied. "Apparently someone doesn't get my sense of humor." He raised his voice at the last part so Jessica wouldn't miss the remark.

"Don't even talk to him," Jessica called from behind our door, voice barely audible beneath the sudden rustling of clothes and other things buried in the depths of our closet.

"Are you going to let her tell you what to do?" he asked.

I stood with my eyes closed, hands resting on the cool countertop, trying to follow the noises coming from the other room while imagining Lenny melting away, skin evaporating into particles drifting out the window. It was a calming technique I had begun using when my anxiety flared.

I opened my eyes. Lenny still stood before me, my mental prodding unable to loosen him from the floor. He smiled, hands still draped with a dozen bras. Jessica appeared in the doorway at my back, my gym bag slung over her shoulder, sunglasses resting on her nose.

"Let's go," she said.

"I need to pack," I stammered.

"I did it for you," she said as her shoulder brushed mine. She knocked the bras Lenny hadn't collected onto the floor, then left, slamming the door in her wake.

"You know what they say about road trips, right?" Lenny said.

"Do I want to?" I replied, looking through the door's slim windows. Jessica was out of earshot, stuffing the gym bag into the back seat.

"They'll make or break a relationship. All that time spent in the car, no one else to talk to. Good luck with that. If she can't laugh every once in a while, I don't know how long I'd be able to put up with her."

"Hey, she's got a great sense of humor. She's just sensitive about stuff like this. Thanks for being a dick," I replied.

"You're welcome."

"Just be nice. It's not going to kill you. I love her. We live together. That's how it is. I don't want to have to choose between the two of you if you keep being a jerk."

I paused, waiting for him to come back with some *bros before hoes* bullshit, but it never surfaced. He seemed to shrink, inches shorn from his legs, his shoulders. It was possible the thought never crossed his mind, that I might prefer her company to his.

In some way, it was sad. We both knew he had never sustained a lasting relationship. His behavior suggested he hadn't peeled back anyone's skin to see the inner workings of their heart. Closeness was an adjective he couldn't define.

"Whatever, man," he said, turning away, walking down the hall. "You left those instructions in the greenhouse, right?"

"Yeah, right where I told you they'd be," I replied, a little shocked by the sad tone of his voice.

"Good," he replied. His bedroom door closed to punctuate our conversation. I knew he wouldn't forget to water the plants, the tone of his voice said so. That fear fell from my mind, replaced with the knowledge Jessica would bring up Lenny moving out as soon as we crossed state lines.

CHAPTER 9

We drove in near silence as the radio looped pop songs. Ballads of lost love and misconnections. I tried to start a conversation about Lenny, how I hoped he'd mature, morph into the guy we always hoped he'd be, but I couldn't get the words right. The background music never fit. My stomach churned an acidic wash when I envisioned the confrontation.

While Jessica never directly spoke of kicking him out, I could feel it lingering on the edge of our words, a specter in the distance. I made jokes while Jessica stared out the window at a passing farm. A big black sign was anchored to a rusted silo proclaiming their harvest of alfalfa.

Once we found the exit ramp, there was nothing but abandoned farmhouses, weed-strewn lots, and downtown streets littered with *for rent* signs in display windows. That was where my family came from. At least my father's side. They had shopped in those stores now home to dust-thick windows and cobwebbed cash registers. I recognized the faded bookstore where my father bought my first Edgar Allan Poe collection, the sole title responsible for my current reading tastes. Their floor to ceiling shelves stood bare, empty like everything else in town.

A green road sign listed the surrounding towns and their distance from our current position. Several were named after European locations: *Paris, Norway, Sweden*. Seventeen miles. Twenty-four miles. Waterford, my father's childhood home, our final destination, was thirty miles west. Down steep roads overhung with thick branches. Pot-bellied boulders thrust their guts over the lane's edge. They were riddled with graffiti, scars from accidents, shattered headlights scattered at their bases. I drove slowly while the dip in altitude popped my ears.

"Is it wrong to wish the Spirits would come for him soon?" Jessica asked out of the blue.

"What?" I replied, nearly skimming the passenger side door across an approaching stone.

"I feel like a terrible person saying this, but what good is he alive? Whoever he's connected to is going to have a horrible death. We both know it."

"Well, his paintings help a lot of people. Maybe it'll balance out all the shitty stuff."

"You know that's not how it works. Think about Rachel, all those other girls. If he was honest with them, that's one thing. The Spirits don't care about sex, but infidelity, that's another issue."

"I hear you, but who really knows how the Spirits look at these things. There's no sliding scale, no reference chart. Maybe infidelity is lower on their list than we think?"

Jessica sighed and shook her head. "You don't need to make excuses for him," she muttered, turning her head to look at the pond on our right.

Out on the calm water, a single boulder disrupted the flat surface, a black blotch over pale blue. The transparent outline of a thin ghost hovered above the rock, no doubt a boating accident or ice fishing mishap resulting in the unusual grave. Ghosts were stuck to their remains. Rescue crews must have missed the body, bones sunk beneath the detritus of the pond's bottom. Spray-painted words and dates defaced the rock, a memorial for the trapped soul. I hoped it wasn't one of my cousins. There was no place to rent a canoe nearby, and Jessica wasn't in the mood for swimming.

***

Half an hour later, my Volvo climbed a ridge in the mountainous road. An orderly stretch of apple trees surrounded by barbed-wire fencing came into view. The farmhouse was situated at the peak of a dirt driveway trickling off from the paved road. Three stories of oak boards hewn from the local forest were doused in white paint, the moss and rot of my childhood sanded away by the new owners.

We took the time to walk under the shading branches of Macintoshes and Golden Delicious. Smooth gray bark guided us through the maze of unblemished fruit, Jessica's hand in mine. We paid for the deep, white bags with the glossy handles, the familiar emblem depicting the barn emblazoned on the front. I snatched one of the apple-picking pole-arms with the grasping metal claws at the end, rubber tipped to avoid bruising fruit. Jessica's height made it difficult to reach even the lowest branches. She grabbed one for herself. Instead of plying it in the trees, she used it as a jousting lance, feigning jabs to my torso and feet. I dodged and parried, poking her back, the dulled hooks comically bouncing off her shins. Other customers stared at us like we were lunatics.

The smell of deep-fried cider doughnuts swept in with each passing breeze. Behind us, pale smoke rose from the main building at the orchard's entrance. A sign said homemade pizza, but the scent said sugared dough and copious amounts of cinnamon.

Once the apples were picked, I told the man in the plaid shirt running the cash register who I was and what my relationship to the orchard had been. He had no problem with us walking around inside the fence line, no problem with me parking my car by the family graveyard and spending a few nights. He even said we could use the outhouse behind the tool shed. He suggested a river winding around the base of their steep hill for bathing. Jessica's frown said otherwise.

"Poland Springs gets some of their water from around here," the man noted.

"So you're saying it's clean?" I asked.

"Nope. Just that people drink it. One bath ain't gonna hurt you."

Jessica shrugged, biting her lip.

I dropped a five into the man's tip jar and returned to the car, bags of apples straining against their handles.

I parked the Volvo in the dirt lot abutting the cemetery. It looked like someone had run a Gravely brush mower around the surrounding area, tearing the shunted undergrowth to pieces and leaving twig-like protrusions poking out from the mulled-over dirt. Just the perimeter. I was surprised they had even done that.

It looked like no one had walked between the stones in decades. Vines and dandelions swayed across the tombstones. Poison ivy crept up fence posts. A fallen pine lay against the left wall, a few orange and brown needles still clinging to its branches. The last Gallagher had moved out of state two years ago, leaving no one to tend to the ghosts' needs. I brought an old fashioned weeding scythe, a single sharpened metal blade at the end of a wooden handle, for the occasion.

We set up camp.

The folding beach chairs piled on top of our mattress were unfolded near the Volvo's hatch as if it was the front porch of our temporary abode. I assembled the charcoal grill. By assembled, I mean I screwed three legs into a metal bowl and filled it with ashy pellets.

The bed was made. Jessica folded back the lip of one sleeping bag, exposing the soft flannel interior. "You're like a furnace when you sleep." She smiled. "Are we going to be too warm in these?"

"We'll be fine. Even if that does happen, we can go swimming in the river. Cool right off. Any chance you want to check it out with me?"

"Possibly...if you play your cards right. I didn't bring a bathing suit."

"Who said you need one?"

"Dave!" She playfully batted my arm. "What about the people up there? I bet they've got cameras hidden in the trees."

"Nah, half the buildings out here don't even have electricity."

"Well, maybe they should think about getting cameras. They're going to miss the show."

***

With our living accommodations set, we wandered into the graveyard. The stones hid in tall, wispy weeds, tips peeking from the overgrowth like prying neighbors. I'd trip over the low ones if I wasn't careful. Four granite posts marked the edges of the plot, a rusted steel rail ran between them. I itched to set the place right, but that would come later.

One corner was covered by oak leaves; another by pine needles. A grave at the center reached a foot or two above my head. It resembled the Washington monument with a crown of ramparts adorning its crest. The twigs and twine of a bird's nest draped over the side of the tower.

I could hear them whisper, the hushed voices of my aunts and uncles, the giggles of my cousin who died when he was twelve. "Look at Dave's girlfriend," he lisped into Aunt Beth's ear. They were packed close, the perimeter of the cemetery confining their walking space. Their thin frames were draped in farm attire, overalls, patchwork dresses. One uncle stood shirtless, his muscular torso devoid of even an ounce of fat. They seemed to bristle and quake as we drew near, unsure of my presence, giddy at the thought of living company. Years had passed since they had answered questions.

The sea of pallid faces receded, opening a walkway to the foot of Uncle Thom's grave. Dried roses and herbs lay cocooned in a disintegrating husk atop his stone. Thom was the first I needed to talk with. I saved Uncle Stephen for second, hoping the time wouldn't arrive. They were the only two with unanswered atonement among the group.

My great uncle's long hair and haphazard beard obscured the better part of his face. His coat caught my eye: stitched together from animal pelts. As he waved Jessica and I toward his corner of the family plot, I waited for a snout to rise off his coat and turn its dull eyes toward us in the same welcome as the man who wore it.

"How've you been, Uncle Thom?" I asked, near enough to see the irregular stitches of his coat.

"It's taken you long enough to visit," he answered.

"I know, and I apologize, work always interferes when I try to sneak away."

"Don't apologize. It's not my life. I've got no say in your priorities," Uncle Thom said, eyes roaming Jessica head to toe. "There's two of us left you need to talk to. How'd you like to begin?"

"Am I getting riddles or are you going to be straight with me?" I asked.

Jessica pulled at my sleeve. She had never been comfortable around the dead, her answers already known.

"Shouldn't you be more polite?" she whispered.

"I know what I'm doing. Uncle Thom's not one to draw things out. He appreciates it when you're blunt," I replied.

"If you think so," she said.

Uncle Thom's forehead spun a web of worried lines as he surveyed our aside. My only memory of him was a brief flash of his self-stitched boots rocking back and forth in a wicker chair, smoking a pipe in his living room. The man's house smelled of rancid tobacco. A taxidermied bear reached a claw over the back of his fraying couch as if to fan away the smoke. The thought of the bear raised concerns, but I wasn't going to bring it up. He hunted for food, not pride.

"You know you'll get it straight," my uncle answered.

"Alright," I said.

"Hunting's never been a sin, but poaching, that's a whole 'nother story. For years I tracked game through our woods. Never went on the neighbors' land. They had their boundary line, I had mine," Thom said, pointing to a rock wall stretching off into the distance. "One winter none of them deer that used to run around these parts made it back. I looked over every trail, every gully. Nothing. That was our food.

"I decided to take a walk onto my neighbors' acreage. Deer just lined up along his back corner. No human prints, snowshoes, boots. I checked the snow. Shot one the first day, right in the heart. Had to kick snow over the bloody mess to cover it up. I felt bad, but I was hungry, my family was starving.

"A couple days later I went back. Still only my tracks circling the trees, they mustn't of hiked back that far, so I shot another.

"It went that way till the herd ran off. And you know what? My neighbor never knew. Their six-year-old son starved. I helped dig the kid's grave, set the stone, but that doesn't make up for my theft. Whoever has to answer for my sins has to keep that in mind," my uncle finished, wrenching his throat as if he was going to spit up a glob of tobacco juice as he had done during life.

"So am I the one who's got to worry?" I asked.

"It's someone, and there aren't many of you left these days. Could be you, could be one of your cousins," he replied.

There were five Gallaghers left, three others with different surnames: O'Sullivan, Hill, Laffin. I saw my cousins walking into bear traps, dangling from snares in a forgotten wood while the Spirits emerged from the underbrush, skinning knives in hand. I didn't want any of that. Clean and unnoticed, seventy years down the road. No one having to cut me down or mop up the mess staining the carpet.

I tried to get Uncle Thom to narrow it down: hair color, height, astrological sign. He refused to push the conversation forward, leaving off saying his heir would be male. So eight dropped down to six. Not great odds.

"Say thank you," Jessica nudged me in the ribs. "Thank him."

"Oh yeah, thanks, Uncle Thom. I appreciate the warning," I said, rubbing my side. Sometimes I forgot they weren't obligated to tell us anything. That it was their kindness that let you live with less worry about Spirit masks appearing in your rearview mirror.

I gave Thom a nod before we moved over to Uncle Stephen's grave. It was much smaller. No polished stone or detailed angels. His looked more like a rock someone dug out of the back yard and painted, the handwriting nearly illegible. Only a few of the letters in his name were still clear. I doubted anyone had ever visited that stone, the grass higher around its edges than the rest. This made me nervous.

Stephen was a round man, his rolling stomach held back by a white t-shirt, grease-stained and crisscrossed with suspenders. In death he wore the same patchy beard he had in life. It looked like a lion's mane torn by the tusks of a feral boar. His eyes were too small for his face, sunken beneath the converging folds of cheek and brow.

"So what are you going to do for me?" was the first thing he asked as we planted ourselves before him.

"I don't know, what are you in the mood for?" I asked. "I've got some things in the car you might like." I had packed a cardboard box full of different knickknacks. A little glass duck, a few months' worth of *Field and Stream*, a tin of Skoal chewing tobacco, a whiskey-filled flask, and a rosary in case he finally found God. We stopped at a convenience store and the local packie before setting up camp. I hid a copy of *Hustler* from Jessica as we left the store, the wrapper crinkling with every step.

I placed the cardboard box of knickknacks at Stephen's feet as he ran his hand through his beard. He bent and perused the assortment, fingers drifting through magazine covers as if he had forgotten his inability to turn a page. He shook his head and leaned back into his slouched stance. I unearthed the *Hustler* from beneath the rest of the accumulated junk, a woman's obviously fake breasts splayed across the cover. He nodded and gave a little laugh. Then he moved to brush it away with his enormous paw.

"Let me see her tits," he said, pointing at Jessica.

She flinched, raising her arms, as if he had thrown a stone at her, eyelids fluttering closed to protect her sensitive blue irises.

"Don't be a dick. Jessica isn't doing that," I replied.

"Then that's all you're getting from me. I ain't trading otherwise," Stephen said.

"Really?"

"A hundred percent. Man's got to have a reason to talk."

"Well, fuck you. We're leaving and I'm taking all this junk with me," I replied, bending to retrieve the trinkets I'd foolishly believed would appease the monster.

Jessica sighed. "Wait one second," she said, shaking her head.

"Why? He's being a perv."

"I'm well aware of that, but we drove so far and no one's around. Just get the rest of your family to look away and I'll do it."

"You don't have to, though. There's so many other relatives to talk to. It probably isn't even him," I said.

"But what if it is?" Jessica asked, eyes downcast.

Out of the corner of my eye, my great-great grandfather shook his head. Thom had moved to the far end of the plot, looking off into the forest, avoiding the scene.

"Like they're going to listen," I said.

Nothing was going to get my cousin to budge from where he sat on top of his headstone. This was his moment to make up for all the sexual yearnings he missed in adolescence. A couple translucent old-timers crept to the lip of their stones, eyes and foreheads revealed.

Jessica ran a hand through her hair. "If it's the only thing that's going to get you an answer, I'm doing it. Just get that kid to look away."

I flashed my hand in a shooing motion toward my cousin. He shook his head before his mother's translucent specter wrapped an arm around his shoulder, ferrying him to her headstone near the entrance.

"You owe her," my aunt whispered as she escorted her son away. I nodded, a mixture of gratitude and sadness swilled in my chest.

Then her shirt was over her head. It was quick; her pale breasts gave a single bounce as the combination shirt/bra jumble obscured her face.

I was glad the shirt blocked her sight so she couldn't see Stephen's smile. I never realized how disconcerting a "toothless grin" actually was until seeing his. I waited for a swarm of locusts to billow from his crumbled jaw.

The enveloping crowd gained a foot or two in the moment, spreading a sudden jolt of claustrophobia through my chest. Their eyes were wide, hands grasping at their sides for something they couldn't hold. As her shirt came down, the wall of men fell to pieces and Stephen's grin gave way. The ghosts hustled back to their stones like cockroaches beneath the sudden flicker of a lightbulb.

"Now tell him," she said, placing a finger underneath her bra strap, twanging it back into place.

"Well, there's not much to tell. A group of them Spirits cornered your cousin Caleb and put the bat to him. You're off the hook," Stephen said, broken grin sliding back into place.

"What?" Jessica stammered, a blossoming pattern of red petals spreading across her pale face and down her neck.

"You should've said something," I said.

"And miss the show?" Stephen replied. "You know me better than that."

And I did. Stephen was barely considered part of the family when we laid him in the ground. "Disowned" was the epithet my parents bestowed. All those hookers and hidden nips in the glove compartment. Back room poker games and harassment charges kept him off the mailing list for family reunions and Christmas cards. The guys at the morgue said someone had to take him, and no, we couldn't toss the body into the ocean or some ditch.

Why we buried him in the family plot, rather than the woods, was beyond me.

"You fucking pig!" Jessica screamed and sprinted to the car, knocking over our portable grill. Its lid spun on the ground, clattering to a halt against a tree stump, as Uncle Stephen laughed. With each mounting cackle, the man swelled like a balloon. He grew in height, chest expanding, shirt barely able to contain his ethereal girth. I had never seen the man at full height. Slouching seemed his natural state. I turned my back on him without a word and followed the bent and broken weeds Jessica left in her wake.

As far as I knew, Cousin Caleb still lived in Florida trying to make his way as a pizza chef. She couldn't have expected me to have known he was dead. His last name didn't match my own, and I never received an invitation to the funeral.

At first, Jessica wouldn't speak to me when I joined her in camp, but after a few minutes, she pulled me into the back of the Volvo, drawing my arms around her shoulders and waist. She nuzzled into me, pressing her face into my shirt as we reclined on the mattress. The fabric grew damp with tears. I rubbed her back in slow widening circles, trying to soothe her startled panic.

For a while, we lay there, bodies pressed together, as if a field of ghosts weren't staring at us from a few feet away. When her breathing slowed and her stomach began to growl, I slipped from her grasp to straighten the grill. Then I lit the briquettes and freed the hot dogs from their plastic wrapping. Jessica watched me turn the little sausages over the flames, rivulets of fat popping as they singed and burned.

***

At night, we spooned through our separate sleeping bags. The flannel fabric was warm to the touch. The seat belt descending overhead jabbed into my shoulder, but I refused to break away from the wall, not wanting to wake Jessica. There was a moment earlier, when she was sprinting away from my uncle's sexual predation, that I worried Lenny's prophecy would be fulfilled, that our road trip was going to shift something between us. He was wrong. Our trip only affirmed the fact Jessica would do anything for me, no matter how uncomfortable it made her. I'd do the same in return.

I breathed deep, sucking down the scent of her hair, floral and sweet, something earthy and verdant beneath.

The night's noises rose around us. Frogs hummed in the trees. A squirrel ran laps down the Volvo's roof. Jessica flinched at the sound, but I whispered calm words into her ear. She didn't wake. White figures moved about the cemetery, a cluster of men imitated the scene from before, one pretending to lift his shirt, cupping his hands over imagined breasts. Others shook their heads, but laughed regardless. After a time, I gave up watching their antics and counted sheep until I could close my eyes. They all sank into the ground before I fell asleep.

***

I woke with a start sometime in the early morning, outside still wrapped in darkness except for a single pale face floating near the window. *Oh, god,* I whispered, heart jarring off my ribs, lungs in my throat. I thought it was a Spirit's mask, the curved beak and empty eyes peering in from the gloom. I almost shook Jessica from her sleep when the being came into focus.

It was my cousin, leaning against a rusted fence rail, trying to get a better look at us. When he saw that I saw him, he ducked beneath the tall grass, leaving me with scenes of my own death playing out until sunrise

CHAPTER 10

Rain forced us inside. A pile of trail maps were stacked on my dashboard, dog-eared and underlined to indicate where we would have gone had the skies held up their end of the bargain. The rain echoed with metallic laughter as it plodded over the broken struts in my roof. The decision was simple: either sit in the Volvo for the rest of the week or explore local shopping plazas and sheltered tourist attractions.

Flea markets and pawn shops lined the streets. Each Walmart we passed had parking lots jammed with dented Jeeps and lifted Fords. We stopped at each, sorting through their five-dollar barrels of DVDs, hoping to find any of the old cult classics Jessica and I loved.

The pawn shop was a hoarder's paradise. Glass cases contained piles of cheap jewelry and video games. Skeletons of small mammals stood transfixed on lacquered boards. Guns lined one wall, broken and on-the-way-to-be-broken skis slumped against another. One wall was composed of flickering tube television sets, all tuned to a news program depicting activists protesting at the Nantahala Forest in North Carolina. Timber companies were attempting to clear-cut a swath of old growth along the Appalachian Trail. Spirits clustered in the trees, hovering above the protestors chained below, waiting to see whose names they'd jot in their books first.

It wasn't looking good for the bulldozer operators and lumberjacks.

If I could have joined the protest, I would have, but distance and vacation time weren't on my side

***

In the next room, the pawnshop owner's son sat among piles of creased paperbacks, scribbling superhero masks across the shirtless men on Harlequin Romance novels.

Jessica pulled a collection of early anime films from a pile of one-dollar DVDs, obviously a bootleg, Japanese calligraphy scrawled with an unsteady hand.

"Would you watch these with me?" she asked.

"Hell yeah," I said.

"You know Lenny's going to make fun of you, right?"

"I'll ignore him."

"You won't have to when you kick him out," she said, eyebrow arched, a smile on her lips. "Then we could watch all the animated movies we wanted without him in the background criticizing brush strokes or how characters are shaded."

I laughed. He was always harping on other artists' techniques.

"I always hate when he rags on the lag between the audio and their mouths."

"See, that's what I'm talking about. No more ruined movie nights. No more screaming girls at three in the morning."

"Yeah. I know. Let's talk about it later. This isn't the best setting to come up with big plans," I said, pointing to a taxidermied armadillo holding a bottle of Jose Cuervo.

"Fine. I'm holding you to it," Jessica said, checking the price tag hanging from the creature's leg. "How would this look on our dresser?"

***

After an hour of perusing aisles of blown-glass lamps and dry-rot guitars, Jessica was ready to leave. She had her armadillo and anime. I found a strip of rabbit hide with an oak tree drawn on it in charcoal, root system intricately detailed. Oaks were my favorite. They supported more than five hundred other species, nearly double that of its nearest competition.

The man behind the counter asked the little boy coloring the dust jackets to run a price check. He didn't believe the artwork was so cheap. The child dropped his pencil, a half-finished Batman logo stenciled across the broadest airbrushed chest I had ever seen.

The owner sported the same style of facial hair as Uncle Stephen, patchy beard matted with sweat. He followed my eyes to where the boy disappeared.

"Don't worry, he can read just fine," the man said, tipping back a can of root beer into his mouth. "Been doing it for years."

"How old is he?" Jessica asked.

"Eight," the man replied.

"Great. It's nice to hear when kids like to read," Jessica said.

Her eyes traced the boy's exit. Jessica and I had planned on having children for years. There were few things either of us wanted more in life. Only one though. Our income was too low to support more, no matter how much we wanted them. She didn't want to raise a family struggling from paycheck to paycheck as she'd been raised.

"He's right, Dad. Five bucks," the boy reported.

The father thanked his son, tossing him a can of root beer from a mini-fridge tucked under the counter.

"Hey, would you mind if I bought one of your drawings?" Jessica asked, pointing to a Fabio look alike painted in a green rendition of the hulk. The kid had crossed out the book's original title, *The Other Celtic Sword,* and etched in his own: *Green Guy Finds a Girl.*

"Yes, please," the boy said, his smile broad. He jogged over and handed Jessica the paperback.

"Thanks," she said. "How much is it?"

The boy stared up at her, his lower lip clenched between his teeth.

"Five dollars," he replied.

Jessica slipped him a ten. He snatched the bill, thanking her furiously before jogging back to his work in progress. Batman needed the rest of his garment penciled in. I paid for the remainder of our purchases. On the way out, Jessica's eyes darted from the child to me, most likely wondering what he would have looked like if he was a mixture of our genes instead of the grizzled man behind the counter and the woman he convinced to share his bed.

I hoped we wouldn't have to wait much longer.

***

That night, our bed was no longer comfortable. Humidity swamped our makeshift camper, making everything I touched feel like a damp spider web. Condensation dripped down the windows. Jessica and I had to put distance between us, the heat too overbearing to fold into each other's bodies. She still reached out a hand, our fingers twined together for brief moments before I had to readjust myself, searching for a cool patch. The flannel-lined interior of the sleeping bag stuck to my back as I rolled through nightmares.

I offered to spring for a night in one of the local hotels: air conditioning, waterbeds, the sharp tang of pool chlorine.

"That would be way too expensive," Jessica replied. "We can't swing two hundred a night after our shopping spree."

Her eyes moved to the taxidermied armadillo propped in the far corner of the hatchback.

***

Somehow, Jessica barely sweated at all. She'd rise in the morning, sweep her long hair into place with a few combing fingers, and wipe the sleep from her eyes. I looked haggard, hardened drool crusted to stubble, eyes puffy and caked with grime. She'd laugh about it then ask me what we were going to do that day, which, in itself, wasn't that exciting. It was a repetitive loop of the previous day: another indoor flea market, a different stuffed squirrel mounted on a different miniature toilet, greasy food at truck stop diners with vinyl seats and fifties jukeboxes.

Lenny was always the topic of conversation. He was never far from Jessica's mind.

***

Jessica and I made love after I promised I'd kick Lenny out when we got back. I said I'd make all the arrangements she requested. Restructure the lease. Throw his things on the lawn if he didn't leave quietly. I felt guilty for turning my back on Lenny, but it was inevitable. Yeah, I admired his personality, some aspects anyway. Creative. Outgoing. Spontaneous. Always fighting routine. I wouldn't have met half the interesting people I had if he hadn't painted them in our living room. I'd miss that, miss his inappropriate jokes when we had guests over.

I wouldn't miss the drug residue on the coffee table though. That was never easy to explain to others. Or the thrum of heartbreak lingering in the air, haunting every room like graveyard specters.

Before we began to strip off our clothes, Jessica did a thorough inspection of the surrounding area, making sure my young cousin wasn't hiding behind a grave, mouth agape at our exposed flesh.

Two lights were on in the farmhouse looming atop the hill. I promised her no one would be watching, that we would catch their shadows as they peered through closed blinds. She said my eyesight sucked. I said that everyone went to sleep early, considering they had to rise with the sun. She laughed. We were both horny, so neither argument really mattered as I tugged off her underwear.

In the cramped space, movements were restricted. Raised legs and arched backs were impeded by the low roof. Faster paces were slowed by rusted shocks and a creaky suspension. We rolled through variations of standard positions: doggy-stuck-in-a-travel-crate style, missionary-hiding-from-carnivorous-wildlife. Her pale skin was chalk-white in the moonlight. My farmer's tan left my two-toned stomach aglow in the darkness. She looked ethereal, spritely. I looked like something out of a trailer park.

Foreign sounds swept in from outside, interrupting her gasps and my groans. Jessica's attention darted out the passenger windows. The scrape of squirrel claws against tree bark, oak limbs sagging in the wind. I laughed when the sudden flutter of turkey wings caused her to scream. They were migrating to the trees to roost.

"If they weren't awake in the farmhouse before, they definitely are now," I said.

Jessica punched me in the chest and told me to shut up, a smile on her face.

When we finished, Jessica lay curled in my arms, the compressed humidity of our backseat sweating through the sleeping bags. Even as my heart rate spiked and my body temperature escalated, I drew her close, my face sinking into the tangle of her hair. Everything felt alright in that moment as Jessica's breathing slowed. Next steps lingered further off, consigned to another day, distant cemeteries. Instead of worrying about death, I lay there, listening to the slow rain of falling apples, like the beat of Jessica's heart at my side.

***

Jessica slept in. I snuck from the hatchback, retrieving my scythe from a nearby tree. Uncle Thom was the only ghost up and about. He leaned against his stone, arching his back in an early morning stretch. He nodded a greeting as I swung the scythe through high grass, shearing it low, creating the appearance of order and symmetry. The metal blade stirred a breeze as I manicured the paths between stones. I picked dandelions by hand, halting the spread of downy seed-heads repopulating my groomed landscape.

Once the grass was shorn, I retrieved the rotting flowers and wreaths, depositing them in a moldering compost pile in the woods.

From nearby fields, I collected tiger lilies, lupine, and daisies to weave into bouquets.

I twisted stems, morphing rigid materials into rounded displays. The buds were in bloom, the scent sweet, a mixture of fragrances from each. I rubbed my palms against my neck, scenting my skin with natural cologne before depositing each floral display on my family's graves.

Lastly I carried the toppled pine into the woods, clearing the last debris from the plot. I couldn't leave my ancestral burial ground in the state I discovered it. Their ghosts deserved something better, not the neglect of years passed. Finished, I retraced my steps toward the car, but Uncle Thom called to me before I could duck through the gate.

"Sorry for what Stephen did to you two the other day. He's not well liked around here," my uncle said as I neared his stone.

"I figured. Death only changes so much. He's an ass," I replied.

"I won't debate that. You've hit the nail. Squarely. I've been thinking about something."

"What?" I asked, peering up the hill to where tractor engines were jolting into life, preparing for a day of carting tourists about the orchard.

"Part of me wonders how certain those things I told you really are," Thom said.

"About the Spirits?"

"Yes. I never get a clear view of the person's face. I'd tell you if I knew, that's how I am. It could happen at age forty, maybe fifty. The timeline's really blurry."

"So you guessed. I thought all ghosts knew what was going to happen?"

"If you're lucky. Some of your relatives knew every detail. Aunt Minnie knew it was her son. She saw the door to their tool shed nailed shut by the Spirits. Even saw the look on his face as he starved, no one but her to hear his screams. But me, all I can tell is whomever it is has got short hair. That's why I say it's a guy. I can't even make out the color."

Every ghost I had encountered claimed to know every detail of their familial fate. But Thom pointed out a dozen cousins and uncles who were or had been unaware of their direct connections to the living. They had greyed visions of their pasts. Thom said it was like the reception on his old black and white television, fixing the antennae in a winter storm. Definition eluded them, which churned my stomach. I didn't need things to be more complicated than they already were.

Ghosts were proud beings. Most weren't willing to change their original predictions. They'd lose their power over the living, the only hold that kept visitors coming back to talk, to keep them from being forgotten.

"Some just make it up to seem holier than thou. It's the only thing you've got going once you're buried," Thom said.

"But you can't mess with people's lives like that," I replied.

"Most don't see a problem with it. That's how it's always been. It works itself out one way or another."

"I've never heard of someone getting it wrong."

"You're young. Give it time. Talk to Aunt Sue if you want proof," he said, pointing to a rectangular stone near the entrance.

"But..."

"Just look at your father. Your great-uncle knew what would happen, but was twenty years off in his estimates, didn't know they were going to lay the blankets on him so soon."

The pneumatic hinges of the Volvo's hatchback opened behind us. Jessica slipped into a pair of sneakers that lay on the ground beneath the rear bumper, moist with dew. She waved to us then moved to light the grill, dropping a lit match into the coals, squirting a little lighter fluid when the briquettes wouldn't catch. Then she unearthed the package of plastic-wrapped sausages from the cooler. After several days of straight sausage, I'd be happy to never see another one again. The coagulated fat within the intestinal casings crackled and popped as I said goodbye to Thom.

"We've got to get going after breakfast," I told him.

"That's fine. I'm glad you stopped by. Thanks for cleaning up the place," he replied, adjusting the stitching on one of the hides adorning his shoulders. I thought I saw him push the snout of some sewn creature back into the garment, but wasn't sure.

"And I'm glad I don't have to worry about Stephen's prediction, not to be selfish or anything."

"There's no shame in it. No one wants to die like your cousin if they can help it."

"Thanks."

"Sorry if I screwed with your trust in ghosts. Better you know sooner rather than later."

"No, I really appreciate it. I'll keep that in mind."

With a few parting words, a reminder of his possible timeframe, and a failed attempt at a handshake, I joined Jessica. My thoughts were scattered as we packed. Questions filtered through my mind as I disassembled the grill and foldable chairs. *If ghosts don't actually know, was I wasting my time asking? What would twenty or thirty years of marriage amount to? What if it was less? What if we never made it to the altar? What about our child?*

Thom's news didn't make my prospects much better. The potential of living to midlife was only marginally helpful with the planning Jessica and I hoped to begin. I didn't mention Uncle Thom's advice to her. Jessica didn't do well with change. I kept the voices to myself, letting them mutter in my ear.

If they could be wrong, what else was a lie?

CHAPTER 11

Jessica's fate had been settled two years ago, etched in stone by the dead and their choices. Her Aunt Helen decreed the pattern and flow for the rest of her life. *Rest easy, life will be long*, Aunt Helen's thin lips crooned. The only trait I could remember were those lips. During life, the woman caked on makeup, thickly smattering it across her face as if she used a mason's trowel for an applicator. Clotted lipstick made her mouth resemble a gash in a ripe pomegranate. The hue still lingered after death, leaving her lips a light charcoal rather than bleached white.

It would be a letter in the mail, Helen said. Something from an old friend, a would-be lover, someone she had forgotten from youth. It would happen two days after she stepped into her eightieth year. The heart attack would be quick, induced by the news scrawled in cursive. It was a love letter never sent. The return address at the top belonged to a house that no longer existed, the postmark stamped 2007. She'd picture his face, the crisp part in his hair, her own reflection in his darkened pupils, then her heart would tremble and cease to beat.

I pictured a Spirit dressed as a mailman, blue button-up shirt, wheeled letter carrier in tow, handing her the envelope. There was never any mention of my name. The address wasn't even close to my home. Jessica had never been to Idaho, but she refused to comment on the matter when I brought it up.

She knew there were fifty-five years ahead; hence the precaution.

When we first met we barely slept, eyes hungry for each other's bodies. Desire never grew old, but eventually we craved different sights too: Nevada's deserts, the swollen banks of the Mississippi, Maine's rocky coastline, all of which were viewed with her hand in mine. Our naturalist wanderings brought us to yearly blooms in far flung botanical gardens, the titanic roots of redwoods, rivers choked with water lilies. Recently, that had slowed, our trips focused on graveyard visits, the necessities of mature life. Paying rent. Avoiding debt. We promised each other new trips when the verdict came in.

The added incentives made Uncle Thom's revelations even more difficult to grapple with.

His words were all I could think about as we drove down the Mass Pike on our way home, passing gas station signs and carved Native American statues, liquor stores bigger than supermarkets. Gypsy moth caterpillars had devoured the oaks along the roadway, leaving their gray skin leafless and bare. In some ways I felt like the blighted growth, my skin stripped away, the laws of my world lessened and unstable. I focused on the curving yellow lines painted on the pavement, willing the thoughts to subside.

"Who else do you need to talk to?" Jessica asked, as I surfaced from daydreams. She had an array of manila folders spread on her lap. Black and white photographs of women's faces adorned their upper corners. She was examining clients' files, comparing backgrounds with job openings in the community.

"A few people on the other side of the family," I replied, shaking off the ethereal blear clouding my eyes.

We never talked much about where my mother was buried.

"Are they on Cape somewhere?"

"Just a couple aunts I talked to a while ago. One was a nun. Cousin Carl has nothing to worry about, just male-pattern balding and arthritis. Aunt Ginny had a few too many drinks during life and Liz isn't going to enjoy her brewery tour as much as she thought. The rest are out in Western Mass."

"Can we stop on the way home?"

"Nope, it's four hours in the other direction. I'll have to ask Mark for some time off."

"That works. The sooner the better, you know?"

She made me promise. You could see her running calculations in her head, those flickering pages on the calendar and my presence on each major holiday. A worried look passed over her face at the prospect of only one more Christmas. Who would be her New Year's kiss in ten years? In twenty?

***

We passed a roadside shrine to a dead woman. Her framed photo hung on a cross mounted to the guardrail. Plastic flowers and garlands were draped about, but the reflective chintz wasn't what caught my eye. The purple petals of a nightshade bloom sprouted at the base of the vigil. When the Spirits claimed a life, nightshade grew on the spot, a symbol of penance paid.

"You think anyone would mind if I harvested that?" I asked, pointing to the flower.

It was my habit to transplant the flowers whenever I stumbled upon them. I kept a single ceramic jar filled with potting soil in the trunk for such occasions. You never knew what secrets a new specimen would yield.

"Really, Dave?"

"Yeah, why not? No one else is using it."

"That's not the point. How would you feel if someone dug up your nightshade?"

"If they were using it for science..."

"Still not cool. If you get permission, that's one thing, but definitely no otherwise. Consider what the Spirits will think," she replied as the purple flowers disappeared in my rearview mirror.

CHAPTER 12

When I stepped out of the Volvo, the repetitive crash of a slamming door resounded from the back of our house. The wind had risen, whipping leaves into a frenzy. Gusts tossed them in somersaults across the yard, plastering them to car windows. I could hear steel and glass reverberate off the jamb, drag open, and then slam closed as the wind hassled everything in its path. Jessica tilted her head toward the noise, eyebrows wrinkled, worry lines creasing her forehead. Had Lenny forgotten to close the back door after another hurried entrance with a new woman in his arms?

Then it hit me. The back door was made of wood. It wouldn't sound like that.

I ran, nearly tripping over the roots pushing through the patchy lawn along the side of our house. I rounded the corner, Jessica's footfalls at my heels. Out back, the greenhouse door was torn open, lock dangling on the bent clasp, useless against the pull of the gale. The brick path was hard beneath my feet. As I reached for the door, it swung open, catching my outstretched hand. The pain was quick, thin metal slicing through layers of skin. I ignored it, stepping through the doorway.

My eyes hurried down the rows of potted nightshade. Many had their blossoms torn by the whip of the wind, stalks bent so their faces lay on the table. Some of the berries had burst, splattering the back wall in a dark purple smear, pieces of their skin black against the sheeting. I inhaled sharply as I noticed the ground. Three sparrows lay on their backs, twig-like feet extended into the air at the base of our prized belladonna. Their carcasses were fresh, as if death had just crept into their bodies. They weren't riddled with maggots or beetles. It was obvious they had eaten the smallest of the berries.

In that moment, I saw myself prostrate on the ground, sunlight filtering over my rigid corpse. It could have been me. I could have been the one, clutching my throat, Clint's promise of safety rotting at the back of my mind. What would I have seen before expiring? The hallucinations of a thousand faces, vines curling around my limbs, my throat swelling shut, the terror walled up within me.

"I can't believe he left the door open," Jessica said, placing a hand on my kneeling shoulder. "He knows how long you've been working on this."

I knew he did, but my mind wasn't on Lenny. I believed the flower would have worked. That the myth wasn't superstition put in place to make people feel better about their mortality. I touched the broken stalks, felt the cold skin of the flowers as they drooped, wilting where they had once swelled full of life. Even if I had been a skeptic, I had faith in Clint. That his madness was founded in concrete truths. I didn't know what to believe anymore.

"Who knows," I replied, plucking one of the flowers from the vine.

"What happened to the birds?" she asked.

"They ate the berries."

"Weren't they supposed to be fine, even for smaller animals to eat?"

"That's what I thought," I said, plucking a bloom off the vine, then another, attempting to keep their stalks intact. I removed all the blossoms until the brown tendrils lay bare, their thin necks headless. It looked like any other plant. Nondescript. Innocent. I held my bouquet at arm's length, not wanting the ruptured berries to get on my skin or the opened wound on my hand.

"What are you going to do with those?" Jessica asked.

"Show them to Lenny. Bring them to Clint. I don't know, put them in a vase on the windowsill. They're quite beautiful when you forget they're toxic," I replied.

"Are you okay?"

Jessica's hand smoothed up my back, tucking beneath my shoulder.

"Nope."

My hands shook. The flowers wavered, as if tremors coursed up their spines. I hadn't been that angry since the day we buried Clint, and I attempted to fight off his entire family. I wanted to burn the greenhouse down. Char the memory until it was blackened beyond recognition. I didn't know where to place the blame. Lenny? Clint? The only recipient readily available waited back inside the apartment, probably balling some drugged-up chick he met over the internet. I handed the flowers to Jessica and walked toward the house.

"What are you going to do?" she asked, looking at me, then down at the flowers.

"I needed a final reason to kick Lenny out, this is it," I replied, moving toward the door.

"Shouldn't we, you know, talk about this? Maybe clean up the birds? See what plants are still okay?"

"No. I'm doing it now."

There was finally something I could control in my life, something unseen hands couldn't morph and mold into whatever shape they pleased. Lenny's disregard for my flowers, the one thing I left him to care for, proved he wasn't much of a friend anyway. I opened the door just as the wind died off. The trees stood still. The whistling that sang through the rusting gutters held its breath.

CHAPTER 13

"Who?" I asked, anger abating as I looked at Lenny in disbelief.

"I can't remember," Lenny stammered. He was sitting at the edge of his bed, red satin sheets wound around himself like a cocoon. His hair fell in his face, visible through a seam in the tangled bedding. It was the first time I had seen him lose hold of his calculated composure. He looked pathetic in sweatpants and a tie-dye tee. The shirt draped around him like a ship's sail on a windless day, his thin frame too meager to fill the space. The contemplative artist was gone. The suave ladies' man was buried beneath bed sheets, tears dry on his cheeks.

I sat beside him, trying to focus on the matter at hand, but it was hard. Lenny's ceiling was painted like a modern Sistine Chapel, divided panels depicting stories of death. He recreated infamous Spirit encounters in minute detail. There was Carlton Shea, the man who had been tied to an anchor and tossed overboard. Helane Grieux, her seven day public starvation in the town center depicted on a sunny spring morning. Alex Jefferson, skinned alive at the pulpit of the old Methodist church. If I looked closely, I could see our old classmates among them, Mia, Brent, Ben, and Mike. Clint was up there too.

Lenny left a few spaces blank, waiting for a new muse to fill the opening.

"You don't remember the girl's name who you got pregnant?" Jessica asked, leaning in the doorway, arms crossed over her chest.

"No, I don't," Lenny replied. "She's in my phone as 'Eyes.' That's it. We were drunk. I can't believe she even remembers my name or where we live."

"And she's sure she's pregnant? That you're the guy?" I asked.

"As sure as you can be," Lenny said. "She says she's a month late. That she took the test and it came back positive. Even sent me a picture of it."

He handed me his phone. On the screen was a photograph of a thin plastic pregnancy test with the pink positive plus sign centered in the shot. There was no arguing with that. Lenny took back his phone and hurled it into a mess of pillows at the end of the bed.

"So what's your plan?" Jessica asked. "You're going to take care of her, right? Set up the doctor's appointments, get prenatal vitamins, go to Lamaze class and all that? I can get you some information from work if you want. A list of providers, some pamphlets on local resources for young parents."

Lenny looked up from the floor, eyes barely visible through tangled hair. The look on his face said he didn't want her there, witnessing this low, likely misunderstanding her concern as mockery. If there was one thing Jessica wanted to avoid, it was the suffering of a child, even if it was the offspring of roommate nemesis number one.

"I don't know. I haven't had time to think about her. I can't have a kid," Lenny said, raising his arms to the paintings adorning the ceiling. "I have so much to do. Such a short life. I thought she was on the pill…"

"You're really thinking about yourself right now?" Jessica asked.

"It looks that way, doesn't it?" he replied, voice dripping disdain.

I was stuck between the two. Yeah, Lenny was being a shit about the situation, but it sucks to be in the situation in the first place, granted he should have worn protection. And as for Eyes, whatever her real name was, I couldn't imagine what it would be like to carry Lenny's child, or anyone's child for that matter.

With the sudden news, I hadn't been able to mention the greenhouse. The wilted flowers dropped from my mind the instant I saw Lenny wrapped in his protective cocoon. It wasn't the right time to kick him out. I wasn't heartless.

"It's not about you anymore. If you've got a kid, you focus on them, even if that means you have to give up your art," Jessica said.

"I'm never giving up my art," Lenny replied.

"You're being selfish."

"At least I'm not forcing her to have an abortion or something."

"You don't get it," Jessica said, her voice underscored with disgust. "Good luck with that."

Then she turned from the doorway and walked down the hall, slamming our bedroom door. I moved from the bed, grabbing a chair from Lenny's desk littered with preemptive sketches for future projects, a heap of innumerable Spirit masks smiling up at me. I swung the chair around, facing Lenny head on.

"She's right about a few things, man," I started.

"I know, and it kills me," he replied. "I never wanted to have a kid. What kind of dad knowingly leaves his son when he's five? I've only got a few more years left, that's it. It's not like I'll be able to raise him or be there when he needs me."

"Or she... But you could be there for a while. That's a start."

"I would have used protection if I knew. It's not like I'm adverse to wearing condoms, but she said it would be fine."

"Things don't always work the way you want them to. Are you going to meet with her anytime soon, you know, to discuss this whole thing, maybe learn her name?"

Lenny chuckled a single forced breath.

"Her name would be a good start."

"And I don't think you have to give up your art. That's how you make your money. It would be more than enough to support your child. Jessica isn't always right," I said.

"That was my plan," Lenny replied.

"Good."

I rose from my chair, returning it to the drawing desk. Lenny unfolded a layer of his cocoon, sitting erect, staring at the painting above his head. He focused on one blank space, white as the original walls.

"When you find out, I want to paint you there," Lenny said.

"I'm flattered," I replied.

"Really though. I'm rooting for you, how else am I going to finish the ceiling?"

"I'll get on it as soon as I can."

Lenny pointed to an adjacent space.

"You know who I'm painting there?" he asked.

"Don't tell me," I replied, knowing the answer. "Just let that go. Jessica's not going to give in. Especially now."

"She might. You never know."

But I did know. Once Jessica set her mind to something, it was permanent, dry cement, a line penciled in the Spirits' book. Nothing short of witnessing her death would unveil his prized material. The last thing I needed was for him to continue to pester and pry. She wasn't going to let the pregnancy affect our plans, not after what Lenny said. But I couldn't do it at that moment, especially not with the news. I hated feeling guilt for something I hadn't done. What kind of guy kicks a soon-to-be-father out of his house? That wouldn't look good to the Spirits, and Jessica wouldn't want that either.

And who knows, parenthood could be the catalyst we both prayed for.

Lenny thanked me for the support. I told him I would cool things down with Jessica, but he didn't care. He called her a few names I would never repeat, but I reminded him he hadn't presented his predicament in the most tactful manner. She sometimes forgot Lenny had feelings, that he was an actual person, not an amalgamation of character flaws. I told him to let me know if he needed anything. He pointed to the ceiling's blank space.

***

The door to our bedroom was locked. I wrestled with the knob, twisting and nudging until the mechanisms clinked in surrender. Inside, Jessica lay in bed, propped up, comforter around her waist. As I began to strip off my gym shorts and t-shirt, she drew her copy of *Women's Health* up between us, a paper thin wall graffitied with toned yogis in fluorescent spandex. I kicked my laundry under the bed and peeled back layers of blankets. Our new air conditioner hummed in the window, the room kept a chill sixty-five.

I moved close to Jessica. She moved close to the wall. The magazine rustled like a theater curtain, signaling the end of a play in a swoop of red satin.

"What's up?" I asked.

She continued to read, or kept up the appearance of reading.

"Is it really that engrossing?" I asked after a moment of slow page turning. I reached out, my hand intended for her bare shoulder. It landed on a vacant pillow. Jessica had slipped from bed, standing at its edge in her red cotton sleeping shorts and tank top. The magazine was abandoned on the nightstand.

"Not tonight," she said. "You said you were going to kick him out, and now this."

"I was, but he's having a kid. I couldn't do it. Let's give it a week. Things will settle down and I'll tell him what's what," I replied, not quite sure I believed my own words.

"You know that isn't true."

Her voice was calm. Muscles tensed, a thin vein pressed against her neck. I could tell she was fighting an urge to yell, to let her built up dissatisfaction boil over, engulfing everything in our room. But that wasn't her. She wasn't the yelling type.

"It is. He's gone. I swear," I began.

"I know you're trying to be a good friend, but what about us? How are we going to move forward if we're always stuck in the shadow of that fucking narcissist? It's not like this is a surprise. When you sleep with that many women, it's inevitable. Would you feel bad for a knife thrower who finally struck an artery?"

"I mean, I'd feel bad for the assistant…"

"And Lenny's not the assistant. I can't stand how he treats women. I see it from their angle. You don't. You can never get pregnant. I can. The guy is ruining some girl's life and you're just there, patting him on the back, telling him it will be alright."

"Hey, I said I'll talk to him, and that's what I'll do. But I can still be supportive. He needs someone pushing him in the right direction," I said.

"He can get support somewhere else. Tell him to take accountability for once and move out. Find his new family a home," she replied, tentatively shifting the sheets, clearing space for her body. She had this look on her face of complete disgust, as if she was looking at a carcass crawling with worms. "You know I love you, but you can't protect assholes. He's like every other guy I've reported at work. The abuse. It seems like nothing from the outside, but it's different when you're on the receiving end."

"Okay. I get it. Can you just come back to bed? It's been a rough day. We both need a good snuggle and some sleep."

"Can you just move over? I need space," she said.

I was in the middle of the bed, one hand planted in her warm outline, staring up in disbelief. My mouth was dry, tongue searching for any well of moisture hidden within. We always slept curled together. I could barely remember a night where she wasn't tucked against my chest, arms forming an impenetrable knot of elbows and skin.

Shifting to my side, I slid away, leaving a stretch of bare mattress between us. I promised I would give her the space she wanted, offering to sleep on the couch. *No*, she mumbled, before easing herself beneath the covers, making sure our bodies wouldn't brush. I didn't think it was possible, but I could feel the air between us, like a body of water hovering there, on the cusp of becoming mist or steam. The temperatures fluctuating ever so slightly, humid, then chill. Gooseflesh spotted my arms, sweat crested my lower back before sprouting along my spine.

I knew Jessica wouldn't let me touch her. And I couldn't blame her. I shouldn't have waited so long to make a move. There's only so many times you can put something off. First cemeteries, now Lenny. I wanted everything to move forward, but now I was waist deep in a stagnant pond, rotting fish floating around me. With the Spirits looming, witnessing every choice and action, I felt choked, left dangling, my feet unable to touch bottom.

At the thought, I reached for Jessica, but let my hand fall short. No embrace was going to fix this. I almost stood, shaking off the sheets to clear my head in the greenhouse, but then I remembered the state of the nightshade. All that black blood coating the walls. I'd have to obtain another specimen to move forward. One or two of our prized plants remained undamaged. Something could be done, but was it worth it?

CHAPTER 14

The first month I worked in the cemeteries, robbers ransacked the tombs. They broke headstones, snapping thin granite, extracting the copper shafts running through their reinforced spines. The metal's scrap value was at a high, employment rates approaching an all-time low. Sections of the cemetery looked like monks in prayer, stones bent to the ground, kneeling with their heads pressed against the earth. Weeds grew around their edges, leaving limp stalks to curl over fallen markers. My mower blades nicked their corners whenever I got close, sending a cloud of gray particles into the air, the taste of stone dust settling on my tongue. They lay in repose until we got the work order to reset them.

We created cement casts, molding protective gray shells around their severed extremities. Others required long screws and steel plates to keep steady. One base had been reduced to rubble by a negligent snow plow driver. I dug a level ditch a foot into the ground, placing the remaining stone upright before filling the groove with instant cement.

The worst vandalism occurred in the Chase mausoleum, the giant marble crypt at the cemetery's center. Bolt cutters mangled the rusted lock. Strong hands pried the steel bars of the door from its frame, twisting the once gilded designs of flowers and thorns into unrecognizable shapes. The same hands wrenched covers off caskets and pocketed a pocket watch and several rings from the skeletal remains. Mrs. Chase still cried over the lost necklace that held a hand-drawn silhouette of her young love encased in a golden frame. Mr. Chase always said he looked better with a little age on his bones, that I shouldn't pay his wife any mind as I trimmed around their home.

We had to weld a new lock in place and wrap a stainless-steel chain through the door handle, sealing it tight against a new generation of grave robbers.

We never found the guys who originally ransacked the Chases' mausoleum. I always looked for her necklace at flea markets and yard sales, but it never showed up.

***

Early one morning, I found the chain stripped from the mausoleum door lying tangled around the base of an overgrown arborvitae a few stones away. I would never have noticed it if it wasn't the time of year to trim back the new growth. The padlock hung from the last link, the steel hinge stuck in place. There was no damage, no dents from hammer blows or scars from crowbars. The locksmith in town said anyone with a slight knowledge of picking locks could have freed the clasp and rattled the tumblers out of place.

Around the same time, the couple's relative I had seen on previous occasions started visiting the tomb more frequently.

I could never place her age, somewhere between the first and last day of high school. Mr. and Mrs. Chase lit up when she sat cross legged on their front porch. The missus would bend close to hear the girl's soft-spoken stories. I waved from time to time. It was always returned. She must have been their great-great-granddaughter, paying respects, maybe searching for an answer to her own fate if she was old enough. I found buttercups clustered beneath their doorway, tiger lilies wrapped with black hair elastics. She made neat piles of gray moss at the base of the marble step. She peeled at it with her fingernails, cleaning the facade of the aged mausoleum. She was not the type of person you would expect to be a burglar.

A month later, Mark saw her hurriedly retracting a clothing line draped with drying jeans and black t-shirts. It hung from the columns of the mausoleum, stretching to a neighboring oak tree. The Levis and crewnecks came down in a hurry. She balled them up in a nest of sleeves and pant legs, sprinted into the mausoleum, and pulled the heavy metal door closed. She wasn't quick enough to dodge Mark's gaze as he sipped his morning coffee from the comfort of the dump truck

"I'll give her another day," Mark said. "Maybe she'll move out now that she knows we've seen her."

"It's not like she's bothering them. Could we just leave her?" I asked.

"It's got nothing to do with the Chases. If the police found out, it would be really hard to explain why we let a minor live with a couple corpses. It's a rough life trying to feed two kids with the wages they pay at Dunkin Donuts."

"Hey, you're more qualified than that. Don't sell yourself short. I hear Home Depot has a great benefits package."

"Regardless, I'd prefer to keep this job."

"You've got a point."

***

One day passed. Two slipped by without her blur of black hair shifting in or out of the mausoleum. But on the third day, I caught her shuffling a grocery bag full of canned goods behind the door's stained glass. Part of me wanted to let her stay, let her enjoy her meals between Mr. and Mrs. Chase's twin coffins, sharing stories of his days at sea and her days waiting on the widow's walk for his return. Mark's daughter's face hovered in my mind, her crowded teeth, the braces they had been saving up for over the past year. She always covered her mouth when she laughed.

I went to get Mark.

***

"You knock," he insisted.

"You're the boss. Shouldn't you handle evictions?" I asked.

"No. I handle the lower staff members, making sure they know where they stand. Now get to it."

I knocked on the bars. Mr. Chase swept through the door, the wine-tinted glass and thick metal bars sifting through his legs and torso.

"What can I do for you, Dave?" he asked, tipping his captain's hat forward.

An engraving etched into the bottom step of the monument, unpicked flecks of moss blossoming in the hollows, read *Lost At Sea*, the tagline that followed many sailors into the grave. He'd been a captain on a merchant ship that ferried whale oil between Nantucket and Britain. He'd tell you the story about his ship going down if you asked. How the waves and the sky became one black mass, seeping through the boards, snapping masts as it surged over the starboard rail.

"Sorry to bother you, but we've seen a girl coming in and out of here. It looks like she's living with you guys," I said.

"Oh, she's just visiting. A welcomed guest. Our, umm, second cousin's great ah...niece. One of my last living relatives. Different last names though, through marriage. Not her marriage, but..."

"We bolt the doors to keep people out," Mark said from over my shoulder. "Health codes. You know that. It doesn't matter if she's related or not."

"Everything's tidy," Mr. Chase said, taken aback.

"Could you ask her to come out here?" I asked. "Make sure she knows we're not angry or anything. We're not calling the police, or her parents, or whomever. It's just something we have to do."

Mr. Chase merely sighed, slumped his shoulders, pushed his hat back to its original tilt, and passed through the door.

"You really should let her stay," Mrs. Chase said, poking her curly head through the stained-glass window to the left of the door. The russet hues tinged her cheeks and forehead a deep crimson as she talked. The woman died at least thirty years after her husband. While he looked in his forties, she must have been on the far side of seventy when the Spirits showed up. Her translucent skin hung limp on her frame. Crows left their footprints in the sand around her eyes.

She dragged the rest of her body into the sunlight, pulling her broad hips through the window as if it offered resistance.

"We can't," Mark said.

"Really?" Mrs. Chase answered. "We paid for the building, didn't we?"

"Whaling's now illegal, isn't it?" Mark replied.

She looked as if she was going to take a swing at him, jaw clenched, fists held taut at her hips.

"It's fine. It's fine," came the voice of the girl from behind the door.

The hinges creaked as the amalgamation of steel and rust swung forward. I had never seen her so close. The shortened distance clarified her age: sixteen, seventeen. No older. Her black hair hung down her back. Thick bangs obscured her forehead. Her face was layered with freckles that were slightly darker than her tan skin. A black t-shirt clung to her shoulders. Above her left wrist was a self-drawn tattoo of a skeleton in a flowing gown, feet performing a dance step as one hand held the hem of the dress. It was good, as if a professional had etched the lines, but she was too young. I'd guess she was right-handed.

My eyes lingered on a fading black and blue bruise on the side of her neck. When she caught me, her hand wandered up to the mark, obscuring it with her palm.

With the opening of the door came the faint waft of mall-scented perfume, the sweet flowers that reminded me of high school romance.

"I figured you guys would catch on," she said.

"It's nothing against you. Just can't have someone staying out here. It can't be good for your health living in the dark like that," Mark said.

"It's not like I'm hurting anyone," she said, looking up at Mrs. Chase. "They should have a say in this."

"Wish I could help you there, but no. The cops would eventually learn you're here and evict you. Maybe even put you in jail for the night: vagrancy, trespassing, defiling the dead," Mark said.

"You call this defiling?" she said, stepping aside so the inner room of the mausoleum was exposed. Inside there was a sleeping bag unfurled between two caskets on lifted podiums. A rickety table draped with a blue checkered tablecloth stood at the back wall, a single place setting on top. A vase with blue irises sat next to the Bible originally entombed with the couple. The bag of groceries sat in the corner. The light from the back window played off the casket's varnish.

"She's got you there," I said to Mark. "We'll help you move your stuff. We can throw all of it in our dump truck and drop it off at your house. The truck bed's clean, I promise."

The girl scanned the horizon looking for the truck with a look of disgust, as if the bed was filled with trash or wet mulch. She shook her head, pivoting on her heel. The door closed in one fluid motion, slamming with the echoing finality of the cavernous granite room within.

"We can't let you—" Mark began to say.

"I'm just getting my things together. Give me a few minutes, okay," she said.

"Of course," I answered, looking at Mark, attempting to pat down his anger with a wave of my hand. She was just a kid. I hated the idea of being any harsher than need be.

The shuffling sound of clothes being shoved into a gym bag came from behind the stone walls. The light swish of canvas sounded as she dismantled her camp. The click of aluminum cans and a muttered "fuck" followed. A single can had scurried across the floor, crashing into the other side of the door with a sloshing gargle.

"Just leave the spill. I'll get that after you leave," I called into the mausoleum, opening the door without an invitation.

The single room was dark, the light tinted from the stained glass. You could see the work done by the grave robbers. Brass handles were now vacant nail holes and crowbarred gouge marks. One coffin had been dragged so it dangled off the slab of stone beneath. It appeared to be on the edge of teetering to the ground. Gashes tore up the light woodgrain resting underneath the varnish where hurried hands had pried the boxes open. With the blue checkered cloth stripped away, the decaying wooden table stood bare between the caskets.

The girl was on her knees between the two coffins, brushing odd beans from her sleeping bag. She began rolling up the flannel fabric once the gravy was daubed up with a stray sock. Mr. Chase paced around her as she finished tidying the space, muttering life advice as fast as it would come. *Now don't mind your mother, I'm sure she means well...*

"If you don't have space in your backpack, I can go grab a trash bag from the shed. Not saying your stuff is junk or anything, just it's the only thing I've got to offer," I interjected from the door.

"I've got it," she replied, rising from her knees, sleeping bag tucked under her arm. "I dragged it all out here without your help."

"Sorry. If you don't mind me asking, and feel free to keep it to yourself, why are you living here?" I asked, leaning over to pick up a forgotten can by the edge of the doorway. I wanted to ask about the bruise on her neck, but didn't know a tactful segue.

"Any reason you want. Mom's a nutcase. Dad's dead. Boyfriend dumped me. Dog got hit by a moving van. I've got a list around here somewhere if you want to read it," she replied, milling about her bag of cans.

"Really?"

"No. Why would I tell you any of that? I've never met you before."

"Oh," I said as she pushed the door open and shouldered by, sleeping bag brushing my chest. It smelled of something sweet. The girl must have emptied her bottle of perfume in the mausoleum to overpower the stench of decay. Even if the Chases' bodies had fallen to dust, the damp smell of mildew would cling to every nook and cranny.

"And don't follow me," she said over her shoulder. She walked down the road between rows of stones. I wanted to tell her we didn't have the time, but held back. Dandelions crept up between the stones, opening their yellow, unwanted smirks to the sun's rays. Poison ivy tendrils had already claimed two stones at the back corner of the cemetery. I'd suggested renting goats to chomp on the invasives, but Mark said it wasn't in the budget.

"What's your name?" I asked as she neared the end of the road.

Over her shoulder, she flipped us the bird, remaining silent.

It wasn't the ideal setting for a first impression, so I avoided passing judgement. She was willing to sleep in a cemetery over staying at home. The backstory couldn't be pleasant.

***

Clint slumped against his headstone, hands placed on top as if holding himself up. Every angle of his body spoke of longing. He looked like a man who hadn't slept in months, even though the dead no longer required sleep. The distance between Carla and himself was wearing him thin. Just looking at Clint made me want to reconsider what I had to say, but I couldn't get around it.

"I think it's going to take longer than we thought," I said, taking a bite of my tuna sandwich. "The flowers don't look like the pictures you showed me."

"Really?" Clint replied, lifting his head. "I thought you said they were looking great."

"I was wrong, the berries aren't small enough."

"Well, that might not matter, the myth only mentions the flowers. How's the coloration?"

"Not great."

Clint sighed and slid from his stone. He moved to my side, feet hovering an inch off the ground.

"I guess another month or two won't kill me," Clint said, charting out figures with his fingers. "Hybridization is difficult, and nightshade doesn't make it any easier, the hard seed coat, the select number of flowers capable of hybridization," Clint said, pausing as if he was watching the flower blossom and wilt in the air.

I already lied to Clint about Lenny's failed watch of the nightshade, claiming he stuck to our procedures, that of course he kept the door locked and that no, of course I didn't find a small flock of sparrows dead on the floor. I couldn't let him down like that. Before I had even spoken, I made up my mind to take the next step into my own hands.

I requested several books on accelerating artificial selection from the library. I'd further the research Clint had already done. I had all of his notebooks in a drawer beside my desk. There was nothing he knew that I didn't have access to. I always thought we could have been doing things more efficiently. My vision was coming into focus. There was just one problem.

"Did Carla's parents ever dig up the nightshade by the pool?" I asked, my voice more hesitant than I intended.

"No. I built that shrine around it, remember? I spent months on it. Why would they dig it up?" he asked.

"I don't know, some people hate reminders."

"Yeah, why bring that up though?" he asked.

"I just wanted to compare our plant to hers. Chart some differences."

"I see," Clint said, scratching his chin. "Just call her mom before you go over there, I heard she hasn't been doing well."

I nodded even though that was the furthest thing from my mind.

With a sigh, I looked over to where my father's grave stood. For a second, his profile was visible, leaning in our direction, hand cupped around his ear. Then he was gone, only the faintest trace of an after image lingering in the air. Most of the time when I visited Clint, he stayed in his coffin. I had only seen him once before when I was telling Clint about the trip to Maine. Other than that, he avoided me.

"Did you see him?" I asked.

"Yeah, he's been listening since you got here," Clint replied.

"Why didn't you tell me?"

"Then you wouldn't have seen him at all. If he doesn't want to talk, he's not going to."

"Have you talked to him?"

"Yeah."

"What did he say?"

"Not much, you know. This and that. How strange it is to be dead. How much he misses a good Western omelet. Stuff like that."

"He always loved breakfast," I said, remembering childhood Saturday mornings, my father's signature cheddar-drenched omelets before us as we watched cartoons. I never understood how the man I'd known as a kid had become the one who presently hid from me every day. I never would have done that to my own child. "Nothing about me though?"

"Nada. Sorry, man, I've tried my best to get something out of him. He won't ease up, but I doubt he'll hold out forever."

"I know," I replied. "I appreciate you trying."

"It's the least I can do. Not many people get to complete their life's work after they're dead. I'm the one who owes you."

CHAPTER 15

The pool filter coughed by the hedges. I parted spruce needles delicately to ensure no branch would snap back in my face. I didn't want Carla's mother to notice my presence. Sap shellacked my palm as I moved through the body of the bush. Leaving the shadows of the overgrown hedge encircling the property, I found the lawn unmowed, a far cry from how Carla's father once kept it.

The house and property had fallen into disrepair since her death. It didn't help that her father followed two years after the Spirits drowned Carla in the hot tub.

The house's nearest gable end leaned outward, as if trying to slouch away from the foundation. Shingles littered the grass, thrown off like unwanted clothes in the summer heat. The porch steps were missing boards. Something with wings roosted in the still fan at the attic's peak.

A single lamp illuminated a second-story window. I could just make out the image of Carla's mother reclined in a chair, back to the dark night. As a child, I had heard rumors about widows and widowers taking to their homes after their partner's death, never to leave again. I never thought it would happen to Carla's mother. I heard she hadn't taken a step off the front porch in years, having all necessities delivered weekly. Her BMW rested on flat tires in the root-devoured driveway.

As I circled the pool, I couldn't help looking down into the green-tinged water. Squirrels, mice, and other small creatures floated on the surface. The only motion was the paddling breath of the filter. I gagged as the smell of rotting flesh and stagnant water met my nose. Lifting my t-shirt to cover my lower face, I moved on.

I remembered seeing the nightshade on the evening of Carla's burial. Her parents hosted a reception. Pizza. Cola. The dividing of knickknacks that had once meant something to their daughter, but would now act as a memento for her friends. The purple flower knelt between the pool and the covered hot tub. Now only the faintest outline was clear in the dark, the moon a mere slit over my shoulder.

Off in the distance stood the shrine Clint had constructed. Garden statues peered out above the tall grass. Flameless candles lay on their sides. Framed photographs of her had grown waterlogged and discolored from torrential rains. It looked like it had been untouched for years. I shifted my gaze from the dulled memorial to the flower, keeping focused.

If I was going to continue Clint's work, I'd need a new subject. My favorite library book, *The Memory of Plants*, said flowers resulting from Spirit contact retained a certain essence of the dead. The book went on to say when herbalists and shamans concocted tinctures, they preferred to use ingredients with ties to both mortals and the dead, that it made them more potent. What tie was greater than the one between Clint and Carla?

I leaned against the wooden wall of the hot tub. I expected to feel a coolness to the wood, but the water was warm, forcing heat through the retaining walls. Did Carla's mother still use the tub? I shook off the thought, unsettled by the overlapping images of her mother's present and Carla's past.

In my left hand I carried a ceramic pot large enough to contain the nightshade's root ball. Inside was a trowel I took from our greenhouse. Glancing up to the illuminated window, I noted that Carla's mother was still there, reading something in her lap, oblivious to my presence.

I began to dig, sifting softly through the soil that encased the plant. I avoided severing roots, running my fingers beneath the ground when I feared damage to the tendrils. The plant felt sickly in my grasp as I lifted it from the soil. Unlike the specimen Clint and I had nurtured since birth, this one lacked the thickness about the vines, the blossoms droopy and scant. With a last tug, the roots' grasp slipped and the nightshade dangled in my hand. Scooping a few handfuls of soil into the pot, I lowered the plant into its new home.

As I began to rise, taking leave of the hot tub's hidden securities, the screen door on the deck slid open. Footsteps plodded over the remaining boards, taking the stairs with care. My heart leapt. I was frantic to bolt, but there was no time. Carla's mother would see me. Instead, I dropped flat on my stomach as the footsteps approached, my line of sight obscured by the bulk of the tub, which I prayed meant I, too, was unseen.

"Another night," I heard Carla's mother sigh as she loosened the ties holding down the hot tub's insulating cover. "How many more?"

I could not recall a time when I had heard someone speak with so much sadness. My heart deflated. Her voice was weary, laden with unimaginable weight, akin to patients on their deathbed, not a woman of fifty.

The cover tumbled over the side of the tub, one edge landing before me as the thick canvas folded in half. The water hummed on the other side of the wooden walls. A bathrobe fell to the lawn with the hushed collapse of linen. Then Carla's mother slowly immersed herself in the chlorinated water. She hummed a disjointed tune, which broke off as a coughing fit stirred in her chest.

"If only..." she said to the night air, "if only I could hold my head down long enough."

Then there was a sudden rush of water spraying over the sides. A hot wave splashed across my back, the sudden jolt firing my muscles in rapid succession. I couldn't see her, but I knew Carla's mother had sunk beneath the surface. I could practically feel her submerged body through the wall at my side. I should have taken that moment to bolt, to sprint out of the yard and abandon the nightshade, but Clint's face appeared in my mind, reminding me of my promise. So instead, I began to count. Ten. Twenty. I reached sixty-three before Carla's mother rose above water.

She sputtered for a moment.

"Then again, it's better I don't. Who'd suffer for my decision? Lois' kid doesn't deserve this. Jenna. No, she's nice enough. Hank's daughter never came to visit like she promised, but is that fair?" she asked.

It was clear this conversation had played out before between the voices in her head. The voices that kept her homebound. The Spirits tolerated suicide less than other sins. Taking your own life when so many others begged to have theirs prolonged, or restored, was an insult.

Time coalesced as I hid. It could have been five minutes. It could have been two hours. Every part of my body felt stretched, ligaments and muscles pulled taut, beginning to fray from the tension. I contemplated showing myself, apologizing for the intrusion, but knowing her state, I couldn't predict her reaction. She might have carried a knife. Or she might have been naked. I didn't know which would be worse.

"Towel, did you remember the towel tonight?" her mother asked.

"No, no, you didn't," her own voice replied.

"Foolish."

"I just hoped tonight would be the night we wouldn't need one."

"As did I," she stammered, rising from the water. I could feel the reverberations through the wall as she groped about, steadying herself to climb from the water. I inched myself back through the grass, retreating from the cover that lay before me, waiting for her to hoist it from the ground, replacing it on top. I held my breath. Only the hum of the filters disturbed the night. Carla's mother was unmoving just beyond the lip of the tub.

Then her footsteps slunk away, muffled at first by the lawn, then hollow and resonant as she crossed the deck. She paused for a moment. I imagined she was taking one last look at the shrine off in the distance, remembering her daughter, the happiness her life once held. Then the door creaked shut at her back, leaving me alone with the dead rodents in the pool and the sickly nightshade clasped to my chest.

I held my position for another minute, making sure she wasn't watching from beyond the screen door. Then I jogged to the hedgerow, opening a gap between the branches wide enough to allow the flowers room to pass. Before I stepped through the overgrown bushes, I turned and looked toward the single illuminated window. Carla's mother was there once again, seated, back turned as if she had never left. I could see that her gray hair was soaked as it clung to her neck and back. I tried to make out the rise of her breath, but she was so still, almost like she was dead.

For her sake, I almost wished she had been.

CHAPTER 16

"Can you please take that off the wall?" Jessica asked, pointing to Lenny's latest painting, a portrait of Clint a few seconds before the bull's horn plunged into his chest. "I know he means a lot to you and everything. It just makes me uncomfortable. I had another nightmare about it last night. If you want to leave it up, it's fine, but…"

She trailed off.

I wanted to say at least she wasn't having nightmares about her own death, but I kept the point to myself. The night before, after returning home from Carla's house, I woke twice. The first a result of an electric chair, currents coursing through my body. The second, a night at the local theater, The Cape Playhouse's rendition of *Twelfth Night*, a gun to the back of my head, Abraham Lincoln style. Sometimes dreams got away from me. According to my mom's family tree, we weren't related to John Wilkes Booth. Anyway, I saw a documentary about the man who was linked to the assassin. Got the poor guy during an off-Broadway showing of *Seussical*.

It had been two weeks since we returned from Maine. Two weeks in which I hadn't brought myself to evict Lenny. It still bothered Jessica. I could see it in the way she looked at him when he walked about our apartment in his bath towel, when he sat across from her at the dinner table. She only mentioned his leaving once since the night of our argument. She never liked to quarrel. Her forced kindness weighed more heavily on me than any outright rejection ever could.

I walked over to the portrait, lifting it gently, freeing the metal twine from the hammered hook behind.

"I mean," Jessica began to say. "You can put it somewhere else. Like, in the basement. Whenever you want to think about Clint, you can go down and look at him. Make a little shrine and everything. I'll help."

"Maybe," I replied, tucking the canvas into the gap between our dresser and the wall.

"Are you still planning on coming to CrossFit with me today?" Jessica asked. "You can fill Cath's spot."

Two weeks ago Cath had met with an unfortunate end. The Spirits snuck up on her in the sauna after a particularly vigorous workout. They locked the door and turned up the heat. When the janitor found her, her skin had become the same as an aged hotdog, shriveled and pocked, tanned to an inhuman orange. She was the only member of their class that hadn't discovered their fate. That was the trend with their members. No one wanted to exercise if they weren't going to live long, wasting hours on ellipticals, throwing backs out over mangled deadlifts. I was unsure if there was even a point of me joining the class, my uncertain outcome clearly separating me from the rest of the group. But my attendance would make Jessica happy, and I'd been failing in that department for weeks.

"Yeah, I'm still coming," I replied.

***

Before leaving for the gym, I checked on Carla's nightshade. The evening before, I cleared space in the far corner of the greenhouse, removing dead flowers, pushing back encroaching plants to give her some room. Retrieving a clean Q-tip, I transferred pollen from the older plants to the new, then vice versa. Hoping the cross-pollination would be successful, I ordered gibberellic acid to speed up the germination process. If the plants produced healthy seeds, I'd be able to quicken the sprouting, force a full bloom in record time.

After watering the plants, I checked the new lock hanging from the door, toying with the key, latching and unlatching the mechanism to make sure it would hold. I didn't want anything else to wander in while I was at the gym. First sparrows, then what? I dreaded neighborhood kids mistaking them for blueberries.

***

Eight of us stretched in the middle of an open gym as the instructor paced about. Workout equipment lined the walls, keeping the center clear. There was a rack of dumbbells. Ten pull-up bars protruded from the wall at various heights. A cluster of kettlebells huddled in the far corner. There were lifting stations for squats, tangled jump ropes, other ropes that looked like they belonged on sailboat rigging. The whole place smelled like sweat-soaked rubber, sour, with that high school gym undertone.

"So we're going to warm up with some Chelsea today," the instructor said. Jessica had mentioned the workouts had odd names. "Five pull-ups, ten push-ups, fifteen squats. Cycle through every minute for thirty minutes."

"What's that mean exactly?" I whispered to Jessica.

"You have to do those exercises thirty times in a row. Just follow me if you get lost. No one's going to notice if you miss one or two. You'll do great!" she replied.

Jessica wore a black sweat-wicking shirt with vibrant yellow side stripes that matched her shorts. Everyone else was dressed in a similar fashion, color-coordinated spandex in neon hues. I was the only one set apart in my black Adidas basketball shorts and Red City Radio t-shirt, none of which was going to enhance my performance.

"That's just the warm-up?" I asked.

"Yup, then we're going to do some lifts over there with the barbells. Don't worry about that now, focus on what's first," Jessica said. "The high you get afterward is so worth it."

"Any chance I can back out?"

"It's your call, but I think you should stay. It will be good for us," Jessica said, pinching my arm.

At that, the instructor walked to a basketball timer on a table. He pressed a few buttons and the clock glowed red, the number thirty illuminated through tinted glass. It echoed a harsh whistle and the numbers began to fall away as everyone around me jumped at chin-up bars, beginning to hoist themselves up and down with unwavering concentration.

I joined in a few reps behind, feeling the textured bar peeling away the calluses on my palms. I jerked myself up, lowering back down slowly, half the speed of Jessica to my right. By the time I was done with the chin-ups, she was already through the push-ups. She was able to rest for fifteen seconds between sets. I only completed ten squats before the timer whistled, signaling the start of the second round. More chin-ups. I told myself it was all for our relationship, to make up for Lenny-oriented disappointment.

At the halfway point, I was fighting back bile and phlegm. I wiped my sweat-soaked eyes whenever I got the chance. The salt burn grew more irritating with each set. By the end, I could feel my classmates' eyes on me as my arms shook, attempting to avoid falling from the chin-up bar.

"Ignore it," Jessica grunted between push-ups. "You're doing great. It's your first time."

The screech of the whistle had grown to a mocking cry. Penetrating, a drill burning hot through my eardrums. I choked on that rubber smell, the taste of my sweat slicking my throat. My hands were raw from the scraping of repetitive motion. On my last set of chin-ups, my hands were too damp to hold the metal and I slipped, sprawling downward, forcing the air from my chest as I hit the floor.

I lay there looking up at the ceiling, trying to relearn how to breathe. Shapes were fuzzy. Forms lacked the solidity I was accustomed to. Then a mask appeared, gazing down at me. It wasn't the conical beak of the plague doctor I had grown accustomed to seeing out of the corner of my eye. No, it was more humanlike. Everyone knew Spirit masks took on a dozen different shapes throughout a lifetime. I wasn't prepared for the new likeness. After the first mask appeared, three more joined, vacant black eyes staring down as I struggled to breathe, a thin scream escaping my lips.

My family had nothing to do with the exercise industry, no professional weightlifters or personal trainers to screw with their clientele. No one designing workout equipment, neglecting to inspect the stability of weighted cables. This shouldn't be how it happens. The faces bent closer. I hyperventilated, my lungs flailing, swelling, quivering inside my chest. I tried to roll to my side, but their legs were there, fencing me in. Death had found me unexpected, sprawled on sweat-soaked rubber matting, humiliated in front of Jessica and her muscle-bound friends.

Then a hand, wrapped in flesh, not bone, pressed down on my chest, forcing me to stop struggling.

"Dave, what are you doing? Just chill out."

The masks that had belonged to the Spirits moments before dissolved, bone overtaken by flushed skin. It was Jessica, her face pinched into lines of concern. As I lay there, the other gym goers moved away, taking their rest before the next workout.

"You should have sat the last one out if you were having a hard time," Jessica said, sitting next to me. "There's no shame in it. I used to die when I first did them, metaphorically speaking."

"I thought I had it," I replied, voice struggling from my throat.

"You've got to listen to your body. If you ignore how it feels, that's how you hurt yourself. I'd prefer if I didn't have to carry you out to the car after all this," she said with a smile.

"You won't," I replied, standing up. The muscles running down the top of my legs stretched taught, refusing to relax. There was a tense wrench in my shoulders, a numb throb about my armpits. "I just wanted to show you I could do it."

"And you did. Honestly, you did more than I thought you would, no offense."

"It's cool. I think I'll sit the rest of the class out though. Are you okay with that?"

"Of course. You can sit on the bench by the door and watch if you like."

"That sounds better than deadlifts."

Jessica nodded, pushing a string of damp hair from her face, tucking it back into her ponytail. She kissed me, a quick peck on the cheek. A few of the other members began to circle near an arrangement of barbells, some collared with twenty-five pound weights, others with forty-fives. Jessica nodded toward the lifting stations and I told her to go for it.

Clearing away a pile of foam rollers, I sat down on the bench. I opened the door to my right, fresh air slinking by, cooling the sweat on my bare legs and arms. I hated when I let myself go like that, when my immediate reaction dislodged from reality and was replaced with Spirit logic. I knew I wasn't going to die in a gym, not because of their intervention anyway. I could always drop a dumbbell on my head, and that would be my fault, not some lingering repercussion from a dead cousin. I let the thoughts of my death get to me, removing me from the present more and more, until I was merely watching myself live, not truly living. The black figures appearing in momentary flashes were more often coats on hangers, street signs, and strangers at bus stops. Not Spirits.

I focused, counting heartbeats, willing them to slow as I watched Jessica lift her barbell to her chest, then thrust it straight up above her head with a grunt. The toned muscles in her legs shifted into oval cuts, pressing against her pale skin. I followed the subtle alterations of her body, not in a sexual way, but in appreciation of something worked for, something honed. She once told me, every time she went to lift, she heard the voices of her old classmates calling her fat, reciting the names of sea mammals whenever she changed in the locker room. I told her it wasn't healthy to keep their ghosts around, but she said it kept her going. Watching her in that moment, I could hear their voices, each catty insult with a heft of the bar, the jabbing fingers pressing into her stomach as she let the weights drop to the mat.

***

After our shower, Jessica retrieved the painting of Clint from behind the dresser. She carried it delicately as I followed her down the basement steps, a few unused milk crates in hand and an old tablecloth draped over my shoulder. The basement was empty besides a washing machine and dryer, Lenny's dismantled drum set, and a stack of cardboard boxes inherited from my father. They contained the remnants of his life I couldn't part with, like the woven baskets he used to gather mushrooms or the old chess set he taught me on. All gathered cobwebs. The damp scent of mold from the rafters mixed with mothballs from the boxes.

Jessica lit a candle to ward off the aroma of age, replacing it with apples and cinnamon. With the added illumination, Jessica pulled the cord descending from the bare bulbs in the ceiling. The orange light flicked out, leaving us with the single flame to guide our steps.

In a blank space against the cinderblock wall, we arranged the crates, two high, two wide, draping the red tablecloth over the top. She leaned the framed painting so it stood straight, resting on the folded fabric. Clint looked out at our barren basement. The tablecloth brought to mind a matador's cape, crimson and billowing, much needed in the moment the painting depicted.

"Should we christen it or something?" Jessica asked. "It is a shrine, after all."

"Clint would think it's corny. It's here, I can look at it. I think that's enough," I replied.

"I'm glad you're okay with moving it down here."

"It's better than dealing with nightmares."

"Anything to help us sleep, right?" Jessica said, leaning into my shoulder as we continued to look at the painting. The flickering candle cast guttering shadows over the portrait. In one moment, Clint's face was distorted, the fear of the moment emphasized by the deep lines and texture. The next he seemed relieved, resigned to fate and the inevitability of it all.

"Can I ask what you saw earlier?" Jessica asked.

"You know what I saw," I replied.

"But why? It was just a gym class."

"Do you remember what it was like before you knew about Aunt Helen?"

She raised her head from my shoulder and turned toward me. Her face scrunched up, eyebrows knit together. Whenever she looked into her memories, her eyes would rise toward the ceiling, as if the scenes from her past were painted there. She scanned through thought, retracing time, pedaling back two years. Then she nodded, biting her lip.

"Stressful, I guess. I remember being anxious, getting indigestion a lot," she said. "Do you remember when it got so bad I'd throw up?"

"I do," I replied.

"Is that how you're feeling?"

"Yeah, since Clint died. I don't throw up or anything, but the feeling's still there."

"And that's how it's going to be until we talk to your last ancestors."

"I know."

"I don't mean to push you, you know that. It's just, when I was looking, no one supported me, not really anyway. I just figured it would help a little."

"It does," I replied, thinking of the ring in my sock drawer. "I want this more than anything. You know that."

Then the candle flickered once as if someone had blown on it. It went out. We were left in darkness. The sound of movement stirred from nearby boxes, a faint rumbling of cardboard and plastic tarps, the wobble of unstable heaps in slow decay. I felt Jessica, still at my side, unmoving. The speculation of earlier flashed into my mind, the constant approach, the masks watching from a distance one moment, then at my elbow the next.

I felt their breath even though they didn't breathe, heard their voices though they didn't speak. My heart rate became audible. I was sure Jessica could hear it, that it would deafen her if it continued to swell. Instead, she reached down, striking another match. The wick caught, and an orange tongue danced in the still air. The scent of cinnamon returned. We were alone beneath our house, Clint's likeness resting before us, the look of fear returned to his face.

CHAPTER 17

"My sister's bringing the twins down," Jessica informed me over a bowl of cereal Saturday morning.

I was torn at her words. Her sister was difficult to deal with, more awkward than anything. The woman spoke with calculated sugar, which I found unnerving. She'd dish out compliments about what I was wearing, how I looked trimmer than the last time she saw me. She would grab my hand as she spoke, never breaking eye contact, then comment on the adorable way my hair curled to the left side of my head. I saw her do it with everyone, which lead me to doubt her sincerity. My replies were mostly stutters and sidesteps around any actual line of dialogue. But her presence made Jessica happy, so I dealt with my unease for her sake.

Her name was Kate. As sisters, she and Jessica looked nothing alike. Her tan was dark and thorough. She stood around six feet tall. Her hair was shorn low in a pixie cut, jagged bangs drifting into her eyes. She lived just over the Sagamore Bridge, visiting cemeteries up that way, speaking with their dead relatives, bringing graveside flowers on the appropriate holidays. Like me, she never got a solid lead into her fate, no matter how many gifts she gave. She even saw a psychic on a regular basis to instruct her on her next steps to clarity, something she suggested Jessica and I try.

"The twins turned eighteen this year," Jessica said before I could reply to her previous statement. "They're visiting Uncle Jeff with Kate. I'm hoping there's no connection, you know?"

"Why? What's wrong with him?" I asked.

"My family doesn't talk about it. Most of us saved him for our last visit. I mean, I never had to talk to him, but the rest... I don't know why Kate's bringing them now."

"You want to fill me in?"

"Just wait until we see him."

I hated cliffhangers. I was about to unearth her old family photo albums, but the requests began. Whenever we had visitors, which wasn't often, I played tour guide. A beach is a beach, but people always wanted to see at least a dozen. A lighthouse here, the fishing piers there. I showed our guests swamped trails that wound through mud flats, cranberry bogs whose edges were lined with poison ivy, the wire-meshed windows looking out from the Provincetown Monument a hundred feet up, preventing jumpers and any unintended slippage. I mentally composed my checklist of sights and the quickest way to move about them.

Jessica dumped her breakfast plate in the sink and left the room.

I could hear her moving things around in our closet.

A minute later she came into the living room with the sleeping bag from our camping trip tucked under her arm. It smelled like sweat and charred sausages.

"You're going to make them sleep in that?" I asked, thinking back to our humid accommodations. The fabric still felt damp in my hands.

"No, you're going to sleep in it. I told Kate we'd share the bed," she answered. "It's better for her back. You don't mind, right?"

"Well, I guess not. Couldn't she take the couch? I always thought it was comfy."

"That's where the twins are going to sleep."

"Right," I replied, taking the sleeping bag, resigned to my week of floor habitation.

***

I pulled the folding bed from couch cushions, straightened the blankets, and cleared a space in the corner where I could unroll the sleeping bag. Their car pulled in. Greetings were exchanged. The twins barely looked up as they shook my hand. Both had blonde hair, dark skin, a smattering of mall-acquired preppy attire, and lips that never parted. Kate mentioned the new cologne I was wearing and the appeal of my farmer's tan. An incessant buzz echoed from the twins' pockets, the hum of electric wasps that would harass my ears the entire week. James had a significant other back home. Lucy had several. Their phones were never silent.

Lenny was away for the weekend, staying at "Eyes'" place, whom we'd recently learned was named Juliet. They were trying to sort things out. Somehow they hadn't dissolved into a mess of slurred insults as Jessica predicted. I tried to talk to her about second chances, but she wouldn't listen. Three days of monogamy never proved anything.

***

The twins' eyes were glued to their screens as we walked around P-town. Tie-dye murals stretched around storefronts and alleyways, but nothing grabbed their attention. A statuesque man wearing a loincloth handed James a leaflet inviting him to see "Naked Boys Karaoke" at midnight. He uttered a *thank you*, without observing the man's attire. Jessica and Kate snatched the flyer from him and whispered behind covered smiles. There was no way we were staying so they could see the show. The twins were too young and I wasn't going to play babysitter if Jessica and Kate wanted to see a young version of Fabio sing an off-key rendition of "My Heart Will Go On" with his junk hanging out.

When they saw there was a cover charge, they let the leaflet drop to the brick sidewalk. I mouthed a silent *thank you* as the flyer was swept up by the wind to mingle with dozens of other brochures advertising similar events.

***

Red River Beach offered no relief from the incessant texting.

"Check out that yacht," I said, as we reclined on beach towels, trying to distract the twins from their phones. "Have you ever seen a whale so close?"

I must have been loud, because sunbathers on neighboring towels dropped their beach reads, trying to catch a glimpse of the approaching behemoth. Others brought out their camera phones to zoom in on specks in the distance.

"It's coming in to beach itself," I exclaimed, pointing to the open ocean in feign surprise. "Oh no, I was wrong. It's Cthulhu. Too many tentacles, too many tentacles! The horror."

Small children began to cry on their mothers' breasts. Disapproving beachgoers scowled at me as if I was crazy. Only a waif-like man in a *Star Wars* t-shirt, heavy sunburn ringing his neck, brought out his camera for that one.

"A shark!" I hollered, jumping to my feet, pointing into the waves. The twins barely looked toward the water as swimmers fled screaming, tripping the nearest bathers so they wouldn't be first in line for the next *Jaws* sequel.

A lifeguard who must have been in high school asked us to leave. I didn't take her seriously until the walkie-talkie came out and cops were mentioned. *Disturbing the peace,* a staticky voice on the other end intoned. I didn't give the twins time to kick the sand from their heels before we crowded into the car. I could clean the floor mats later.

***

"Did you bring anything to give your uncle?" I asked James and Lucy.

James shrugged.

"Didn't think of it," Lucy said, the slightest twinge of anxiety in her voice. She fastened her seatbelt as we turned onto the highway. The streets were congested with Connecticut and New Jersey license plates all hesitantly flipping on blinkers to warn me about turns they neglected to take. I drove faster than I should have, my curiosity about the uncle building with each passing second. I felt terrible for the twins, their introduction to the ghost world starting on a sour note, but there was a story there and I'd been dying to hear it.

"Get him a Big Mac. Something fried and covered with cheese," Kate said, sitting next to me in the passenger seat. "Fast food always seemed to get to him."

***

Uncle Jeff was buried in the low-rent district of Hyannis. Rundown shopping plazas lined the road with Dunkin Donuts, liquor stores, and twenty-four hour convenience marts. Two abandoned gas stations stared at one another from across the street, prices reflecting the trends of 2008. A man in a flannel jacket slept on the bench outside a church whose windows had been shattered.

The graveyard was nestled on a small plot amidst fast food wrappers and parking tickets. Trash bags were woven into the metal links of the surrounding fence. The tombs were directly overlooked by an abandoned hotel, blackened boards covered the second-story windows. Holes in the roof appeared hacked by a firefighter's axe. The lower levels were nothing but char.

A dirt road ran down the middle of the cemetery, dividing one cluster of stones from the next. Ghosts hung their heads as we walked between their pale shadows. Some seemed to shiver as if they had grown unfamiliar with the living. Others coughed and hacked trying to clear countless years of detritus from their lungs. A gaunt specter lunged at Lucy as she stepped from the road.

"Hey! My body's down there. Keep your feet on the road," he said, his voice thick with cigarette smoke.

"Yeah, yes, sure..." Lucy stuttered as she fell backward into Kate.

"I've never seen them like this before. Ghosts down our way are happy whenever visitors show up," I explained, looking around the ill-kept grounds. Someone had spray-painted an illegible name across the face of one of the stones. Many lay flat on their backs, the names of the deceased staring at the cloudy sky overhead. "It's probably the lack of respect this place gets."

"He shouldn't take it out on me," Lucy said.

"Who else, then? It doesn't look like anyone comes here. Maybe you remind him of his daughter who never visits," I said.

Lucy's eyes fell.

No one knew exactly where Uncle Jeff was buried. We split up, picking our way through the rows. Most names were difficult to read, causing me to stoop and peer at the stones. The markers were squat, rarely reaching past my knee. I had to peel away gray strips of moss and damp newspaper from the faces of several to reveal the occupants lying beneath. A handful had no name at all. I asked the ghosts standing next to the stones what their names were, but they couldn't answer, memories faded with the paint.

In the neighboring row, James kicked puffs of dandelions as he walked.

"You gonna come back and weed the place when those start growing?" an old woman in a ratty tube top asked.

"Um, I hadn't planned to," James replied.

"Think about that one again. I'm not tryin' to have my lawn ruined," she said.

"What do you—"

"She's talking about the dandelions," I called to him.

"Oh..."

"You gonna answer me or am I gonna have to curse you?" the woman said.

"Can she do that?" James asked.

"No," I replied. "Just ignore her and keep walking."

The woman yelled after us, translucent arm flesh swinging in the air. She rattled off curses and condemnations from old horror movies, a line or two from *Evil Dead* verbatim. Impressive, if it hadn't been for the fact the woman truly believed the devil would drag James to hell.

Uncle Jeff's grave sat between a jagged shard of gray stone and an alabaster crucifix with one of its arms sheared away. Neither of the ghosts spoke as we approached. Only their eyes showed any sign they took notice of our arrival. Uncle Jeff had a standard, rectangular stone. Three feet tall. Nice little epigraph below his name: *An entrepreneurial mind never lays dormant.* The guy seemed like the only respectable soul in the place. He was middle aged. Still had his hair cropped short in military fashion. He wore a loosened tie askew around his neck. His resemblance to a lawyer just out of work was uncanny. No smile though, his eyes were half closed as if sleep called to him.

"So you've finally come?" he said as we crowded around his stone. "Who's this one?" he asked, pointing at me.

"My boyfriend," Jessica replied.

"Does he have a name?"

"Dave."

"Well, Dave, you've got no right to hear what I have to say. Get out."

"I want him to stay," Jessica said.

"And I want him to screw off. Family only. That's how I operate," Uncle Jeff replied.

I took out the Big Mac I purchased on the latter half of our drive. I laid the red and white cardboard box at his feet, unfolded the top hatch, and let the smell of diced onions and Thousand Island dressing permeate the air. The man's eyes drifted over the offering, then up to my face. A smile cracked the corners of his mouth, even though his senses could no longer experience the calorically dense beauty.

"Reminds me of a good meal. Haven't had one in must be ten years. You can stay right here," Jeff said, bending down to inspect the food.

"Glad you like it," I replied.

"So you'll be wanting my side of the story then? See who's got what coming?" Uncle Jeff asked.

"That's the idea," Kate said.

"You're not gonna like what I've got to say. How about I just give you a timespan and leave it at that?" he asked, still hovering over the burger.

"No, we need the whole thing," Kate said. Unlike Jessica, Kate didn't know how many years she had left or what shape the Spirits would take when they knocked on her door. She had visited almost all the relatives Jessica had, but never at the same time to avoid generalities and misleading twists. In groups, ghosts tended to be more vague to ensure that the living would return for follow-ups.

"Well, you got it. One of ya will die within the year," he said, looking over Jessica, Kate, and the twins. "The Spirits will come in the night. They'll board your room up a week before they set the place on fire. You won't get out. Or maybe they'll just smother you in your sleep. Asphyxiation. CO_2 poisoning. Something along those lines. Don't know exactly when. Can't say it will be quick or clean. Live while you can, 'cause that's all there is."

My stomach dropped. I didn't want to hear the story after all.

"What the fuck?" James yelled. "What the fuck did you do?"

"I owned that hotel," he said, pointing to a burned-out hulk at the edge of the cemetery, next to the church. "And three others down in Yarmouth."

"What's wrong with that?" Lucy asked, tears in her eyes, the images of her death dancing before them.

"They all burned," I replied, remembering the headlines. Dozens of men and women were trapped inside. The hotels were run down, frequented by addicts, drunks, and sex workers. I'd heard rumors of arson, suspicious insurance money, and the fact that none of the victims had anyone looking for them.

"Got to make your money where you can," Uncle Jeff said. "Not that I ever worried about the repercussions. That's the beauty of capitalism."

From my side came the sound of Kate hacking up phlegm. She spat. It dribbled down Uncle Jeff's stone after passing through his body, leaving a slug trail over his engraved name.

"Now that's disrespectful," Jeff said.

His words were followed by two more globs of spit sliding down his headstone. Lucy wiped her lips on the shoulder of her shirt. James used the back of his hand. I wanted to tell them to wait, to hold off until we got all the information we could before they offended him. A vague, "One of you," wasn't going to help anyone. Maybe another hint. Gender? Hair color? Anything to narrow it down. But no, his screams followed our footsteps as we found the car. You could still hear him with the windows up and the engine churning.

***

The two remaining days of their stay were spent in silence. I continued to ferry them from one attraction to the next in an attempt to distract them from the dark forecast. My jokes weren't landing any better than they had at the beach. Wrong time, wrong place.

Lenny's return did nothing to raise morale. I found him on the couch when we returned from Cuffy's Souvenir Shop, two bags full of Cape Cod paraphernalia in tow. He sprawled over the cushions, sketchpad in hand. I barely made out the shape of a woman's body, dark hair sweeping across the paper. Large almond eyes, round cheeks. I assumed it was Juliet, the newest inspiration for his masterpiece.

He overheard our conversation about the meeting with Uncle Jeff as he shaded the woman's hips. He tried to comfort Kate, offered up his shoulder for the proverbial cry, attempting to rub her back as he got close. Jessica stepped in, causing Lenny to retreat toward the couch.

"Has anyone ever painted your portrait?" he asked, looking at Kate.

"I got a caricature done when I visited the boardwalk in Jersey. Does that count?" she replied.

"Not in my book," Lenny said before rushing into the kitchen. The sounds of chair legs dragged across linoleum preceded his return. He planted the chair before the couch and quickly unfolded his easel. It seemed like he had pulled the canvas out of thin air, the white rectangle magically appearing atop the easel.

"Just sit here," Lenny said. "Get comfortable."

A slight blush rose beneath Kate's deep tan. She lowered herself onto the chair, flattening her skirt over her lap. Jessica grabbed her arm, insisting nothing good would come of it, but Kate shrugged her off, crossing her legs, exposing a stretch of bare thigh.

"Maybe it's what I need right now," Kate said. "Is this okay?"

Lenny looked around the side of the canvas and nodded. "Perfect."

"I always wanted to be a model," Kate replied.

"You're made for it. You would be perfect for one of my anatomy studies," Lenny said. "Well, actually, would you be up for something like that?"

Kate looked down at her exposed calf. "Maybe, what would I have to do?"

"Take off your clothes," Lenny said with a smile. "I swear it's just for the art."

"Do you really think I'd do that?" Kate asked, rising from the stool.

"You never know…" Lenny replied. "I've had plenty of models line up for the opportunity."

Kate sighed, straightened, and pushed past us. Jessica followed her toward our bedroom, apologizing for our roommate. I lost track of their conversation as they disappeared through our doorway. My heart sank even further. He was digging a grave I doubted I could pull either of us out of.

"That's where I usually lose my subject," Lenny said over my shoulder.

"Not a good time, man. Just leave them alone. You can't do anything to make bad news like that go away," I said. "Especially not harassing Kate."

"Hey, it was all in good fun. No harm, no foul," Lenny replied, returning to his original sketch of the woman with the dark hair. I was left alone to scan my list of remaining stops on the Cape Cod tour. I drew a line through *laid back dinner with Lenny*.

***

Another trip to the beach changed nothing. A lunch of fried clams and codfish only left grease stains on shirt fronts. Comfort food failed at its name. James and Lucy managed to capsize their paddleboat on Swan River. Drowning would have been one way to avoid Uncle Jeff's predictions if it hadn't been low tide. I never realized how hard it was to get mud out of someone's hair.

***

The sun had begun to set as our day's festivities dried up. Returning home, we walked toward the front step. Lenny's voice blasted through the speakers in the living room, rattling the door on its hinges. Beneath his jarring vocals, I could hear the sounds of synths and an electronic drum set, reverb on high. He wasn't bad, actually, just not balanced with the rest of the instruments, overpowering them with his lyrics.

James and Lucy stood at my back, cradling beach chairs and a folded umbrella coated in sand, uncertainty lining their faces. Jessica and Kate were still unloading the car. The rear hatch slammed, followed by the sound of rolling coolers dragged across asphalt. A creeping dread swam into my mind.

"You've got to be kidding me," Jessica said. "'Time After Time'? What is he trying to do?"

I looked up at Kate, worry worming holes through my chest. "Is that really a question?"

"No, no, it's not. I just thought with the baby, maybe he'd grow up," she said, dropping the handle to the cooler and taking my keys. She jammed them into the lock with frustration.

"Why love songs?" Lucy asked. "Shouldn't it be something like *Oh baby, I'm sorry you're going to die...you got so little time, why not give me a try?*"

Her voice wasn't suited for an Elvis impersonator. James laughed anyway, so did Kate, but Lucy's song did nothing to stifle Jessica's rage. She threw her shoulder into the door and bounded into the living room. We followed, beach accessories clinking off the walls, rattling the framed photographs hanging there.

Lenny stood in front of the television, karaoke machine at his side, lyrics bouncing across the screen. He continued to sing as Jessica attempted to snatch the microphone. He lifted it out of reach, belting the final measures of the song. Another swipe, another miss. She caught hold of his shirt, tearing the top button just below the collar. He refused to stop. She heaved once, landing heavy on her feet, before pulling the plug on the karaoke machine. The screen sputtered and died.

"This is so inappropriate right now," Jessica seethed, her face growing red. "Do you honestly think you're going to woo her with this bullshit? I thought you were going to be faithful with Juliet."

"Hey, she's cool with me living my life the way I want, at least until the baby's here. We're not married. It's my last hurrah. Figured I'd start it off with a little compassion," Lenny said in an aside directed toward Kate.

"I can't—" Jessica began before Lenny cut her off.

"The whole situation with your uncle sucks," he said into the muted microphone. "I thought I could ease your tension."

"Maybe if you weren't being a perv, but you are. None of us want to talk about this," Jessica said. The group had come to an unspoken agreement about the matter. No more speculation. Not a single mention of Jeff's name.

Lenny dropped the microphone and moved toward Kate, arms hanging low, stretched to the side to receive a hug. Jessica slapped his hand. The resounding noise of skin on skin echoed through the room. The twins slunk from the hall and moved to the couch, backs straight as they sat in silence, looking at the laces on their shoes.

"You're a control freak, you know that?" Lenny yelled at Jessica. "I never understood why this shmuck doesn't dump you."

"And you're an immoral asshole who can't relate to other people. That sounds fitting, doesn't it?" Jessica asked. "You ever think about all those girls you gave VD?"

Lenny cocked his arm back, palm flat as if he was going to strike her. The moment slowed before me, as if in freeze frame. Anger blurred my vision, a flush of hatred pulsing in time with my heartbeat. I stepped between them, wrapping my fingers around his wrist and pushing him back.

"Get out," I said.

"What?" Lenny asked, shaking off my grasp.

"Get out. Seriously. Get your shit and move out. You can't live here anymore."

"You can't make that decision."

"I'm pretty sure I can," I replied, fists clenched, all the exasperation and fear of the past month rising to my face.

"Fuck you. There's still two months on the lease. I'm not leaving," Lenny said as he retreated to his room. "You're stuck with me."

He slammed his bedroom door and cranked his stereo as loud as it would go. The distorted guitars of AC/DC's "Hell's Bells" played on loop for the rest of the night. He knew I hated classic rock.

It was that song we fell asleep to hours later. I in my sleeping bag, Jessica and Kate in our bed.

The twins murmured in their sleep, asking questions I couldn't answer, no matter how much I wished I could. At one instant, James would moan as if the Spirits were before him. The next, Lucy would beg them to change their minds, to take her brother instead, as if they shared the same dream. I wanted to tell them that it would be okay, that only one of them had to worry, but it sounded insensitive any way I phrased it.

***

Jessica tried to talk to Kate in the morning, but Kate wouldn't listen. She shrugged Jessica off as she finished packing her luggage. I heard her mutter something about Jessica's "nice, cushy life." How she "couldn't possibly understand what they were going through." Jessica tried to fold her beach towels, to organize the toiletries the kids left in the bathroom, but Kate grabbed them from her.

"We don't need your sympathy," she said as she zipped her suitcase.

The certainty of Jessica's future put them at odds. When Kate drove off after lunch, they barely exchanged a word, their hug appearing forced and stilted. Kate left distance between them as if Jessica's body was covered with thorns. The cousins had gone back to their cell phones. We shook hands between their texts and then they were gone.

Lenny cut the power to his stereo as their car pulled from our driveway. Jessica cried at my side, waving at their taillights.

CHAPTER 18

The reverberation from the brass door knocker echoed down the hall, rattling the few poorly framed pictures that hung on the walls. Family portraits. Lenny originals. Jessica had already left for work, leaving bed sheets crumpled in the shape of her body. Lenny was probably hungover. Several muffled voices slipped beneath his door, the quiet aftermath of an all-night orgy. I couldn't tell how many people were on the other side, but it was enough to let us know Lenny wasn't going to leave peacefully.

I was jabbing popsicle sticks into moist soil, synthetic spines for oak and spruce seedlings destined to reforest my cemeteries. Conditions had been right: nonstop sun, plenty of warmth. Their first leaves had begun to unfurl. That was how I relaxed, letting the nightshade slip from my mind, those distant familial graveyards slumbering silently off in the periphery.

Abandoning my project, I tiptoed down the hall, avoiding the thought that once I pulled back the curtains I'd find a mob of Spirit masks staring back at me. I gulped and wrapped my fingers around the rough canvas curtains, tugging back the fabric.

It was only Jerry, the guy who owned the junk shop across the street.

Looking out from our front step, beyond the sea of rusting lawnmowers, were the rest of his treasures. Bath tubs with pink rings to plant tulips in, statues of Mother Mary, golf clubs, rungless ladders, bike frames. A sign hung at the edge of his driveway, *Jerry's Treasures*. Beneath, in smaller script, was written, *Open 365 days a year. Never a better time or place to buy than the present.* He wasn't kidding. I saw men unloading trailers of armchairs and grandfather clocks just the night before. Two a.m. had flashed on my bedside alarm clock, the clatter of their hollow bodies and dislodged chimes rang into the night. When the Spirits arrived unexpectedly, Jerry's shelves slumped a little more, the maze of tangled metal sprouted another passage, another wing.

He saw me through the glass. Unfortunately, there was no retreating to my window garden, pretending the rooms were vacant. I turned the deadbolt and let the door swing in on itself.

"Ah, Dave. How ya doing? Good morning I hope?" Jerry said. He wore a denim shirt tucked into a pair of faded blue Wranglers, the hue nearly matching in color. Clean shaven skin clung tight to his sun-scarred cheeks.

"As good as any, I guess. What's up?" I asked.

"Big things, big things, m'boy. Got a large shipment in last night. You wouldn't happen to be interested in a La-Z-Boy recliner, would you? We got leather."

"I don't think we have room at the moment, but thanks for asking," I replied, starting to swing the door closed.

"Too bad, real prime models," he said, sticking his foot in the doorway. "Got another question for you, if you don't mind?"

"Sure, go ahead." The quicker he got it out, the quicker I could get back to my seedlings. I needed to snatch as much time as I could if I was going to get enough trees in the ground to matter. Carbon sequestration took years, years I worried I didn't have.

Jerry reached into the breast pocket of his shirt and unrolled a hand-written list.

"I've been keeping notes of all your father's old possessions I asked for. Remember when you told me you'd look for the scalpel kit? Or the stethoscope? Did you find them?"

"No, can't say I have. He willed a lot of his stuff away. I don't know where half of it went," I lied. All that stuff was stashed in the basement, hidden in that pile of corroding cardboard boxes. Of course I hadn't looked for them. There were only so many hours I could wander this earth, why spend them picking through a dead man's possessions so they could become another dead man's trash? I wasn't willing to part with the few remaining objects reminding me of the brighter moments of my childhood.

Jerry's finger ran farther down the list, tracing more valuable items.

There must have been a hundred things. Most were from his old medical practice: thermometers, copies of the DSM IV, gurneys and stretchers. I didn't keep any of that stuff. They had no value to me. I couldn't remember how many times Jerry had asked for them, how many Sunday mornings found him on my doorstep instead of kneeling in a church pew. I kept telling him no, no idea, maybe Cousin Ruthie took that one. With each response he placed a check next to the article. He paused when he reached the last item on the list.

"What about your father's old blankets?" he asked. "The ones with those Native American designs on them?"

First of all, I had no idea how he knew what my father's bedding looked like; second of all, those linens were what killed him. The last thing I needed first thing in the morning was Jerry reminding me of how my father died of smallpox when it was barely a recognized disease anymore. It hadn't been widespread since 1977 thanks to vaccination.

The Spirits laid infested blankets over my father's shoulders while he slept. He'd wake and see their slack-jawed masks hanging above his face, could feel the disease wash over his skin, the prickle, the itch, the crawling microbes that tunneled inward. If he burned them quick enough, treated himself quick enough, he could catch the pox before it spread and took root. He wrote about it in a journal, detailing each excruciating detail as the ordeal unfolded.

His great-great uncle was one of the men that marched under Jackson's Indian Removal Act of 1838 along the Trail of Tears, doling out free blankets to the Choctaws and Cherokee. As the blisters rose, my father would reinject the vaccines, stalling for another day, another night. His blood wouldn't hold the antibodies and the Spirits would bring a new blanket to replace the old. He gave up the routine after three months. He had started to treat himself more than other patients, a medical Sisyphus of syringes and recurring diagnosis. Someone needed to atone for the sin and he wasn't going to avoid it.

He requested a closed casket at the wake, not wanting his blistered, swollen skin to be seen.

"So how about it? You still got those blankets?" Jerry asked again, pencil tip tapping his list.

"Who are you trying to kill?" I asked.

He laughed. "Ah, my boy, they'll be sanitary now. The disease was only meant for your father."

"I burned the last one," I replied, remembering the scent of charred wool and yarn the day after his lawyer read his will.

"That's a shame. Real collectors' items these days. People are obsessed with getting their hands on some genuine Spirit memorabilia," Jerry said, flipping back through his list, searching for missed items. I knew what would come next and my mind ran through the rooms of our apartment. Jerry wouldn't leave unless I placed something in his arms that could perch on his crowded shelves.

My mind swam through the accumulated debris that a long-standing relationship gathered, trying to pull one item free from the current that wouldn't be missed.

"I got it," I told Jerry. "Give me one second."

I dug into the cabinets above the stove, delving through odd appliances. Panini maker. Garlic press. Waffle iron. Until I reached the bottom of the pit, unearthing the food processor my mother had given us. It was now yellow, its blades dull. When I returned to the door, Jerry's smile was immense, as if I had brought him something belonging in a museum instead of a hunk of discolored plastic.

"Now there's quality," Jerry said, stuffing the list back into his breast pocket, sweeping the processor from my hands in a flash. He cuddled it to his chest, a newborn in his family of discount deals. "I'll get a pretty penny for this one."

"Glad I could help," I replied.

"You always do. Say hi to your dad for me when you see him," Jerry said as he walked down the driveway.

The insult stung. He was two for two that morning: a reminder of my father's death, a reminder of our lack of communication. Jerry was good at making me regret lying about searching for medical equipment. He placed an inordinate amount of religious fervor into his junk collection. Any piece of rust left alone, a sin. I always wondered what the Spirits would do to his offspring. Would it be suffocation under a pile of corroded metal bed frames, or a subtle turn of phrase to trigger a stroke? My money was on the second.

CHAPTER 19

The sign glowed neon purple: the outline of an eye staring out from parted blinds. At her sister's prompting, Jessica suggested we visit a medium to get answers for my dilemma. *Even if she doesn't tell you anything, at least it will be an interesting date, right?* she said, a little more insistent than jovial. The shop appeared to be in a person's single-level home on the other side of Harwich. The screen door hung open on rusted hinges. It clattered against the doorframe as we pulled into the driveway, swept forward by my Volvo's exhaust.

The parking lot was an opened garage door with "park here" spray-painted across the back wall. The words psychic, medium, or fortuneteller appeared nowhere. In fact, there weren't any words at all, as if the eye was enough indication.

"Kate said this woman talks to the Spirits?" I asked.

"Yeah, that's how she put it. She's not her regular mystic, but she's the only one in the area," Jessica replied, emptying most of her money and credit cards out of her purse. She opened the glove compartment and stowed it beneath the copy of my registration.

"What are you doing?"

"Just being prepared."

"You think she's going to rob us?"

"You never know."

The whole thing seemed hokey, but I ignored judgment for Jessica's sake. I imagined an arthritic psychic, floral head scarf, hunchbacked, ill-equipped to pickpocket or wrestle a wallet from anyone. She'd have her own way of getting people to dole out the bills. *Oh, there is just one more thing, but my mind grows cloudy. Maybe another ten dollars will clear the fog.*

I knocked on the screen door. The familiar buzz of nineties punk was audible for a moment, then cut out. A record player's needle lifted out of a groove. From inside the house came the sound of a rocking chair gliding back and forth, recently emptied. The noise ceased as my rapping echoed through the rooms. Then came fumbling footsteps across hardwood, before the door swung open.

The girl who we evicted from the Chases' mausoleum stood before me. She had deep bags under her heavily mascaraed eyelids, a Rancid t-shirt hanging off her thin frame. Her skin was paler than before, as if she hadn't seen the sun in weeks.

I swallowed hard, a thousand questions trilling in my ear. She chewed her lower lip, one hand running through her black hair. The bruise on her neck had faded to a dull yellow.

Jessica was the first to say anything. "Are you the psychic?"

The girl looked relieved. "Oh, you're here for my mother. She's in the middle of her morning meditation, she'll be out in fifteen minutes or so."

"Should we come back?" I managed to ask, finding my tongue.

"No. She lets clients sit on the couch and wait. Make yourself at home."

With that, the girl let us into her house. The shuffling sounds made sense. The floor was strewn with old newspapers and shoe boxes stuffed with mystic paraphernalia: crystal balls, dreamcatchers, bent tarot cards, a voodoo doll whose stitching was coming loose. My foot brushed one of the boxes stuffed with minor gemstones, sending it whispering across the uneven floorboards. The smell of incense masked the scent of pizza grease and tobacco from the next room. A thin layer of smoke hung below the ceiling.

The once vocal record player sat in the corner, a milk crate crammed with vinyl LPs lay beneath. The girl cleared a stack of VHS tapes from the couch, all labeled with a woman in bright spandex raising her knee to her elbow and smiling. They were aerobics videos. She placed them in a box by the door labeled "free with your first consultation."

"Do some crafts or something," the psychic's daughter said, gesturing to the superstitious charms. She pointed to a bowl of shredded paper and another filled with a liquid glue concoction. Then she looked to Jessica, whose face was drawn back, squinting at the heaps of junk, head tilted in a way that said she didn't want to get her hands dirty. "Or you could read."

The only reading material I could see were the outdated newspapers at our feet.

"We're fine," Jessica replied. "I think we'll just wait and think about questions to ask your mom."

"Suit yourself," the girl said.

We sat as the girl walked down the hall. Jessica and I spent the next fifteen minutes looking at the walls and tables stacked with woven twig structures and papier-mache Spirit masks. There was a plague doctor, Mexican sugar skull, and Japanese Oni. A half-finished knight's helm, horns curved like a goat's, lay on plastic wrap. We didn't speak. I could tell we were both nervous. Only the occasional rustle of bodies moving in the neighboring rooms disturbed the silence. I picked up the knight's mask, the paper still damp beneath my fingers. I began to examine it, raising it to my face to see if it would fit.

"She'll see you now," the girl said, returning to the room.

I dropped the mask in shock, hurrying to put it back in its rightful place on the coffee table.

"Don't worry about that," the girl said. "What's the point of masks if you aren't going to wear them?"

"Don't mind him. Thanks for letting us wait," Jessica said. "What's your name?"

She hesitated, looking at me, then sighed.

"Lenore," the girl replied before walking away.

"Well, thanks, Lenore," Jessica said to her back as she led us down the hallway. The walls were lined with photographs of a young girl, maybe three or four. The child shared similar, less-defined features with Lenore, baby fat rounding out her cheeks. In the pictures, she rode a tricycle, sat on a blanket beneath a maple tree, wore aerobic sweats and leg warmers in turquoise and purple eighties fashion. Each photo was faintly faded with the yellow tinge of cigarette smoke.

Incense cast a haze about the room.

A thin woman sat at a table facing the door. Her neck looked too slight to hold up her head. Her cheeks were sallow. Nearly sucked dry. Her silver-streaked hair was pulled into a loose configuration of tangled curls. She was the same woman on the VHS tapes, just drastically thinner. Skeletal, almost. Her thickly veined hands tapped on the table, multiple rings clanging off the hard surface. There was nothing else on the tabletop except a sheet of paper and two pens.

"You must sign this before we begin," she said, pointing to the paper.

"What is it?" Jessica asked.

"A release form," the woman said.

As they spoke, I caught Lenore's eye and mouthed the word, "Sorry."

She shrugged and whispered, "See?" before disappearing from the doorway.

Jessica was already signing the paper.

"Your turn," she said as she pressed the second pen into my hand.

"Why do we need a release form?" I asked.

"Confidentiality," the woman replied. "I can't have you speaking to others about what you see and hear today."

"Sure... I guess that makes sense," I said without reading over the pages of minute print.

We took our seats as the woman began to hum deep in her throat, ranging through high and low notes. The resonance echoed in my chest.

"You've come to see me about your futures, have you?" she asked, her eyes closed. "Your interactions with the Spirits, to be more precise? Are you sure you wouldn't like a little love advice first? I can give you a discounted deal, package them together."

"No thank you. I think we can stick with the Spirits. Only Dave's though," Jessica replied, laying a hand on my own, a heavy blush across her cheeks.

"Are you sure you don't want to hear both? Your Spirits seem to be quite interesting. There could be something to learn—"

"Yes," Jessica said, cutting off the psychic. "Yes, we're sure. I know all I need to know about my future."

The woman shrugged and began to tap on the edge of the table. A slow beat of ones and twos in time with her humming. Then she cleared her throat in a harsh, guttural stop. At first she told me about my job, about the burials that were coming up, the poison ivy I would have creeping up my legs. She talked about uncomfortable encounters with Lenny, our disrupted sleep patterns, the fight he'd put up to prevent expulsion.

More minutia about everyday life slipped by, nothing illuminating. I began to lose focus, my eyes no longer anchored to the woman's quivering mouth. Jessica nodded along with every word. I found myself staring at her gnarled hands. The only finger lacking a ring was the actual ring finger; the others were weighted down with rubies and pearls. My mind went back to the day we kicked Lenore out, what she said about her father's death. Before I could look away, the woman paused in her speech.

"Eyes up here, please," she insisted as Jessica's hand fled my own. "Am I boring you? Do you not find this enlightening?"

"No, it's just... I mean, we were wondering if you could tell us about the Spirits," I said.

"I'm getting there. You have to wade through necessities before you reach your destination," the woman replied. She stomped her heel on the floor and a ghostly moan echoed from beneath the table. Smoke began to issue from the incense at a more rapid rate, filling the room with a thick fragrant fog. "It seems they don't know your name. They don't recognize your face. Do you plan on getting plastic surgery in the near future? A nose job perhaps? No? Is there anything you would like me to ask them?"

She looked straight at me, her pupils narrow, the white eating inward.

Then there was a brief clearing in the smoke. I could see the curtains flutter, the image of a bone mask hovering in place, then two, then an innumerable horde piled on top of one another trying to catch a glimpse through the window. Black skeletal fingers brushed the glass, rattled the panes as if prying at the lock. My heart leapt, fear thick in my throat. There was only so much strain one window could take. Then the curtain fell, cutting off the view of the attempted intrusion. Footsteps resounded where there were no feet. Hushed whispers crept through the floorboards, a laugh, a chorus of chuckles. The Spirits flooded every available space outside the room, fingers running over drywall, pawing at insulation, skittering across beams in the attic. A scream welled in my throat.

Then all faded to silence.

In the mirror to the woman's right appeared a single plague doctor. He looked in at us, head tilted, examining, before he, too, was gone as the smoke wafted back into place. Jessica's fingernails dug into my forearm, the pressure indenting my skin. Her eyes were fixed on the window. I tried to shake her off as she whined for the woman to stop.

"Ask them about my father. Ask them why he won't talk to me," I said, my voice catching at my teeth.

The humming in the psychic's throat grew, building until it seemed we were surrounded by sound. It rose in a crescendo so loud I needed to cover my ears. Jessica did the same, freeing my arm, her eyes beginning to water. Fear was painted on her face. Then there was silence. The smoke faded, returning to the four narrow stems smoldering in the corners. The psychic sighed, her eyes returning to normal, breath steady.

"It seems there's nothing they want to tell about your father. You have to talk to him yourself. No short cuts. Your relationship wasn't always in shambles. There is still much to do to mend the divide," she said, rubbing her hands together. "They did say you must go to where your mother's family is buried. There may be something for you there."

"When?" I asked.

"Does it matter? Go when you can, the ghosts aren't going anywhere," the psychic said, pushing her chair back, rising to her feet. She walked to a stack of cushions piled against the far wall. She lowered herself onto them with her back toward us, staring at the smoke swirling around the ceiling. She drew a pack of cigarettes from her pocket. "Leave the three hundred dollars with my daughter before you go. And don't forget your complimentary aerobics video."

She lit a cigarette and exhaled.

We rose, Jessica swiping at the smoke hanging in her face. Her legs struggled to remember steps, muscles seizing. I reached to steady her before she could pitch forward. The psychic's words made me feel worse, the ominous creep of death approaching at a rapid clip. From the swarm that buzzed outside the window, I was beginning to doubt I'd make it as long as Jessica needed me to, our shared vision of happiness shredded beneath skeletal hands.

"How much did you say we owe you?" Jessica asked, brushing off my aid.

"Three hundred dollars," the woman replied.

"But the paper says one hundred."

"The rate has changed. You were a more difficult customer than most."

I made my way to the door, no longer desiring to stay in the same room as the woman.

"What do you mean? You didn't tell us anything. Shouldn't we get a discount for that?"

The door slammed shut as Jessica followed my steps, the woman refusing to reply. Lenore was sitting on the couch once again, hands laying the last strands of newspaper over the knight's mouth, an old Operation Ivy song playing on low from nearby speakers. She looked up and followed my eyes to where they rested on the assorted masks.

"I sell them on eBay. You'd be surprised what people will pay," Lenore said, holding up the plague doctor and rotating it beneath the overhead lights.

"That's the one I always see," I said.

"I know," she replied, a smile on her face. "Just kidding. Lucky guess. A lot of people see this one. It's those high school history classes. They spend way too much time on the Black Death, well, death in general. We went over it two weeks ago."

"I don't know if I can believe her," Jessica said, joining my side. "Does your mother really talk to the Spirits, or is there some smoke machine beneath the table?"

"Didn't you see them?"

"I don't know," Jessica said. I felt the half-crescent gouges in my arm. They were still there. I wasn't imagining it.

"Believe what you want," Lenore replied. "She's been right in most cases I've followed up on. Not saying that's a good thing."

"Has she always been like this?" I asked in a muffled voice, not wanting her mother to hear.

"No, not always..."

Lenore went on to tell us how her mother was once a famous workout instructor in Los Angeles, the kind that appeared on television at five in the morning before the regularly scheduled programing. She thought she was bettering peoples' lives by helping them get skinny, and for a while she believed it. Then her manager showed her the ratings and the reviews she got from call-ins. A woman had broken her back during a stretch of vigorous cardio. Another man tore both his ACLs in a prolonged lunge. Two or three said they lost the desired weight, but the rest reported no change. That's when she revamped the show, turning it over to talks with the dead, interviews with the Spirits and such. The ratings soared, but the stations refused to air her program after a while, what with the shrieks and nightmares accompanying her readings. They didn't want to fund predictions of death, no matter how many callers they were getting.

"Doesn't really seem like a logical progression," I said to Lenore. "No offense."

"My father didn't think so either," she replied, eyes returning to her work. "Some people can't choose what they're good at."

Jessica nudged me in the side. Lenore's story had softened something in her.

"Sorry," I said.

"Don't worry about it. That was years ago. He seems to be happy now. Death suits him better than living with her."

I wanted to mention I was also sorry about what happened in the cemetery, but I didn't want Jessica to think I was being a creep. I tried to think of a secret code I could use to express my thoughts, maybe say something about the Chases sending their regards, but it all sounded wrong.

"Did she have you put that Spirit mask in the window? Be honest," Jessica asked.

"This one?" Lenore asked, holding up the plague doctor.

"Yeah."

"I've been sitting here the whole time working on this one," Lenore said, jabbing the knight with her finger. "It was probably the real thing. They come around all the time. Usually I think they're coming for Mom, but they just go away after a few minutes. It's wicked creepy."

"We can't pay the full price your mother's asking. We didn't learn anything," Jessica said, standing in the doorway.

"That's not unusual. How much do you want to leave her?" Lenore asked.

I fished out my wallet and separated a hundred dollars in odd bills from the accumulated receipts and business cards crammed within. I left the money jammed between two hunks of polished agate sitting on an end table. Jessica nodded and slipped out the front door with a wave to Lenore.

"Cool. Mom'll probably put a curse on you for being cheap, but I wouldn't worry. She did the same to the cat and he just ran away. I saw him living beneath the neighbor's porch. They feed him better," she said. "Can you do me a favor?"

"Depends," I replied. "I can't let you stay in the mausoleum, if that's what you're wondering."

"I figured," she replied. "Just tell the Chases thanks for letting me stay."

"Sure. I'll mention it when I go into work tomorrow."

"I appreciate it," Lenore said, returning to laying strips of damp paper across the mask.

"Sorry for kicking you..." I said. "I see why you'd prefer the crypt."

"Don't worry about it. A job's a job," she said, smiling. As she eased the sodden strips over the frame, I watched her work. Halfway down her forearm were five circular bruises in the shape of a grasping hand. Before I knew what I was doing, I reached out, stopping her from fleshing out the mask.

"Did she do this to you?" I asked, gently rotating her arm to get a better look at the bruises. There they were, purple-black against her skin. Lenore yanked her arm away, shaking her head. She was calm in her movements, as if she expected my reaction. She went back to her task without stopping.

"Don't worry about it," she said.

"I can call someone, someone who can help," I replied.

"Don't. I'm fine, really. You can leave now unless you want to buy one of these," she said, sweeping her arm across the inventory of her online store.

With a pen I found stuck between stacks of old newspapers, I scribbled my phone number on a scrap of paper, pushing it toward her across the cluttered table.

"Seriously, call me if you need help. Jessica and I will figure something out. It's what she does for work," I said.

"Gracias," Lenore replied, sarcastically. "See you around."

Then I left. I knew nothing I was going to say would change Lenore's mind, and I didn't want to impose. I never wanted to be that guy telling a woman, or anyone for that matter, how to live their life. As the door closed behind me, the neon eye blinked out, the purple glow fading in the glass tubes.

CHAPTER 20

Aunt Erin's son had been a heroin addict, an affliction coursing through Cape Cod's arteries for the past decade. Newspapers were full of overdose obituaries, court orders, and arrests. Our local hospital had the highest rate of heroin-addicted babies born in all of Massachusetts. Passing through neighborhoods and cul-de-sacs, it wasn't uncommon to see police and EMTs wrestling a revived addict, struggling to force them into an ambulance. I knew because I watched it happen to my cousin Milo, Erin's son.

Shirtless, three police officers dragged him across his apartment complex's parking lot, pale skin and black tattoos rubbed raw against cement. Face bloodied, he spat at them, swearing, promising ruination, lawsuits on forced hospitalization. *You had no right to stop me*, being the only line of dialogue I caught. I was dropping off a movie he'd asked to borrow. They wouldn't let me speak with him. I'd never seen eyes so wide. Mouth frothing, veins swollen like mountain ranges, they strapped him to a gurney and wheeled him into the ambulance.

I left the movie between his screen door, a hand written note jammed inside the case: *I'm sorry I couldn't help or make this better.* Four months later, the Narcan failed and there was no breath to pump his flailing fists. He was buried in a Yarmouth cemetery next to his father, neglecting the spot picked by his mother in our family plot. Those were the memories I considered while driving toward Western Massachusetts. Aunt Erin was one of the last ghosts I had to speak with. Her, a half-dozen other odd relations, and my father.

The concept of nature versus nurture unnerved me. The Spirits punished child abuse vehemently, grotesque with gore and retribution. They filled headlines, *Pedophilic uncle's nephew suffers gruesome death.* The color photos depicted a dismembered corpse tagged with seventy-two yellow evidence markers. I didn't know what Aunt Erin had done during Milo's life, but rumors failed to flatter.

***

"Who are we going to talk to?" Jessica asked from the passenger seat. The highway unwound out the window. Mountainous forests were carpeted in deep green. A river mumbled below the radio's voice. The carcasses of old paper mills littered their banks. She left her work folders at home. Her recent grant to fund a battered women's shelter in Harwich had been due three days prior. Things were supposedly on standby until the email arrived regarding whether they got the money.

"Let's not talk about her until we get there, if that's alright with you?" I replied. "She's kind of like Uncle Jeff."

"Well, that's a little ominous, but sure. No worries," she said, frowning.

The ride had been going smoothly. Jessica and I listened to a program on NPR detailing trends in ghost romance. It seemed more of the dead spent their nights below ground in shared coffins rather than sleeping alone. First it was retirement homes and Viagra. Then it was mausoleums and the longing for forgotten flesh. I'd have to ask Clint about it, see if Mrs. Jones had made any passes yet.

"Why did your parents get divorced?" Jessica asked when the program cut to an advertisement.

"What?" I asked. It wasn't a topic I enjoyed discussing. Jessica usually kept away from such conversations. Never prying, always letting information come to her freely.

"Your parents? I was just thinking of them and realized you never told me what happened."

"Well, I always thought it had something to do with Dad's work. He was never around. Long hours. Worked weekends. I remember they used to sleep in separate beds. I can't imagine they had much of a sex life."

"Ew. Let's not talk about your parents like that," Jessica said, a snort of laughter escaping her nose.

"Why? It's the thing that keeps relationships going. Once that dies, everything else seems to go with it."

Jessica cocked an eyebrow, tilting her head inquisitively.

"And you've never asked them directly?"

"No. That would be awkward. *Hey, Mom, why'd you stop loving Dad?* Or, *Hey, Dad, can you recount your sex life in those last few years?*"

"You wouldn't phrase it like that."

"No, but you get the drift. There's no way to avoid the awkwardness. And Dad doesn't talk, not anymore, so that's out of the question."

Jessica began to weave a thick braid through her hair as we pulled off the exit ramp, drawing long strands in cross-hatched patterns, only to loosen them and start over. Amherst was a college town teeming with skinny jean-clad undergrads milling about brickwork bookstores and cafes. Avant-garde cinemas and music shops were nestled between bars and Asian eateries. Jessica spotted a sign advertising a showing of her favorite anime movie about a girl and a river dragon. I promised her if we had enough time, we'd get tickets on our way back.

The town common spread out along our right side, couples lying on the grass, others tossing frisbees or reading books. The library tower at UMass loomed above the tree line in the distance, twenty-six stories tall. They were one of the only schools I applied to before I promised to remain on Cape with Jessica.

Two miles from town center, my ancestors' cemetery occupied a corner of a four-way intersection. Black, wrought-iron gates yawned open at the entrance. The road leading between stones was simply two dirt tracks dug by passing tires with a few buttercups and sprigs of spearmint poking through the soil. Little planning went into designing the layout of the place. Gravestones didn't form straight paths. No one could get a mower between the twists and turns of the macabre maze. A rotting willow lay on its side, root ball intact and pointing skyward.

Jessica unraveled her last experimental braid, leaving her long hair wavy from weaving. Stepping from the car, she stretched her back, palms toward the sky, the elastic material of her running shirt lifting to reveal a section of pale midriff. A twinge of desire pulled at my spine as she moved through several yoga poses, her joints cracking with each motion.

My mother's voice snapped me out of my reverie, eyes shifting from Jessica's sun salutation to the translucent woman in front of me, body striped by the fence's bars. Her hair was cut short, styled in a swoop of spikes. She was thin. A swallow tattoo was emblazoned on her forearm, peering out beneath the cuff of her three-fourths t-shirt. A pair of jeans completed the outfit.

"Long time no see, mister," she said, opening her arms.

"You know that doesn't work anymore," I replied, walking around the fence.

"And you know what I mean."

I let her arms encircle me. A wave of cold swept through my veins, raising goosebumps over exposed skin. I longed for the reassurance of her embrace, but knew I'd never feel it again.

"That wasn't so bad, was it?" she asked.

"No," I replied.

"That's what I thought."

"How have you been, Mrs. Gallagher?" Jessica asked, jogging over.

"Fine, Jessica," my mother replied, avoiding eye contact. She never liked Jessica, always insisting she was too white-bread, too nice for her own good. My mother wanted an adventurous son, month-long trips to Spain or the Amazon. The chance to study orchids in their natural environments, the hedge mazes in Versailles. *How are you ever going to be more than a landscaper?* she would ask, assuming I only stuck around because of Jessica, never considering my own anxieties about the change of scenery, or the pull of love. I told her she didn't know Jessica the way I did, that it was all worth it.

"Hey, who's that?" Jessica said, pointing to my grandfather, who stood beneath the boughs of a maple tree. "He looks just like you."

"That's my father," my mother replied.

I was surprised to find him there, smiling at us, his grease-stained Dickies and button-down work shirt the same as I remembered. He split his time between haunting the riverside dam near the old paper mill where he had worked and loafing about the headstones. One lunch break, after the steam whistle blew, my grandfather and his work buddies took their meals to the water's edge. My grandfather, finishing early, climbed the dam, hoping to get a view downstream. He stumbled, performing an awkward swan dive off the cement ledge seventy feet down. His body surfaced days later, one leg missing. It had gotten stuck in the riverbed, snagged on downed trees and rocks, which is why he was permitted to travel between the two. Only three fourths of his body was buried beneath his tombstone.

Jessica was right, he looked like me, only with a beer gut and thinning hair. He possessed the same cowlick on the left side of his head, forcing his hair to rise in a wave, coursing over his forehead.

"You're not here to talk to him though, right?" Jessica asked.

"So this isn't a friendly visit?" my mother asked, eying me suspiciously. "I thought you already talked to everyone here."

"Well, not..." I began.

"Erin? Are you serious? You haven't talked to Erin? Really, Dave, that's irresponsible. The one person you wouldn't want and you left her for last?"

"Yeah, I guess so," I replied, feeling childish, like my mother was about to banish me to my room without supper.

"And here I was thinking you just came to say hi," my mother said.

"Well, that's part of it," Jessica interjected. "Dave's been talking about how much he misses you, how he feels bad he can never get away from work. He's been drafting a proposal to get new dogwoods and cherry blossoms for one of his cemeteries, oaks and maples to act as carbon sinks. Taxpayers are so stingy though."

I was proud she remembered the specific trees. I was flattered. I watched as my mother's countenance brightened, her lips folding into a smile. She had a soft spot for cemetery maintenance and beautification. Every ghost did.

"I get it, I get it," my mother said apologetically. "Life gets away from you sometimes. At least tell me you've gotten something out of your father?"

"Can we just leave it at the trees?" I asked.

"Dave, you know you need to—"

"Who are the flowers from?" I asked, pointing to her small stone. A bouquet of browning roses lay in a heap, moldering at the foot of her grave.

"You know they're always from Aunt Janey," she replied.

Aunt Janey had been mom's best friend since middle school. They played sports together: soccer, volleyball. Accompanied each other to prom when neither had a date, not because they were unattractive, but because they had too many suitors to choose from, or so they said. During my teenage years, they took "mommy vacations," leaving me at home with Dad, traveling to warmer climes, sunning on the beach, fruity drinks in hand. Aunt Janey had no children, so I was like a second son to her for a time. She never really stopped by after Mom died. I knew she still visited Mom's grave from time to time. Unlike me, she prioritized my mother's afterlife over her own.

"I figured. Has she been around recently?" I asked.

"Those are from last month. I expect she'll be by sometime this week. She usually arrives like clockwork."

"Well, I'm glad you've got company," I replied, moving to the grave, lifting the wilted flowers. "You want me to drop these on the compost pile?"

Over the back edge of the fence, a mound of rotting Christmas wreaths, flower stems, and a variety of organic material slowly melded into a uniform black sludge. I moved to carry the bouquet away until my mother yelled for me to stop. It was sudden, a burst of breath and anger, a tone I hadn't heard in years.

"Sorry, but leave those there. Jane will take care of it when she gets here," my mother said when she calmed down. "You should go talk to your aunt. She gets less lucid as the day goes on."

Jessica and I took our cue, leaving my mother staring down at the flowers arranged at the foot of her grave. Aunt Erin stood before the central spire of the family's plot, stock still, staring at the sky. She was over six feet tall. She wore a hooded burial shawl wrapped about her emaciated frame. The curling edges dangled an inch above the grass. It was torn about the sleeves, frayed along the stitching. It gave her the look of a specter from old horror movies, draped in sheets, the breeze causing the fabric to dance as if there was nothing beneath. As we approached, she lowered her head, leveling partially closed eyes at us. My stomach dropped, dreading the questions I'd prepared. Her hair slipped from beneath the veil, falling about her shoulders in matted clumps, as if she hadn't cleaned it the year before her burial.

"How many times have you skipped over my grave?" she asked before we could greet her.

"Um, I don't know exactly, but—" I began.

"Seventeen. You have been here seventeen times without speaking to me. What makes you think I'll answer your questions, seeing you saw fit to ignore me so many times?"

"I wasn't avoiding you or anything, I just had to talk to the others. I can only manage so much in a day," I said.

Aunt Erin's palm flew through my face, the arc of a backhand swat sending frost through my sinuses, chilling the fluid in my brain. I nearly fell over the headstone at my heels, hands scrabbling, latching onto a neighboring granite spire.

"Don't lie. It will get you nowhere," she said, dropping her hand to her side. She walked a circle around the clustered family stones. The fabric of her shawl billowed out for a moment, exposing scarred skin around the nape of her neck and wrists, pinprick holes and grooves where flesh had rotted away. She tightened a hand around the cloth, cinching it up, censoring the damaged flesh. "You brought me nothing. No offerings. How am I to show respect when respect isn't shown to me?"

"I didn't say I brought nothing," I replied.

"But we didn't," Jessica whispered at my side.

Aunt Erin's eyebrows ascended, her head lowered, laugh lines creasing her cheeks. She moved closer, standing before Jessica, looming, looking down at the shorter woman.

"I feel sorry for you," the ghost said.

"Why?" Jessica managed through pressed lips.

"It's not something I will disclose, seeing, as you said in your own words, you brought nothing."

"What I've offered I couldn't bring," I said, stepping between the two. The cold front of my aunt's shawls whispered about my face, a sea of ice shifting beneath my skin. "I visited your son three times last week. I mowed his plot, planted fox gloves around his stone, weeded, even bought one of those ceramic deer statues. You know he loved animals."

Aunt Erin stepped back, straightening her spine. The fabric of her garment stretched taut over her bony frame. She looked to the sky as if searching for something.

"How can I know you aren't lying?" she asked.

I produced my smartphone from my pocket and scrolled to the pictures I had taken of my cousin's grave. Milo stood next to the headstone. The pink and white bells of foxglove flowers danced about his feet. The lawn was shorn low. I had been keeping up with the grave, knowing no one else would.

Erin wiped at her cheeks. Eyes fluttering, the faintest hint of tears welled in their corners.

"He has no one else to visit him," she moaned in a throaty warble. "Thank you."

"I figured he deserved something nice," I replied. "I don't have much to offer, but there it is."

"Which is enough. Do you plan on having children?"

My glance flitted to Jessica, who was anxiously flexing her calves, rising up and down in place.

"Yeah," Jessica began to say. "If it's a boy, we're going to name him Albrecht, if it's a girl—"

My aunt cut her off before she could continue.

"That's not good. My heir will answer for the mistakes of my youth. I'd prefer not to relive those days, so I will keep my reply brief. I brought men into my house while my husband worked. There were drugs, blackouts, too many hands. At the time, it felt right. We needed money. I remember hearing Milo cry from his crib, the body of a faceless man standing over his tiny frame. The cries grew louder. The rest is lost to time. A broken memory," Erin said, slumping back against her headstone, swooning in a near faint. She was being dramatic. Ghosts didn't suffer the same bodily lapse as the living. I knew she wanted to end the story before the real reason to summon the Spirits arrived, but I wouldn't call her on it. No one deserved to relive their greatest mistake.

"What does that have to do with us having children?" Jessica asked.

"That is the trigger, if it is you, David. Once the child no longer needs its mother's milk, they will come, more than you can ever imagine. Waves of masks, skeletal fingers tracing every line of your body, stripping away clothing, dignity, peeling back layers of skin and muscle...until, until..."

"I get the picture," I said, swallowing the organs that had risen to the back of my throat. I gagged, tasting acidic bile beneath my tongue. I had never felt so sick, an entire flu season crammed into a single second.

Jessica had wandered off completely, sobbing. She opened the door to the Volvo and dropped into the passenger seat, closing it heavily behind. The sonorous thud echoed through the cemetery, causing several ghosts to jump. The sound drew their eyes toward our car. Then they wandered over to me, heads swiveling from one end of the graveyard to the other, my mother's included. I could tell from the look on her face that she knew Erin's story, the bleak prediction she spoke of.

"Thanks for the honesty," was all I could muster, my voice drowned beneath murdered desires, the hope of our future child snuffed out with the lightest breath.

"There's no guarantee it'll be you. If there is no child, there are no Spirits. You have other cousins, distant and close. It may be one of them," Erin replied.

"I wouldn't wish that on anyone," I said.

"But think of her." Erin's thin finger rose, pointing toward the Volvo. "Would you leave her alone with your child?"

My mind shifted to Lenny, the decisions he was having to make at that very moment.

"No," I replied, turning my back on the gaunt woman, retracing my steps toward the gate.

"I never wanted any of this to happen," Erin's voice floated over my shoulder. "Sometimes you invite evil into your life without intending to. Forgive me. Give my love to Milo."

"I'll think about it," I mumbled under my breath.

As I walked the weed-strewn road, my mother fell in step beside me. She didn't speak. The curved metal of the gate opened before us. I turned, gazing back at the scarecrow of a woman in her battered shawl. I imagined her sprawled out on the living room couch, the same drug that sucked the life from Milo's veins coursing through hers, ending her life ten years before her son's. It was unnerving. My stomach wouldn't settle. Joints ached. My head throbbed. I knew the woman had done terrible things, but having them laid bare before me, I couldn't wrap my mind around it, couldn't fathom how she shredded our plans of parenthood so quickly.

I managed to mumble a promise to my mother, swearing I'd visit again soon. She only smiled, told me everything would be alright, and waved me off. It was like condolences at graveside services. There was nothing anyone could say that would make things better.

I climbed into the driver's seat, a hollowness spreading through my limbs, reversing down the singular road. Jessica wiped at tears, cheeks flushed red, a patchwork of rash and irritation snaking over her pale skin. She stared straight ahead, as if looking into her future, sifting through eighty years of childless existence, just the two of us, barren. I placed my hand on Jessica's knee. She clasped it with both of hers, heaving a deep breath, mentioning something about adoption and how we'd be alright. Her forced optimism was well intended, but I reeled from Erin's words.

Even if my aunt was wrong, who's to say I'd even make it into my thirties, leaving the snapshot of a singular aged woman sitting alone in her father's old armchair. Dad was still silent, Uncle Thom unsure of what was to come. I could feel the root of an anxiety attack blossoming around my frontal lobe, climbing my chest. It was too much all at once. Jessica wanted a healthy family, something I was unsure I could give her.

Backing out into the street, a black Audi took my place at the mouth of the cemetery gate. For a moment, as our windows aligned, I could see Aunt Janey, a pair of thick sunglasses covering her eyes, a baseball cap constraining her curling hair. She waved as we passed, until she noticed the tearful woman at my side. Then she placed a foot on the gas and sped into the cemetery with a squeal of tires. Mom must have spoken to her about Erin. It was always the worst being the last to know.

CHAPTER 21

A month after cross-pollination took, Carla's nightshade began to bud, black berries developing in pods of six and seven. Wearing gloves, I plucked a dozen from the plant, gently carting them into our kitchen. I read if you boil the seeds briefly, you could speed up the germination process, killing off unwanted pinworm embryos. They bounced around the boiling water, scalding bubbles shifting their dark skin from one side to the other. With a strainer, I syphoned the water, a cloud of steam rising from the kitchen sink.

Growing trays stretched across the empty greenhouse table, soil filling the pockets. I lined the base of each with a mixture of stones to ensure proper drainage. Dipping the needle of my pH reader into the dirt, the meter fluctuated momentarily, settling on a six, perfectly centered for the acidity level.

I dug finger-sized holes into the soil, depositing each berry a few inches apart to create an equal dispersion of nutrients and sun. Lastly I sprinkled the gibberellic acid from the capsules I ordered over the soil, creating a thin powdered snow over the dark sediment.

In two, maybe three weeks I would have my first sprouts. Another month and I might be able to make out the markings on the leaves. *The Memory of Plants*, a book I got at the library, instructed me to crush up the leaves from the mother vine and knead them into the soil. It was supposed to accelerate the growing process in the same way hormones can make a tadpole metamorphosize in days. The plants would attain full height long before others showed signs of flowering.

I sat down on the stool, leaning over the soil, praying under my breath. With everything else crumbling around me, I needed this. The gardening and pollination experiments were the only things calming my nerves.

I drew the engagement ring with its inlaid sapphire from my pocket where I kept it most days. After Aunt Erin's prediction, I didn't know how Jessica would take my proposal, but I had to ask, to know whether she still held hope.

She had said that it wasn't a big deal, that there was always adoption, but I could see it in her eyes. Something had faltered and cracked. She held distant stares for moments on end before I would call her back to the present. Questions swam through her mind, questions I didn't know whether I wanted answered.

The ring's orbit was cool beneath my fingertips as I examined it in the greenhouse light. Perfectly smooth. The ring was a reminder of a path chosen, one I wanted to walk to the end more than anything else. And I would, I thought, depositing the ring into its tiny envelope. When Lenny was finally gone, I'd ask. I had been telling myself that for so long, it was hard to imagine things any other way.

***

Pushing through the back door, I found Lenny on the couch where he hadn't been before. His easel was set in the middle of the living room. I wanted to douse it in kerosene, burn the canvas before anyone else could see.

Lenny had finally done it. Jessica was rendered on the canvas, her long blonde hair now gray. Shoulders stooped, a layer of loose skin padded her neck. She clutched a letter, seated in her father's old armchair, a sweeping fire engulfing the room as she read. He had never heard the exact connotation of the letter, and the subsequent heart attack, but had attempted it anyway, hypothesizing the connection between postage and mortality.

"Was I close?" he asked from the couch, staring at the portrait. He wore a white tank top spotted with red and orange flecks of paint. "I think she's really going to like it."

"Put that away, man. You don't need to be a dick about this," I replied.

"Nope. I spent an awful long time on this one. I need to show it off. I mean, if we had a little discussion before the whole *get out of my house* bullshit, then maybe we could compromise. But no."

A harsh flurry of his paint brush and the fire swept further across the canvas, creeping over floorboards, licking at her shoes. The expression on Jessica's face was unchanged, still engrossed in the letter.

"Remember when you used to get along with Jessica? Before you found out about your death? She's not the one that changed. I just want to throw that out there," I said. "Now you're having a kid. Shouldn't you want to move out?"

"Yeah, on my own terms. Not hers," Lenny replied. "But honestly, I don't want to be around for this. She's got you whipped and you've gotten boring. Maybe it's better you never learn how you're going to die. There needs to be a little surprise left in your life," he said, adding another stroke to the canvas.

"You're really going to say that?"

"Yup. The way I see it, this is going to be monotony central. Don't you ever wonder what it would be like to be with someone else? Or to actually go do that forest restoration thing you talked about? This cemetery thing you're doing is pretty small scale."

"Hey. Maybe if you actually loved someone as much as I love Jessica, you'd understand. I feel bad for Juliet."

"Don't bring her into this."

"You're taking shots at Jess, why can't I?"

"You know you're kicking your last living friend out of your life, right?"

"You're not my—" That's when I realized, he was right. With Clint gone, Lenny was the last connection I had to the corporeal world. I spoke to the dead more than the living. Mark was a co-worker. We never got drinks after our shift. I only met Lenore twice, and she was the last person I could bring to mind having a conversation with. With Lenny gone, it would be Jessica and I, alone, in those rooms. "You're my last friend."

"*Was* is more accurate."

"Don't be like that."

"Forget it, I'll be out of here in two weeks. After that, don't call me or anything."

I hadn't heard the front door open, but Jessica stood behind me, her floral print blouse tucked into her neatly ironed black skirt.

"You're leaving early?" she stammered, unable to keep from smiling.

"Don't get too excited," Lenny replied. "You've still got two weeks to get through first."

"I think I'll manage."

"Oh, and by the way," Lenny said, shifting his easel so she could view his painting. "What do you think of my latest portrait?"

Jessica's smile slid from her face. I swear I could hear the expression hit the floor, heavy and wet, like a waterlogged sponge. She lunged forward, hands grasping at the canvas. Lenny was too quick. He swept the painting up, hoisting it above his head, inches out of reach. She hopped in awkward jolts, high-heels hampering upward lift. She swore in rapid bursts. Lenny only laughed, lowering the painting a hair, enticing further attempts, only to lift it high as she gained altitude.

"Nope, this one's going to be a centerpiece for my art show. You should be flattered..." Lenny said.

"You had no right to paint me. This is sick. People aren't meant to see their deaths," Jessica replied, out of breath. I would have thought from all those box jumps at CrossFit she'd have a higher vertical leap.

"Then I guess I'm a sadist," Lenny replied, gently pushing her aside, one hand eased into her shoulder. He carried the painting over his head, careful not to scrape it against the light fixtures or ceiling as he moved down the hall. His door closed and I was alone with Jessica, who steamed and stamped over our carpet. I found myself saying words I didn't completely believe. Comforting her. Assuring her it would all be over soon. That we were on an upswing.

"He's going to leave. It's just two weeks. All we have to do is exist for two weeks, then it will be us, together, like we've talked about," I said.

She nodded and leaned in to kiss me. Her lips were warm, her open mouth tasted like the tropical fruity gum she'd been chewing. Tongues traveled, skin pressed hard against skin. For a moment, I felt good about my decisions, then I saw the horde of Spirits over Jessica's shoulder, their hands reaching out to me as Aunt Erin had promised, skeletal fingers searching for something inside. I broke from Jessica's embrace, a cold sweat spotting my forehead.

"Is everything alright?" she asked.

"Yeah. I'm great. Two weeks and we're on our own," I replied.

CHAPTER 22

I expected the orgies from nights before. Naked bodies dripping sweat over upholstery and carpets, unfamiliar names howled into the night from beyond Lenny's wall. Cacti arranged by my bedside, an unnavigable maze of spines and bristles. But Lenny did none of that. Instead, the last two weeks of our cohabitation were marked by subtle inconveniences, minute pranks that snuck up on me, ones I might have missed if I didn't look close enough.

He moved my houseplants an inch or two out of the sunlight and smoked weed from every fruit Jessica bought for her lunch breaks. I had never seen so many biodegradable bongs in my life. He hid toothbrushes in sugar jars. Exchanged my cologne with Jessica's perfume, switching bottles, ensuring I would smell like lavender and violets instead of Old Spice. I didn't really mind. They were more comical than offensive.

The only woman he brought over was Juliet, the slightest baby bump pressing against her shirt front. They never said anything to us, just closed their bedroom door, made vigorous love as was commonplace, and discussed the layout of their new apartment. I saw the way he looked at her. It was the same way I looked at Jessica.

***

On the night Lenny finally moved out, the same night his art show opened, I found myself donning a shirt and tie. Even though Jessica said I shouldn't go, that I'd miss an episode of our favorite show, I walked out, planting a kiss on her lips, a promise of *I love you* in her ear.

I needed to see his paintings one last time before they slipped from my life. Even though Lenny was occasionally a dick, I didn't want my last living friendship to flicker out on such a sour note. Not everything fit neatly into a morality test.

Shades of gray, I reminded myself.

***

At the gallery in downtown Dennis, the walls were hung with portraits of men and women I didn't know. The small crowd meandering from canvas to canvas peered at names as they examined artist statements tacked to the wall. Small bulbs above added texture and shadow.

The paintings had been arranged in simple black frames, leaving the full emphasis on the subjects, the captured seconds. There was a balding man wearing a Hawaiian-print shirt submerged at the bottom of a pool. A middle aged woman with blonde hair entering an elevator filled with Spirits, the lights to various floors all extinguished. There was an image of a woman I recognized as one of Lenny's late-night guests, fluorescent hair extensions and subwoofing headphones no longer around her neck. She was older, slimmer, falling from the heights of a skyscraper, staring up at the sun as she plummeted toward the sidewalk. The portrait of Jessica hung prominently in the middle of the room.

The back wall housed a single frame, larger than the rest. It was of Lenny looking at his reflection in a gas station bathroom, the mirror's image showing a group of Spirits waiting by a urinal. The room's light was tinged green, the bathroom tiles a faded teal. Remingtons lingered in the Spirits' hands, not yet raised for the final moment. Lenny's hair was clipped short, no longer unruly or slick with gel. He was still thin, long arms bare beneath a gray and red striped tank top. His eyes were rimmed black, sleep eluding his future self. Under the portrait stood the man himself, nearly five years younger, a tailored suit, flat black, with a pale blue undershirt beneath.

He greeted fans, shaking hands, doling out business cards and consulting on future commissions. It was strange to see him in that light. Professional. Respected. He painted most of the portraits in our living room shirtless, listening to some alternative reggae band through our shitty speakers. This wasn't the image I associated with my soon-to-be ex-roommate. He wore more clothes at that moment than I had seen in months. Jessica refused to accompany me to his art show, especially after the whole unsolicited portrait debacle. I understood why she was angry, but it would have been nice to have her at my side, examining his brush work, the message behind his paintings.

I spent a moment scanning the walls before I parted the crowd and approached Lenny. Three people, two women in their thirties and a man in his fifties, surrounded him, nodding with enthusiasm as Lenny described his process. Juliet stood beside him, a sequined black dress draped over her body, brown hair let down in orderly curls.

"The only time I'll pass on a commission is when the patron smiles when they tell me about their death. There's a certain type of person that fetishizes it. I can't handle that," he said.

"I don't think I could manage a smile saying something like that," a red-haired woman said.

"I should have told Jessica that," I said, breaching the edge of their circle. "I didn't know there was a loophole to get out of your portraits."

"Nothing would have held me from that. She was overreacting anyway. Look at all these people. They love my work. I'll never understand what her problem was," Lenny said, ignoring the hand I extended for a shake, his head cocked to the left. "What are you doing?"

"Trying to be supportive. I wanted to see the show," I replied, letting my hand fall to my side.

"Supportive? If you wanted to be supportive, you shouldn't have kicked me out of the house. That seems logical, right?" he asked, turning to Juliet.

She pulled him down by the collar of his shirt, forcing him to stoop to her height. She whispered into his ear, covering her lips with a cupped hand. I could tell she was trying to get him to be cordial, if not for the sake of our fragmentary friendship, then for his appearance in front of his fans. He sighed deeply as she released his shirt. He took one step forward and wrapped a hesitant arm around my shoulder in a semblance of a hug.

"Thanks for coming," he said, with a smile that seemed to say he regretted everything that had happened.

"Didn't want to miss the show. You've got some of my favorites around here," I replied, looking over my shoulder toward Jessica and the creeping flames that ate away at her armchair.

"It did come out pretty well, didn't it?"

"Yeah. It's not accurate, but the detail's perfect. That's really what she's going to look like when she's eighty."

"I hope you get to see her at that age," Juliet interjected.

"I do too," I replied.

After a long silence, Lenny slapped me on the back, hard, forcing me to stumble.

"I don't want to be a dick," Lenny said, "but I've got a bunch of other people to talk to. You don't need to run off or anything. Enjoy the paintings. It's what they're here for."

"Yeah, I will," I replied, beginning to put distance between the two of us.

Lenny turned and kissed Juliet, holding her there as if waiting for a camera flash to capture the moment. It seemed honest, their connection. It was odd how things unfolded, the way a future could be decided by something so brief. In a way, the instant resonated. Maybe Dad would finally talk to me. Maybe Jessica and I would be happy, our long lives stretching out before us. Our child birthed without the Spirits looming over my shoulders, their hunger for my flesh forgotten.

Jessica made me happy, regardless what Lenny said. I couldn't imagine my lips locked to another's, my arm around someone else's hip. After all, travels to distant forests were only distractions from a search for love.

"Hey, when you go home, I left something in my old room for you. Check it out. Everything else is gone. I promise," Lenny said, turning to a group of teenagers. They examined a portrait of a woman stuck beneath a sewer grate, fingers wrapped around the metal bars, eyes darting off to the left, to something unseen and unsketched.

I let the crowd swallow him, allowing myself to drift toward the far wall, the line of portraits hanging there. A large group of people stood around Clint's gored body, the bull wandering in the background of the canvas, blood-smeared flowers in the foreground. It was the sister shot of the painting he gave me, the one hanging above my basement shrine. I caught clips of dialogue, a general consent that no one gathered around wanted to meet their end in a similar fashion. I couldn't bring myself to breach their circle and speak on my friend's behalf. They said the same thing most said about whichever portrait they stood before.

Can you imagine what their ancestors did?

At least that one's quick. Starving for a week, now that I'd prefer to skip.

I hope there's less blood when I go. I can't believe anyone could lose so much.

I found myself pushing through the crowd, quickly scanning over the arranged paintings. A woman wading into a half opened iron maiden, a man losing his footing at the edge of a mountain path. There was a young guy in tight jeans and a flannel shirt strapped to an operating table, an arrangement of every sharpened medical tool imaginable lying on a neighboring tray. As my heart rate began to spike, I took one last look at the image of Jessica, her letter, and the encroaching flames. The look on her face was far more serene than I remembered, eyes half shut, mouth peaked in a smile of acceptance. I hoped my own demise would be so peaceful, but at the moment I seriously doubted it, surrounded by the most gruesome deaths imaginable.

***

Instead of going home, I swung my Volvo down the narrow cemetery roads of Mt. Pleasant, headlights illuminating graves in the dark. I parked on the grass before my father's headstone. Mark hated when I pulled up on the lawn, the embedded tire tracks marring the manicured cut. I sat behind the wheel for a minute, thinking over how to approach my father. Being a doctor, I figured he couldn't fight the urge to help someone with a medical inquiry. I could fake an accent, claim some sickness in need of diagnosing. He wouldn't deny a sick man relief. He wasn't that kind of person.

Looking around, I scanned for lingering ghosts, those who refused to sink with the sun. Only a distant specter stood out against the night, pale skin luminous in the dark. Thankfully, it wasn't Clint. I didn't want to hear whatever jokes he would devise after hearing our interaction.

Opening the car door, I altered my step, plodding heavily across the grass, emphasizing each footfall. My moment of dissuasion had to be convincing. With one hand on the cool marble, I coughed into my free hand, clearing my throat.

"Aye, you think this could be cancer?" I asked, directing my improvised New York accent toward the ground. My heart rate hadn't slowed since I left the art show, the paintings of bloody dismemberments and torture devices etched in my mind. "Thing used to be the size of a dime. Now I'd say it's more of a quarter. Real asymmetrical."

I waited, listening for any stirring beneath my feet. I went to clear my throat again, but my father's face peered up at me, blades of grass rimming his countenance like a lion's mane. The lines on his face lacked emotion; no smile, no frown. It was the first time I had gotten close to him in nearly three years. Nothing had changed, as was the case for every ghost, hairline still receded, an extra pouch of skin developed under his chin, eyes clouded and distant.

"But seriously, I need to talk to you about—" I began to say, as he bobbed beneath the surface of the ground, descending as if into a pool of water, out of sight.

I followed him down, dropping on all fours. I attempted to grab his hair, to hold the skin of his cheeks before he could drift away. I tore up grass, digging trenches in the dirt with my fingernails. A single punch to the packed earth left my wrist shot with pain, a quick flash rippling through the joint and up my arm. I lost my footing and fell headlong into the stone, connecting forehead to solid slab. I rolled onto my back, staring at the night sky, swearing, cursing my father, the knives of his abandonment sinking deeper into my shoulder blades. My fingers fumbled over the raised lump, pressing as a dull throb swept from the spot. Stars drifted in and out of cloud cover. Wet grass dampened my shirt. I lay there and muttered promises to my father, swearing I'd get him to talk. He could hear me, I knew it.

Scare tactics rarely worked on ghosts.

CHAPTER 23

Jessica met me at the door half naked, her toned body backlit by the hall light, pale skin nearly as translucent as ghost flesh. She leaned forward, grabbing my arm and forcing me up against the wall, all those CrossFit classes putting weight behind her stiff arms. As she slammed the door, she pressed her lips to mine, tongue wandering through my mouth. Her flat stomach and breasts pressed against the front of my shirt. She didn't speak, allowing her movements to lead mine. I left a trail of discarded clothes as we stumbled toward our bedroom, past the closed door to Lenny's room. Whatever Lenny left could wait.

It was our first night alone in the apartment.

***

I forgot every sexual experience I'd had up to that moment. Her blue eyes hung on mine, never looking away, focused, keen and intense. For a moment I could have sworn I stepped out of my own body and watched our lovemaking from the ceiling. Eventually, the silence slipped away, replaced by my name cascading off her tongue. I had no idea how it lasted so long. I figured it would be over in seconds, given my recent anxiety, but the clock flashed two in the morning. I couldn't have walked through the door any later than nine. With a final gasp, she fell back, sinking into my arms.

"I love you," she whispered, nuzzling into me.

"I love you too," I replied, twining my fingers through the expanse of her hair.

She fell asleep within minutes. I was left awake, staring up into the darkness. A slight headache sent dull throbs through my temples, dehydration from the previous hours. A thin layer of salt coated my skin. Muscles in my abs tightened uncontrollably, cramping, making it hard for me to roll out of bed. I slipped Jessica's head onto the pillow. Her eyes remained shut as I stole off to the kitchen to get a glass of water.

The tap trickled as I filled my cup. Jessica deserved to sleep soundly after the last few months. I looked out the kitchen window into the darkness outside, toward the streetlight a distance down the road, sipping my water. It illuminated the corner of Jerry's junk heap, the light reflecting off an upturned lawnmower, a rusted amalgamation of bed springs and wires. Then the light disappeared into surrounding trees, their thick limbs like giants in the dusk.

My mind wandered to my planned marriage proposal. Lenny was gone. It was time. I had the night picked out. The ring now rested in my bedside table. I could practically see the look of pleasure on her face as I said those words kneeling in the sand. As long as Aunt Erin's predictions truly didn't weigh on Jessica's mind, things would go smoothly. I hoped. Finishing my water, I washed my hands and forearms, splashing my face in the process. Then I moved off down the hall.

Parked before Lenny's door, his parting sentiments reminded me of the gift within. I hadn't looked inside since he left, the final confirmation that he was gone, the life once lived on the other side now continuing elsewhere. With a little hesitation, I twisted the handle, flipping on the light as I walked in.

The only object left in Lenny's room was a small portrait of myself. It leaned against the far wall, nearly devoid of detail. In the painting, I stood with my hands in my pockets, gazing out at the viewer. He placed me in my work uniform, stained jeans and an orange t-shirt, the town's emblem emblazoned on my breast. I wasn't older. He didn't add the extra pounds of age, the hint of frailty that came with time. This unnerved me. Was it a prediction of an early demise? Hopefully not. The rest of the canvas was an untouched white, all except a faint shadow in the upper right corner. Looking closely, I could see it was a Spirit peering down at me, examining, searching. Its skeletal fingers gripped the edge of the canvas, the plague doctor's beak detailed to historic specifications.

Attached to the bottom was a sticky note. It read:

When you find out how it's going to happen, let me know. I'd be happy to finish this for you. Good luck with your search.

Your friend,

Lenny.

A lump rose in my throat. I hadn't thought I'd be so torn at his departure. Predicting emotions was never my strong suit. I sat on the floor, pulling the canvas into my lap, examining the brush strokes.

The pain in my wrist had yet to dull from punching my father's tomb. Lenny's words, while well intentioned, emphasized the discomfort, prodding my anxiety into being once more beyond the canvas. The figment stood before me in the guise of a young boy, myself, somewhere between the ages of twelve and fourteen. The young me cracked a braces-laced smile, tipped his baseball cap, and asked, *What if this was middle age?* Then he vanished, sucked deep into the depths of my mind. My fixation on lifespans was unhinged for the evening. No calming breathing routines helped. The image of my younger self disappeared, but I could still hear his question reverberate in my ear. Lenny was gone. It was official. Jessica and I were the sole inhabitants of our apartment, and it didn't make me feel any better.

I looked up at the ceiling. The paintings Lenny toiled over across the last three years were now gone. A thick layer of smooth white coated every inch. Clint and Carla were missing. Carlton Shea and Helane Grieux were left to the distant past, their portraits now indistinguishable from the rest of the bleached expanse. Besides the indents in the rug where his bed posts and writing desk had been, I could barely tell anyone lived in the room just the day before. I left the painting where it leaned against the wall, not wanting to extract the last remnant of Lenny's life from the empty space.

CHAPTER 24

My mower was bogged down from wet grass gathering beneath the deck. It rained for three days, making the lawns more puddle than dry patch. Still, the grass needed to be cut. We hadn't been able to mow for a week. At that rate, we'd be so far behind when things finally dried, we'd never catch up.

Even though I was wearing a raincoat, I was soaked to the bone. My jacket was plastered to my back in a cold damp suction. Ghosts shook their heads in sympathy as I navigated between headstones. Grass barely cuts when it's wet. Mostly it bent down, matted beneath its fellow green comrades. The few blades that were sheared shot out of the catch and splattered across the nearest stones, leaving a dark green tint to the pale granite.

I dipped down into a gully. My rear tires slid sideways, leaving two tracks of mud in my wake. As I attempted to regain control, my forty-eight tipped into a divot at the base of Mr. Doane's twin angels. The ground held for a second before the whole front end fell straight down, dirt and mud erupting in a geyser of sediment, launching me off the sulky, nearly landing in the angels' arms. The safeties caught and the blades died in an instant, the rear half of my mower still above ground, while the rest was interred. I hit a sinkhole, a grave whose slate had cracked beneath the erosion of rain, leaving an empty cavity beneath.

Mr. Doane bent over me, holding his top hat in hand, inquiring if I was all right. I lay on my back, breath knocked from my lungs, water sloshing in my ears. He held his hat over my face as if it would keep me dry, but the droplets continued to descend. He was calm for a minute before he looked at his stone. He began to mutter angrily. The murmur evolved into a howl, becoming a full scream in seconds. He moved from my side and stared down into his grave, looking at the unearthed remains that had once been his body.

"You fix this, you fix this right now," Mr. Doane bellowed.

I sucked in as much air as I could manage, every muscle in my body aching as I joined him by the grave. The slate covering the tomb was halved. One jagged side had slipped down into the crypt, the other hung over the mouth of the opening, supported by the walls of brick. The casket's lid, or what was left of it after years of rot, offered no cover to the bones. The skull was yellowed, dark marks from rotting tissue stained around the eye sockets and cheekbones. The ribs were raised in a hollow cave, each pointed peak bare, scraps of clothing disintegrated years ago.

"Why are you waiting? Does this not matter to you, boy? Go, go!" Mr. Doane said, waving his arms, flourishing them as if to slap me from the edge of the hole. I backpedaled, trying to think of a solution.

I ran to find Mark, Mr. Doane's wails following my steps. Looking to my side, I saw the other ghosts gather around the cave-in: some to offer calming words to Mr. Doane, others to look at his exposed carcass. They shambled slowly, all urgency sucked from their step years ago.

***

Mark sat in the shed sharpening mower blades. Molten orange sparks showered from the grinder's abrasive disc, cascading over the floor. His smartphone was tuned to a weather report: *Rain... Rain, not going to let up until next week.* He stacked the sharpened blade on a neat pile of others as I entered the room, cutting the grinder's motor, silencing the spinning engine.

"Looks like we're not going to catch a break," he began to say.

"No, no, we're not. I got a cave-in over at Doane. The mower's pretty far in the hole. He's screaming," I said, catching my breath.

"Did you try to get him to stop?"

"Nothing I was going to say was going to stop that guy. You'd think I killed him again. To make matters worse, all the other ghosts are heading that way."

Mark shook his head, rose, and unlocked the closet at the back of the shed. He withdrew a length of towing chain from inside.

"Get some shovels. We've still got a few yards of loam in the back of the dump truck. It will be wet and heavy as hell, but we got to fill it somehow," Mark said.

I sorted through the pile of shovels, pickaxes, crowbars, rakes, brooms, and other landscaping tools, trying to find the right implement. Only the pointed spades would be able to dig into the muddy mixture. I grabbed two, tossed them in the back of the truck, and hopped in, the uncomfortable dampness of my pants more evident pressed against the vinyl seat. Mark drove as fast as the narrow roads would allow, avoiding stones leaning precariously over the paved path.

When we arrived, more than a hundred ghosts surrounded the hole. Some had coaxed Mr. Doane to step away from the mouth of his grave. They stood beneath a copse of scrub pine, attempting to distract him from the mess. One of the only questions left to a ghost was what happened if their grave was destroyed? Rumor had it they would be forgotten, dying another death of obscurity. Some claimed it was how you finally made it to heaven, once the last earthly remnant of yourself eroded completely. It was in the Bible. If bones remained, so would the ghost. The Spirits caused anxiety in the living. The deterioration of a grave caused it in the dead.

My father's outline hovered at the top of a hill, leaning against a maple. The familiar slouch of his shoulders and hang of his head were clear against the dark sky. He stared down at the crowd, shaking his head at the scene. I waved. It wasn't returned. He vanished before I could part the sea of ghosts, trudging up the incline toward him.

"That your dad?" Mark asked as he tossed me the end of the chain.

"Yeah, that's him. I thought about running up there, but we've got to get this done before anything else happens," I replied.

Mark hooked his end of the chain to the truck's ball hitch.

"What else are they going to do? Yell some more? It's not like they can start knocking over stones in protest. Go catch him."

The hill was now devoid of my father's silhouette. I could have caught him. He was never very fast, even before the lethargy of death took over. But I didn't. More ghosts crowded the grave from the surrounding stones. I wasn't going to leave Mark to pull the mower out by himself. It would take him forever to fill the hole in the rain.

I shooed away gathered ghosts. Their bodies rose like flies off raw meat. I wrapped the chain around the handlebars and hooked the metal claw onto the exposed portion of the deck. With a thumbs-up, Mark stepped on the gas. The slack in the chain disappeared. The engine sputtered and revved as the mower emerged from the chasm. With a final jolt, the mower slid across the grass, gouging deep furrows. The ghosts retreated to the hill where my father had stood, getting a last look before we filled the hole.

Mr. Doane left the ghosts by the scrub pine. He floated over to his stone where we were dumping the contents of the truck bed into the chasm. Mark had the bed raised to the sky. The loam slid down in one solid heap, spreading across the grass, clogging one corner of the hole.

"I never thought this would happen. The mason who set my vault was a competent man. Not like the fellows who constructed some of the shabbier monuments around here," he said, a hand running over his bushy mustache.

"It's not uncommon. Ground's always so wet. High water level. Displaces all the dirt so you can't predict how sturdy the ground's going to be on any given day," Mark said, lowering the truck's bed back to its original position, the entirety of its contents now scattered.

"I thought death would be the last shock of my life," Mr. Doane said.

"You'd hope so, wouldn't you?" Mark replied.

I shoveled loam, tamping it into place so there wouldn't be any air pockets when it settled. The last of Mr. Doane's bones disappeared from sight when the bed was emptied. It was now just a matter of making sure it didn't happen again.

I walked over the fresh loam, flattening it until it leveled out.

"I really apologize for all this," I said.

"I believe this would have happened whether it was you on the mower or anyone else. I'm embarrassed at my overreaction," Mr. Doane said.

"Don't worry about it," I told him.

"Go start up the mower," Mark said to me as he returned to the truck. "Take your break once you get it back to the shed. We can't leave it out here to get rained on."

What else had it been doing all morning? I wanted to ask him, but what good would it do? I was already drenched. The five-minute mower ride back to the shed wouldn't make any difference. Once I got it started and said goodbye to Mr. Doane, I took the center road leading straight to the end of the cemetery. My father didn't linger beneath the trees along the path. He was gone. Most of the other ghosts had retreated to their coffins. Even though they couldn't feel the rain, it did nothing to improve the atmosphere of the place.

***

The line at Box Office Cafe was long, nearly winding out the door. The restaurant's walls were painted a light orange, every inch of available space hung with old movie posters in glass frames: *Jaws*, *Star Wars*, *Return of the Living Dead*. It was the theme. Items on the menu were named after famous movies or actors. *My Big Fat Greek Wedding* was a meatball sub. *Reign of Fire* was a buffalo chicken pizza. The heat spiked every time an oven opened, scenting the air with melted mozzarella and oregano.

In the seating area a large flat screen protruded from the wall, the first scenes of *Edward Scissorhands* snipping across the surface. Everyone was there for lunch, another dose of caffeine to keep their eyes open, but more so as an excuse to stay out of the rain.

Somehow, above the commotion, I heard the door open and a familiar voice sigh as she merged into line. I turned and there was Lenore, just as drenched as I was, an inverted umbrella in hand as she tried to recurve the spines and stretched canvas.

I stepped out of line and walked to her side, the eyes of other blue collar men following me.

"You want help with that?" I asked.

For a second, it seemed she couldn't place my voice, eyes focused downward toward the umbrella's refused cooperation. After shaking it several times out of frustration, she looked up, and uttered an unsure *Ohh*...as if I wasn't the person she wanted to see.

"Yeah, here, see what you can do," she said, handing me the umbrella.

In the midst of all the people, I wrestled the spines back into shape, tossing thick drops of water on everybody within a six-foot radius. The grumbling grew worse. One man threatened to kick my ass. I shrugged and he went back to contemplating which coffee would get him through the afternoon.

"How have you been?" I asked, handing the umbrella back. "Probably not a good week to visit the Chases, right?"

"Yeah, terrible time for it, but it's not often I can get away from my mother. Take the chances when you get them, you know?" she said, looking down at her soaked apparel.

Her band t-shirt and skinny jeans were even more plastered to her than usual. Even wet, they had the look of being slept in. Her bangs were pressed against her forehead in damp clumps. Only the dancing skeleton tattoo seemed unfazed by the inclement weather. I didn't notice any odd bruising for once, which made me glad.

"I left a few minutes after your little incident wrapped up," she said. "I saw the whole thing from the mausoleum. How'd that fall feel?"

I hadn't thought much about it, but my shoulder killed. "Could be worse. If I hit the stone, it would have been easier to just roll me into the grave and save everyone the trouble."

"I think that would be against health codes," Lenore replied.

"Hey, that's not..."

She laughed. "I'm just giving you a hard time."

It took a while for us to reach the front of the line. Most of the tables had emptied. All the Fords and Chevys had pulled from the parking lot, drifting back to the job sites they had abandoned. We talked about the weather, what the Chases thought about the cave-in, and how they never had to worry about such things. They hadn't been among the crowd that swarmed Mr. Doane.

"*Alexander the Great* and a Jack Nicholson, light on the cream and sugar please," Lenore said to the woman behind the counter. She rang it up, green numbers appearing on the digital readout. Ten-fifty. Lenore rummaged in her pockets and drew out eight dollars in damp bills. She counted them with a last hope there might be a five hidden among the ones.

"Cancel the coffee, I guess," Lenore said.

"I got you," I said, handing her three more ones. "Don't take the coffee off her order."

The woman behind the counter nodded and placed a Styrofoam cup beneath the burbling coffee maker.

"I don't know if I'll be able to pay you back anytime soon," Lenore said with a frown. "Mom's increased my weekly mask production quota. The Spiritual items market is in decline. Money's tight."

"No worries, just eat lunch with me and we'll call it even. It's not much fun to sit here alone," I said, pointing toward the tables of middle-aged men scanning through smartphones, ignoring Tim Burton's masterpiece on the TV.

I placed my order, retrieved my *Club Dread* sandwich, and joined Lenore at a table next to the window. The surface was covered in actor's head shots pulled from tabloids and the internet, all covered in a thin layer of shellac. Lenore's umbrella rested against the glass. She was already halfway through her buffalo chicken sandwich, leaving the remainder lying on top of the foil as if she were full. I ate a few bites in silence, waiting for her to say something. She only looked at the TV screen. Someone changed the channel to the news. Protestors continued to block bulldozers before an old growth forest. The Spirits lingering in the boughs appeared closer than before, breathing down machine operators' necks. I was glad the Spirits placed such emphasis on conservation, that they were there for the trees.

"Is she always like that?" I asked.

"Who?" Lenore replied without looking at me.

"Your mother, you know, from the other day?"

"Yup. That wasn't the worst. Not even close. She once told this guy he'd die right after the reading, and what do you know, they killed him the second he tried to get out of his seat. I'm pretty sure she saw the Spirits sneaking down the hall and didn't mention it."

"How'd it happen?"

"Slit throat. Did you notice there wasn't a carpet in there?"

"Yeah."

"Well, there was one a few months ago. She's jacked up the price since then so she can buy a new one."

"I thought that was a bit much to pay when she didn't really tell me anything," I replied.

"I can try to get you your money back if you want."

"Naw, it's fine. Jessica wasn't happy about it, but what can you do?"

"And how's Jessica after all those predictions, or lack thereof?"

"Well, she's alright. We had a bad time in Western Mass with my aunt."

In truth, since Lenny's exodus, our lives had been great. We were having insane amounts of sex. Jessica walked naked through the halls at all hours of the day. It was like the first months of our relationship, bodies new, a constant desire to run fingers over exposed flesh. The night before, after making love, we talked about the future, our wedding, having a child. When I mentioned the last topic, Jessica's eyes wandered away from mine, drifting toward the windows and the greenhouse by the woods. I knew she worried about Aunt Erin's words, but my looming meal of nightshade was beginning to overshadow other concerns.

"What happened?" Lenore asked, finally meeting my eye.

"Basically, if I'm connected to my aunt, when Jessica and I have our first child, a mob of Spirits is going to skin me alive," I replied.

"That's rough. You sure you really want kids? Maybe it's a blessing."

"I don't think so. We've always wanted one, but that's only half of it. I'm not sure about the connection. I could still be linked to my father, or a dozen other ancestors who've given me next to no info either. Can I ask you something?"

Lenore nodded, a leaf of lettuce protruding from her lips.

"Would you want to stay with a guy who was going to die next week?"

"Sure, if they were a worthwhile person," she replied without pause.

"Well, that goes without saying, but what if we could never get married? What if my aunt was right about the kids?"

"If Jessica's talking to you like this, then she's neurotic. She should want to live whatever life she can with you. If it's three years, whatever. Twenty? Even better. I dated this guy, he was a year older than me. He died after we dated for five months. It sucked, but I'm glad we had even that long."

"I get that, but did you know ahead of time about his timeline?"

"He had a vague idea. Neither of us cared. There are only so many happy moments in life, you know? I figure you've got to take them when you can, even if it's only for a little while."

After saying that, we grew quiet.

Lenore folded the foil back around her half-eaten sandwich, twisting the ends together to keep it from falling apart in the rain. She opened the mouth of a small drawstring bag slung over her shoulder and placed the sandwich inside. She finished the last drops of coffee, but didn't throw the cup away.

"It's what I've done my whole life. I've been conditioned to worry. Dad was big on the idea you need to do what's right so you don't screw anyone else over," I replied.

"And you don't have to. Just don't be a sleaze and the Spirits aren't going to lynch your kids. That's all you can control. The rest is already decided. It sounds like you're doing right by Jessica, so why worry?"

"Sage words from someone so young."

"I take most of it from the crap Mom tells customers. Every few weeks she says something worthwhile," Lenore said as she stood, retrieving the umbrella from the window. "Thanks for the coffee. I'll pay you back sometime."

"You can give it to me when you're visiting the Chases. Just stop by the shed. We're there first thing every morning."

"Yeah, maybe. I don't visit much anymore, but I'll think about it," Lenore said, pushing in her seat. The metal legs screeched as they dragged across the hardwood. "Remember to relax a little."

"I'll see what I can do," I replied. "Do you want a ride?"

"Thanks, but I'm all set. I don't mind the rain," Lenore replied.

She walked out the door and back into the downpour. With the umbrella open, she crossed the parking lot, dodging puddles swamping the cement. With her free hand, she held the coffee cup outside of the canvas awning, letting the raindrops fill the Styrofoam. I followed her steps as she walked in the direction of the cemetery, the same way I'd take after cleaning off the table. It was a long walk. I had a feeling she was lying about her current sleeping arrangements, but I wouldn't call her on it.

When I looked up after clearing the crumbs from my sandwich, Lenore disappeared, a screen of rain washing out her silhouette.

CHAPTER 25

Clint's notes were splayed on the greenhouse table, water spots and soil smears marring the paper. Comparing the image he sketched on the page to the slender stalks creeping from the soil, I could tell he was right. Internet resources claimed flowers couldn't be present. Contemporary botanical texts said more months were needed. But there were my twelve freshly potted nightshade vines, each with recently budded flowers, all baring the early marking of children's teeth. I only had to wait for the berries to swell. Doubt left my mind. Toxicity had fled the plant's veins. Ingesting the ripe fruit would be harmless, Clint's voice whispered in my ear.

Early that morning I stopped at his stone to find him hunched over, weeping, his face in his hands.

"What's wrong, buddy?" I asked, stepping off my mower.

"Do you know how long it's been since I've seen her?" he whispered.

I did the math in my head, tracing calendar pages back to the day of his death. "Five months?" I guessed.

"Close," he replied. "You know I never went more than a week without visiting. I need to see her face. I'm losing my mind."

Clint, up to that point, had seemed well adjusted. Our conversations had taken on a familiar tone. Mostly jokes about high school friends and speculation on what species of plant would survive the end of the world. His money was on algae blooms in the ocean. I knew it would be mushroom spores and their miles of mycelia. If they could travel through space, they could survive the implosion of a planet.

"I know it's rough, but really, I have a good feeling about the plants. Give me another week or two and I'll take the final step," I said, botanical pride thrumming in my veins.

"You're that confident?" he asked, face appearing from between his hands. At that moment, as despair flashed to hope, I got a glimpse of the desolation in Clint's eyes, the identical way he had looked at the mental hospital.

"Yeah. No doubt about the markings this time. None at all."

He rose to his feet, brushing nonexistent dirt and grass clippings from his pants, old habits still clinging to life. He straightened his flannel, sucked in a deep breath, and aligned his spine.

"I don't want you to rush into this. Be sure before you pick the berries," he said, remnants of tears in his eyes.

"Of all the things I'm going to rush into, this isn't one of them," I replied.

"Are you going to ask her?"

***

Water trickled down my arm, dampening my sleeve. I hadn't been paying attention to where the watering can was pointed, slowly emptying its contents over my skin instead of the rootball. I brought myself back into focus and topped off the last pot, the slightest stream dribbling over the ceramic edge. Yes, I told him, yes, I was going to ask Jessica to marry me. He seemed excited, but not as excited as he did about the plants, which made sense given his current state of affairs.

Folding the notes in hand, I hung the watering can on a hook near the door. Then I left. Jessica had just stepped out onto the back porch, a piece of paper in one hand, a pen in the other.

"I figured you were out here," she said, moving to the glass table we purchased from Jerry two weeks ago. She sat in one of the mismatched chairs we arranged around the table, the mesh seat whining as the fabric stretched taut. "Come look at this."

I sat in the plastic chair beside her, looking over the rudimentary diagram she had sketched. My name appeared at the top of the sheet, six lines drooping below like squid tentacles. At the end of each were the names of remaining relatives. My father. Aunt Erin. Thom. Cousin Calvin, whom I hadn't spoken to. Aunt Cori and Aunt Diane, both left for last minute meetings. Beyond my father, the odd assortment of relations had already given a few answers away. Most seemed like improbable matches, but couldn't be ruled out completely. Each had a date stretching over the next two months scribbled below their names. Jessica mapped out each of our upcoming weekends to correspond with a visit.

"I've worked it out so we can get this done as soon as possible. With my days off and your vacation time, it should all line up," she said.

"God, I love you," I said, leaning across the table, kissing her on the mouth.

"Now hold on," she said, breaking away from my advance as soon as our lips brushed. "I wanted to talk to you about something before we continue with this."

I drew back, hesitant at what would come next.

"What's up?" I asked.

"I don't want you to keep working on Clint's nightshade. It's just a myth. It's stupid to put this much effort into keeping you alive," Jessica said, gesturing to the piece of paper, "to waste it on poisoning yourself."

"But it's going to work," I replied.

"No, it's not. You need to stop or…" She trailed off.

"Or what? I'm not going to die."

"You don't know that. First Aunt Erin's prediction, now this? If you want to live, you have to work with me, not Clint."

"But he's my best friend."

"And he's dead. Nothing's going to change that."

"This could."

She shook her head.

"This isn't a difficult decision," she said, pushing the piece of paper across the table until it rested directly in front of me. "I don't want to find you on the kitchen floor like the sparrows."

"But you won't—" I began to say before my words were interrupted by the sudden screech of her chair's metal legs scraping across the deck's wooden boards. Jessica stood and turned without a word, returning to the house. The screen door crashed at her heels, emphasizing my poorly chosen argument. Leaning back in my chair, I drew the sheet of paper from the table. All the time she spent on me. I didn't know if I had ever done a decent job communicating how much I appreciated it. Simple sentences never carried the emotion I intended.

I traced the six lines with my index finger, from my name to my aunts, then back again.

I'd stop if that was what she wanted.

The wedding ring pushed against the denim of my jeans. She hadn't noticed. If this was how she felt, she should have said so earlier. I pushed everything else aside for the sake of our relationship. Why wouldn't I do the same for this? My time in the greenhouse could have been spent traveling, talking to ghosts, working on my other gardens, or planting my latest crop of birch and cherry in the cemeteries.

What could I say to Clint to break the news? Pushing it off into the future wouldn't make things better. My anxiety wouldn't appreciate it. A replay ran on loop in my mind, Clint on his knees, weeping. He'd have to understand, though I knew he wouldn't.

***

I hardly saw Jessica the rest of the day. Before I could apologize, she slipped out of the house and went for a two-hour run. She locked the door to the bathroom upon her return, no shower stall conversations through banks of steam. With a plate of sweet potato chili, she moved from room to room, uprooting herself from one table to the next whenever I slid across from her. In the end, she went to bed before me, locking the door, the resounding click causing my heart to sink even lower than it already had.

***

I tripped the lock. Jessica didn't say a word as I entered the room, relocking the door behind me. I said goodnight, but it wasn't returned. I said, "I love you." Her reply was an unintelligible grumble into her pillow. I turned the light off without even searching for the book on my bedside table. After a moment, Jessica rolled onto her back. Her shoulder brushed my own.

"I didn't mean to sound controlling," she said. "I've just been stressed lately. Talking to Aunt Helen was easy. She just told me what was going to happen. I never expected your side of things to be so difficult. I just want things to work out, you know?"

"I'm sorry, Jess, I really appreciate your help with everything," I said, placing an arm around her. She wound her fingers through my own, pulling them closer, tucking my hand beneath her breast. "I was trying to tell you earlier that I'd forget the flowers. If that's what you want. It just came out of the blue. I wasn't expecting you to ask me to quit."

"I didn't expect you to keep this up for so long."

"Really?"

"Think of how it sounds to me. *Hey, Jessica, I'm going to eat these poisonous berries to bring Clint's girlfriend back to life. I'll probably die, but at least I'm being a good friend. You'll be okay after I'm gone, right?"*

Her imitation was spot on. I heard similar voices at the back of my head each time I walked through the greenhouse door. Endangering my life seemed far off, the final act more a theory than a tangible possibility. I wanted to help Clint, remain loyal to our agreement, but now the last scene was opening before me and reality had slunk on stage. The potential to beat out death also held its sway. The possibility of using another plant to alleviate the problems Jessica and I faced was so tempting. If I was going to die young, Jessica could plant another nightshade and, *tada,* I'd be back. No more predictions to dread, our dreamed-of life stretching out before us. But that all hinged on the whole not dying when I ate the berries thing. Statistics said there was little chance of that. Uncertainty loomed over me, doubt spreading its roots, the voices growing louder than ever before.

"I never thought of it quite like that," I said.

"Well, it's hard to look at it any other way. I plan on spending my life with you. The last thing I want you to do is eat nightshade."

"It's hard to argue that logic."

"See."

"I'll get rid of the flowers tomorrow. I'll plant them in Mount Pleasant. Mark won't mind."

"Good," Jessica replied, her limbs constricting my torso, pulling us closer together. "I worry about you."

"Someone has to," I replied, caressing the back of her arm.

"I love you," she said, before nestling into the joint between my shoulder and chest.

"I love you too," I replied.

***

The rattle of the door handle woke me from my dreams. Someone was shaking the knob, getting the mechanism inside to vibrate and spring free. I thought it was Lenny. I didn't know if he'd turned his extra key in to our landlord like he promised. He could have knocked and I would have let him in; it's not like I held a grudge. I'd checked all the doors before I went to bed. No one could have gotten in unless they jimmied the locks. Maybe Lenny forgot something. His portable easel, blank canvases stored in the basement, that purple amethyst necklace he left by the sink?

The lock popped in near silence, the dull thud echoing around our room. Jessica slept on beside me. A black hand reached through the opening of the door, pushing it back with unmoving fingers too long and narrow to belong to a human. It wasn't Lenny with his faded mood ring and paint-stained palms.

My stomach dropped, breath smothered in my throat.

In a hushed rush, five figures slouched into the room, their outlines only a few shades darker than the rest of the gloom. They faded in and out of sight, my eyes still crusted with sleep. Their bodies were camouflaged, leaving only their white masks hovering in the empty air. The red glow from my alarm clock reflected on the five bleached plague doctors.

One Spirit dragged a clear tarp behind him. It looked like the same material constructing the skin on my greenhouse. The sheeting brushed over the carpet with the faint sound of plastic rustling against itself. A cloying scent drifted in on the hem of their shrouds, rancid like the loading bays at the town pier, dogfish and grouper gutted on the planks. Beneath that was the faint smell of smoke and char, faint yet specific.

The things I had heard about life flashing before my eyes wasn't an exaggeration. Memories flickered in front of me like movie stills unspooling over a drive-in screen. I saw my father untangling my fishing line from the beak of a snapping turtle at the creek beside our house. My mother and I weeding our vegetable garden. The sand dunes where I first took Jessica on a date came into view only to be replaced by our first kiss, the first time we had sex. Clint's hammock hung from pine trees in the summer heat. Grampa's funeral. Lenny's first art exhibit. Blurred transitions from one to the next, faces melding, emotions splitting down the middle.

Then the projectionist set fire to the reel. Faces melted with the blackening film, charred and indistinguishable. The taste of burnt fear settled on my tongue. I needed to run, but there was nowhere to go.

The five figures encircled the bed, the tallest holding the polyethylene sheet at the center, directly between my feet and Jessica's. I wished I knew. I wouldn't have been there sleeping next to her. I would have slept on the couch. I didn't want her to wake to me suffocated beneath the plastic sheeting, the choked scream on my lips, my bowels given out, all the blood speckling our blankets. I couldn't fathom how she slumbered. The reverberation of my heart erupting in my ears was enough to shake the bed frame.

I kept silent, promising myself I wouldn't wake her. It would be one of those images she wouldn't forget, and I didn't want that. I was crying.

"Why now?" I asked.

The center shadow shook its bleached crown of bone.

"What?"

The Spirit lifted a finger and pointed at Jessica.

"Don't wake her. She doesn't need to see this," I whispered.

It shook its head once again and passed the tarp to the Spirit standing by Jessica's side. It bent down and wrapped the stifling material around her face, her features still clear through the translucent window.

"What are you doing!?" I screamed, jumping out of bed. "You're here for me. She's got more time. Years! Years!"

Jessica didn't stir. She seemed to be under a sleeping spell, something out of *Grimm's' Fairy Tales* before Disney edited their darker undertones. Then, as the Spirit tightened the tarp, the material suctioned to her mouth and nose, swelling in and out as she struggled for air, eventually growing taut. Jessica kicked and thrashed, limbs wild, grunts muffled by the covering, frantic, pleading.

I lunged at the nearest Spirit, hands outstretched, trying to pull them off her. My fingers swiped through their fetid robes, unable to latch onto the body beneath. I flailed and scrabbled again and again until a hand shot out and pressed into my chest. A radiating wave of cold swept from the Spirit's palm. I fell back, ice water clouding my vision as Jessica continued to convulse. I collapsed onto the bed, sweeping most of the sheets about my body in a tangled web.

"What the fuck! What the fuck!" was all I could say, the tarp's seal cutting off Jessica's last breath.

I couldn't move, couldn't look at Jessica, who shivered inches away.

I threw up, wretched and heaved, covering the bed with a thin layer of bile. I couldn't wipe the mess from my lips, clear it away from my forearms and thighs. The moist slick was sinking through my boxers, leaving them plastered to my leg. I felt helpless, my inability to protect her crippling, cement replacing blood in my veins.

Something soft brushed my ankle.

It was Jessica's foot.

I threw up again.

My vision wavered in and out.

Time dragged. I waited for the sun to streak through the blinds, but it never came.

A bone-hued mask dropped into view. The shadowy specter stooped to bring its bleached face level with my own. It tilted its head as if confused, unsure of what to make of me, of who I was. The empty blackness of its eyes yawned before me. There was nothing inside. Just expansive darkness and distant pinpoints of light resembling unfamiliar constellations, a cosmic vastness I couldn't comprehend.

The second wave of cold was more excruciating than the first as the Spirit placed a bony hand on my shoulder. My back snapped into rigid alignment, as if a solid icicle had pushed its way up my spine. I could feel each disc separate from its neighbor, then compress as the cold pushed onward. Each bone followed suit: knee, thigh, collar. Pain and paralysis. I wouldn't be able to walk. My hands would never uncurl, tap a shoulder, bring food to my lips. The list unraveled. All the things I'd never get to do again. The last was kiss Jessica, slipping the wedding ring around her finger. As the thought appeared, the cold passed and I was alone, the Spirits having retreated down the hall and out the front door.

Jessica lay at my side, cold and motionless. Her face was frozen, mouth gaping, unblinking eyes focused on the ceiling. I wanted to puke, but there was nothing left to expel. A welling dread filled the space food once occupied, something foreign and cancerous swimming through my guts. I felt as if I would tear open, loss seeking my seems, spilling organs, draining blood, two lives extinguished in unison.

The sour smell of tomato sauce and beer hung in the air, on my sheets. My limbs moved like they had before, allowing me to wave the acrid scent from my face and clean some of the vomit from my body.

I nudged Jessica, I don't know why, but I did. No reflex stirred; the fingers of death had slipped quickly through her frame. With shaking hands, I tried to hold her, my arms wrapping her rigid body. She was cold. The electrical fire within her, the subtle hum of breath, was drained like a silent radio. I leaned over and kissed her on the lips, regretting not doing so before we went to bed. The taste of sour blood came away with me as I sat up, unsure whether it belonged to her or me. My face was awash in tears, entire oceans draining down my neck. My entire world ended over the course of an evening.

On the dresser stood a single potted nightshade flower, evidence to show the authorities I hadn't strangled Jessica while she slept.

I got out of bed, my bare feet sliding across the bile lying stagnant on the carpet. I found my way from the room, unlocked the door the Spirits had so thoughtfully locked on their way out. I sat in Jessica's armchair. I couldn't clean up the mess. I couldn't cover her body with an untarnished sheet. I couldn't do anything except hold my head in my hands, tears welling heavier than before.

That's where I remained, hunched over, covered in filth, until I called the ambulance at four o'clock. They took her body away, took the flower, and left me with a handful of consolatory words and paperwork that needed to be filled out.

The last EMT to depart left a business card with the number for the morgue and another for a coping-with-loss hotline.

"Call the morgue after forty-eight hours. They should have all the results they need by then. They'll also connect you with someone to arrange the funeral," he said.

I nodded from the armchair, unable to form words.

"I'm sorry you had to see that, kid."

I removed my hands from the sides of my head and looked at the short EMT with his reflective defibrillator hanging from his waist. A slight paunch pressed against the front of his white shirt. He looked to be my father's age, if he was still alive. Same build. A different style of glasses, but that was the only divergence between the two.

"What do I do now?" I asked.

"I'd clean myself up and get out of this apartment. You can fix your room later. There's no rush. Find someone: friends, family, anyone who will be awake right now."

"Yeah, that's... Yeah."

We fell silent. He looked down at me. I looked up at him. I could see the pity in his eyes. He turned away.

"Make sure you call that number," the EMT said as he began to close the door. "If you forget, the state takes over the proceedings. I don't know what happens from there, but it probably isn't something you want."

"I'll remember," I said as the door closed.

CHAPTER 26

I did what the EMT said: I went to Lenny's new apartment downtown above the pizza shop, vaguely remembering the address he gave me to forward his mail. I knocked on his dented wooden door, and waited for a reply. I wasn't in control of my movements. My body lurched and swayed in a semblance of organized motor functions, but there was no thought behind my steps. I saw each motion over my left shoulder, following my body down the street, to his doorstep. I saw me knock, wait, another knock. I wondered if my body would ever leave his doorway, if the hollow spreading deeper into my chest would swallow me whole.

The light tread of bare feet approached from within. Someone squinted through the peephole at the door's center. Then the steps retreated. The door stayed shut. Only the peephole's black rounded glass remained staring out at me. Had I misremembered the address?

I leaned forward and put my eye to the age-worn cracks in the door. A single light burned inside the apartment. It fell over a living room wall, illuminating familiar portraits. The faint buzz of a TV came from within. Juliet's black coat hung from a chair. It was five in the morning. Either he was still mad or he hadn't sobered up from the night before and couldn't recognize my features in the early morning light. I rapped my knuckles on the door once more, praying someone would hear me before my mind completely unraveled, my last ounce of cognition bled dry.

A neighbor, an elderly man in a white t-shirt and sweatpants, opened a door from the other side of a fence.

"You need help with something?" he asked.

"No, no, I don't think so," I replied, my hand hovering inches away from the door, letting the third knock fall away.

"Well, let people sleep then," the old man replied. "No one likes to be woken up this early."

"I'm sorry," I said as I climbed down the steps behind the pizza shop. The old man slowly disappeared from sight with each step until I couldn't see him anymore. My feet carried onward.

***

Clint's parents' house was abandoned. After he died, they packed their belongings and moved to Florida where his uncle owned a condo near Disney. Everything looked the same from the outside except the lack of lawn furniture and vacant driveway. A *for sale* sign groaned in the wind. I found myself on the front porch, hand clearing a coat of pollen off the handrail wrapping his deck. Through the window, the bare hardwood floors were stained from the silhouettes of absent furniture. A newspaper from a few weeks after Clint's death lay at the end of the driveway.

I walked around back to the unkempt gardens. Flowers had dried and browned. Fall weighed heavy on their petals, dragging them into the mulched beds below. I could still make out the muddy tracks where the bull uprooted the lawn. It was hard to believe the family reunion happened seven months ago.

I spent all morning searching, but never finding a friendly voice.

So I went to the cemetery. Mark wouldn't be there. His family had taken a long weekend to visit a cabin his uncle owned in the Berkshires. Only a dozen ghosts roamed about. The early risers waved at me in the dull glow of the rising sun. Sweat crusted my skin, the thin layer of bile still coated my lower legs. I hadn't noticed the smell until that point. Maybe it was better I hadn't run into anyone.

Clint's grave was vacant. He only rose after ten. I knelt at his grave and knocked as if it was a door. The marble was cool on my sore knuckles. He didn't answer.

"Clint," I muttered, at first quietly, then rising in pitch and frequency, desperation creeping into my voice. A few ghosts rose from their graves around me, fingers reaching through the grass, pulling themselves up. Their fingers sifted through the dirt like the fruiting bodies of mushrooms, translucent and desirous. They wanted a taste of living emotion.

"He'll be up soon," Mrs. Jones said, hand hovering over my shoulder. "Heavy sleeper. Are you okay?"

Ghosts don't truly sleep.

I didn't answer.

A shadow crept around my father's stone. I could see it at a distance, vague and shifting. I rose and jogged to his grave. A flash of shoulder blades and loose-fitting fabric descended into the earth beneath his name. No breeze accompanied the sudden movement, no voice was left to soothe my cored-out emptiness.

The keys in my pocket jingled as I walked between stones. The sharp metallic points dug awkwardly into my thigh, pressing their teeth into the seams of my pocket. The Chases' mausoleum sat atop the neighboring hill, the early morning sun glinting off the stained-glass windows. I unlocked the door with my utility key. The dead couple were sitting atop their respective caskets, reliving shared memories from a hundred years before.

They only looked up after a minute of me standing in their doorway. I let the chain fall to the marble. A sleeping bag lay balled up in the center of the shadowed space.

"She left it here," Mrs. Chase said. "I swear she hasn't been back in days. Weeks even."

I remember muttering something about not caring before I unrolled the bedding, drew back the zipper, and crawled inside the flannel womb. It smelled like a clothing store in the mall, polo shirts hanging on one wall, toeless sandals on the other. It was sweet, alluring, the opposite of the fetid cloth wrapping the Spirits. The memory of their scent dimmed, drifting beneath the waves of synthetic perfume.

Then I slept.

***

A foot prodded me awake, gently tapping my shoulder. It was light at first, growing more insistent as I refused to stir.

"Is he still alive?" Lenore's voice whispered.

"He's not dead," Capt. Chase said. "You can see him breathing."

"He was muttering something awful while he slept. Burning hotels. Suffocation. He didn't stop," Mrs. Chase said.

Light from the prismatic windows fell over my body. I stared at my hands, the vibrant blue veins snaking beneath my skin. I must have looked dead, undead, living-dead. Something out of a Dracula movie. The smell lingering around me suggested the same: bile, decay, and the overpowering scent of Abercrombie & Fitch.

Another kick landed in the center of my back.

"Cut it out," I coughed, my dry throat begging out a choke.

"That's all I needed to hear," Lenore said, walking to the opposite side of the tomb. I could see her shoes, her calves, but nothing higher. "Can you move?"

I lifted my head, bringing the rest of the room into view. Her cell phone chirped. The screen flashed 911, waiting for her to hit send. She placed it back in her pocket without dialing.

"Maybe."

I flexed my toes, rolled my shoulder blades in a single rotation. Unfortunately, life still clung to my bones.

"I didn't think this place could stink worse than the first time I opened the door. Good job on that one. I'll need to get an air freshener if I'm going to sleep out here again," she said.

"You shouldn't—" I began.

"You can't use that logic anymore. The pot calling the kettle black and all that," she replied.

"I have reasons."

"And so do I."

I propped myself up on my elbows. Lenore stared down at me as if she were observing animals in a shelter, worry lining her forehead, lips pursed. A series of bruises in the formation of five fingers marked her wrist. She didn't cover them when she noticed my gaze.

"You saw my mom. She's not really with it. She was in a trance and doesn't remember anything. Happens a lot. She made this prediction when I was younger, some sort of Oedipus killing his father kind of thing. But inverted. Daughter killing mother. She puts too much stock in hallucinations. I'd never kill her. Violence isn't my thing. Occasionally it crosses my mind when… Well, usually I'm able to look past it," Lenore said.

"I'm sorry…"

"Whatever. It happens. Everyone has their own crap to deal with. Why are you here? You've got a bed at home. It's got to be more comfortable than this."

I winced at her words. Jessica's body lying on the covers floated through my memory. Cold. Quiet. I wondered where her corpse rested, sightless eyes staring at the plastic wrap of a body bag, the retractable steel of a morgue chamber.

"Are you going to tell her?" Mr. Chase asked.

"You said something about it in your sleep," Mrs. Chase said, eyes averted.

Lenore was the only living person that had ears for my story. Lenny wasn't around. Clint's parents lounged in the Florida sun. Clint and my parents were dead. The words came out in torrents. Lenore stood there, frozen, towering over me. You could see it on her face: she hadn't expected what I had to say. The Spirits, the tarp, Jessica choking at my side. The vomit, my inability to move. The Spirit's frigid fingers running across my chest. By the time I was finished, Lenore had sunk to the floor, placing a hand on my shoulder as tears found their way onto my lap.

"I'm so sorry," she began.

"You've got no reason to apologize," I replied.

"Still. What else can you say to something like that?" Lenore said. "There's no decent reply."

"You don't say anything," Captain Chase said. "You let things rest. Nod along. Let them know you're listening, that you're concerned. Anything more and the sentiment is forced."

Mrs. Chase looked at her husband with a scowl. "No, you've got to be comforting. Compassion is the only—"

"It's fine, it's fine. We don't need to discuss it. Really," I said.

I stood up, the sleeping bag falling about my feet in a jumbled heap. I stretched, cracked my spine, craned my neck until it popped. Inside the crypt, many of the accents Lenore had taken away were back: the tablecloth, the vase of flowers. There were new books piled in the corner, a larger supply of canned foods and dried fruit. The Styrofoam cup from our Box Office lunch stood on the table, half filled with rainwater. She had obviously been living there for a while.

"Did she know it was coming?" Lenore asked.

"No. No, she didn't. She thought she did, and that's what I can't get my head around," I replied.

The prediction was so precise, so clear. Eighty years old, letter from a forgotten lover, heart attack. Twenty-five was never mentioned. Jeff said one of the group would be answering for his crime, but I never believed it would be Jessica. Probably one of the twins. Her sister, maybe. Through the haze of shock and loss it hit me. Uncle Thom's words. His conviction that ghosts were liars. That some of them muddled predictions in fear of being forgotten, of showing themselves as weak.

I drove Jessica to her aunt Helen's grave years before. She had the old woman's ghost repeat the prediction to prove what she said. It was her way of getting me to think about our future, and to hurry my own process. She didn't call Jessica by name, only referring to her as *Dear*. I figured it was normal. Jessica never called her anything besides *Auntie*. No proper names. The old woman stuttered a lot. Squinted as if looking into the sun as she spoke, nearly blinded.

"Is there anyone you can go to?" Mr. Chase asked, interrupting my contemplation.

"Her dead aunt," I replied.

"I meant for support."

"Everyone who can give me support's dead. I need to know the answer, hear it from her aunt's lips."

The Chases and Lenore nodded in accordance. It made sense. It wasn't a long drive. I rolled up the sleeping bag, trying to keep the damp sections off my bare skin. I felt bad Lenore had to smell the rank stench of my stomach acid and chili. I carried it through the metal door into the sun after I said my goodbyes to the Chases, thanking them for their hospitality, despite the chill that hadn't left my veins.

I looked down at the lock and chain lying outside the door like a coiled snake. For a moment I considered fixing it in place, winding it through the broken hinges. Instead I left it where it sat. Lenore stood with her back to the mausoleum, arms crossed.

"I don't mean to bring up trivialities, but you never gave the Chases my message," Lenore said, one hand resting on a stone pillar, a sarcastic smile on her lips.

"Sorry. I've been a bit preoccupied lately," I said.

"Don't worry about it. Just don't mention me staying here to your boss and we'll call it even," Lenore said.

"Well. I mean, you shouldn't. Health codes and whatever. Just don't let him see you. We're always here first thing in the morning, but we always get out by five. Remember that. Mark doesn't need to lose his job over this. If you start to get sick, go see a doctor. Be smart," I said.

"Thanks."

"How'd you get the lock off?"

"You can learn anything with enough YouTube videos."

"Figures."

I promised Lenore I would drop off a new sleeping bag soon. Mark wouldn't kick her out. He wouldn't notice her. I was the one who usually noticed anything in the cemetery.

"Buy one with a flannel lining. It gets cold in here at night," Lenore called from over my shoulder. "If it's not too much to ask."

"It's not," I replied, walking down the center road dividing the cemetery. More ghosts had risen in the time I had been asleep. This time, none waved. I knew they knew. Someone must have been listening beneath the stained-glass window. They held a solemn vigil as their eyes followed me out of the cemetery. I could feel them on me even as I rounded the bend in the road. Their gaze would follow me until I figured out what had happened to Jessica.

CHAPTER 27

I wanted it to be a bad day, dark skies, gray in every way possible, but it wasn't. It turned out to be a day for postcards and Impressionist painters. Pink veins lined the clouds. The ocean curled in picturesque breaks, light surf lapping across the beaches, plovers and gulls sifting through the wash. The faintest wind blew across my face as the sun slouched toward the horizon.

That morning, after dropping off Lenore's new sleeping bag, I attended Jessica's wake. Kate planned the whole thing. I was barely able to string words together. Contacting every living acquaintance would have been impossible. Her co-workers at the non-profit managed to reach a handful of the women she helped over the years. They huddled out front of the building in black mourning attire, ringed close together, remembering the times Jessica had aided them in locating jobs or paying for vaccinations for their children. I caught snippets of conversation as I passed. I wanted to thank them for coming, but couldn't muster the syllables required.

Kate met me at the door of the funeral parlor. She escorted me to the room where Jessica's body lay, flowers ringing her mahogany casket. An overhead light shone down on her upturned face. That was as far as I got. A podium standing to the left of the door supported a stack of prayer cards with Jessica's photo on them. I turned one over in my hand, reading over the birth and death dates. My mind refused to connect the numbers, to believe they were true. She was still alive inside my mind, waiting for me to return home. The body in the casket was a doll, a poorly painted replica of Jessica's beautiful face. Before seeing the supposed mannequin, I considered looping the wedding ring over her finger. Her ghost could walk around with the memento for the rest of eternity, knowing I had been honest about my intentions, that our love hadn't been a farce.

But my thoughts moved in rapid bursts, jostling one image into the next: Jessica's screaming face beneath the tarp, the casket, the night Lenny moved out, Jessica's nude body in the doorway. I stumbled. Kate tried to support me through the doorway, dragging me into the ceremony room, but I couldn't move. I didn't want to see her body again, the affirmation unavoidable under closer scrutiny. I kept telling Kate I'd wait. *For what?* she asked. *For her to come back*, I replied.

I sprinted out of the funeral home, knocking the stack of prayer cards across the parlor floor in a sudden flurry.

***

I hadn't changed out of my funeral suit before driving to Aunt Helen's cemetery. I needed to speak with the woman before I moved forward.

The ride to Provincetown was slow, the single lane highway congested by countless cars plodding past sheltered inlets stuffed with sailboats. Catboats and Sunfish bristled like long grass swept by the fall wind. I honked at the cars in front of me, but there was only one lane. No room to pass. My thoughts wavered between rage and numb removal. I wanted to have a calm conversation with Aunt Helen, but the testosterone thrumming in my veins said otherwise.

When I arrived, one car sat in the gravel parking lot. My Volvo slid into the only other space directly next to it. On the hill before me, steepled headstones prodded the skyline. Ornate crosses and sculpted angels mixed their gray granite with the deep blues and soft yellows marbling the heavens.

A young couple crossed my path as I walked through the graveyard's twisted metal gate. He wore plaid. A yellow blouse fit loosely over the woman's shoulders. She smiled quick and assuring. The man had a dried-up wreath of flowers clutched in his hand. A new wreath bloomed on a nearby stone, daffodils and daisies, a symbol for a successful match, long years and a happy life. Jessica had placed an identical wreath on Aunt Helen's grave two years before. Dead and decayed, it rotted in a distant landfill, appropriately stripped of meaning.

Helen's stone was plain, the angel in the upper right corner simply carved.

She floated over the stone, as if sitting on a bar stool. Her lips were painted, a swath of charcoal against her light gray form. Her head crooked to the side at my approach, as if she was searching her memory for where she had seen me before. Her well-plucked eyebrows raised in recognition. I was glad she remembered.

"Jessica's dead," I said as she began to wave.

"Oh, I'm sorry, dear. She was a nice girl. I swear I saw her only a week ago," Aunt Helen replied, face regaining its confusion.

"Jessica hasn't been here in two years."

Aunt Helen drifted off her stone, thin feet skimming slow steps over the grass. She stood before me, barely five feet tall, peering up into my face. It looked like she wanted to call me a liar, her deep-set eyes pressed tight. She raised a finger beneath my chin before speaking.

"But she was here last week. Her sister, the one you're thinking of, hasn't visited in two years."

"No, that's Jessica. Kate's her sister."

"I told Kate two years ago about that letter from the Spirits. I wouldn't have said anything about that to Jessica."

"But you're not getting it. You're attaching the wrong names to the wrong faces. Just listen! Jessica's dead. What the hell do I have now?"

A howl rose in my chest and tore through my throat, escaping into the night air. The animalistic cry was harsh, shaking the remaining leaves of nearby trees, causing all the ghosts within the cemetery to turn in our direction.

My calm demeanor crumbled, words coming out in cruel barks. The voices of the young couple were audible between concussive snarls. I couldn't make out their words, just the concerned tone. Who were they to judge? Each had a hand to hold, a partner to replace loved one's wreaths with. They didn't have to visit one another's ghost.

The faint chirp of a phone's dial tone met my ear accompanied by a half conversation. Then their headlights flashed into life, illuminating the entire cemetery in a brilliant flash before returning to the gravel road.

"I think I know which is which," Helen said, her voice rising to meet my own.

"I've been with Jessica for seven years," I replied.

"You're lying."

"Why would I do that?"

Her mouth hung open. Her pale tongue curled back on itself as if wrestling to free her next line.

"Honestly? I got them mixed up? She's dead? No, I..."

"You did. She is."

Helen stumbled back to her stone, leaning against it for support. One hand clutched her head, the other groped blindly behind, searching for solidity she would never find. She stared at the ground, at the bed of spent tulips wilting around her grave. I paced the circumference of her plot, hands balled in aching fists.

"I never meant to," her voice had become childish in apology.

"I mean…" I faltered, hatred waning. "I guess they look similar."

The two stood side by side in my mind, Kate looking down over her pale sister. Their hair shade: polar opposites. Jessica's thin face and Kate's high cheekbones created unmistakably different countenances. I couldn't fathom the mistake, but I didn't want to crush the old woman's heart anymore, wrath bleeding out of me.

"When did it happen?" Helen asked.

"A few days ago. They came for her in our bed," I replied.

"That's horrible. Were you…there?" Her words became garbled. Tears fell from her face and cascaded down around the dried husks of faded tulips.

"It's not your fault. Uncle Jeff—"

"Not him," she broke in.

Blue and red lights strobed across the face of Helen's grave, illuminating her form in a frenetic blaze. The brief whir and yelp of sirens bayed from the parking lot, a clipped howl then silence, followed by the click of car doors opening and shutting. The couple must have called.

Two police officers took their time walking up the path, their measured steps kicking loose gravel. I began to sweat. I pictured myself handcuffed in the back of their cruiser, being read my Miranda rights for the accusation of disturbing the peace and harassing the deceased. Then they were there, a new sorrow pushing up from the well in my chest.

"We got a call about someone yelling up here," one of the officers said. "You're the only guy around that's breathing. Something wrong you'd care to tell us about?"

"No, everything's fine. We just had a misunderstanding," Helen said, wiping the last tear from her eye.

"Never seen a ghost cry before. Has he been harassing you, miss?" the second officer asked, putting a hand on my shoulder, fingers digging into the hollow of my collar bone.

"Please don't touch him. It's my fault."

"Why was he yelling at you? No point getting angry at a ghost. You can't do anything to them, they can't do anything to you. So why?" the first asked.

"Tell them what happened, Dave," Helen said.

I shook my head. The cop's fingers burrowed deeper between muscle and bone. I didn't want to tell them. It was hard enough to talk to Helen, let alone complete strangers. They didn't need to know. There was no warrant. No subpoena for the information. I had rights. They could screw themselves.

"We've got to investigate every call. You want to come for a little drive? We've only got one other guy in our holding cell. Pretty drunk, but he'll be good company," the first cop said.

With that, Helen burst into a second wave of tears. She told them about her mistaken prediction. How I had been in bed with Jessica when the Spirits arrived. The eighty years she should have had. Suffocation. The wake. All of it.

In the darkness, I could barely make out the officers' frowns. It was probably the first time they ever heard a ghost admitting to being wrong. It was earth shattering in a way. The hand left my shoulder. It brushed off nonexistent dirt as it left its perch in an unspoken apology. The tears pressed harder against the corners of my eyes, my throat tightening. A tear jostled free. I tried to avoid crying in front of strangers, but it couldn't be helped.

"Didn't mean to upset you," the first cop said.

"Sorry for the interruption," the second said, tapping the first on the shoulder.

Not another word was said. They moved off into the glow of the headlights as if they were the ones who had done something wrong. Shoulders hunched, they made it back to their car. The lights cast their outline in shadow, black like the bodies of the Spirits, just huskier, more bloated.

The tears continued to fall.

Helen tried to place a hand on my shoulder, but her fingertips passed through my shirt. A cold twinge shot from the source as if I had leaned up against a freezer in the back of a grocery store. The police car disappeared. The only light left was a yellowed streetlamp hanging at the mouth of the cemetery, that and the slight gray phosphorescence of the ghosts milling about.

Helen's stone held a touch of the day's warmth. I reclined to the ground, resting my back against it, a dull heat radiating through my t-shirt replacing the sudden chill. I wanted to leave, to not be sitting in a graveyard crying, or at least be sitting in my car crying, or better yet at my house. Alone. No crowd of ghosts looking over my face with inquisitive eyes.

"I know you loved her," Helen said, hovering above me.

"I still love her," I replied. "There's no past tense."

"Well, I know you do, but she's gone. You can't love her the same way anymore."

"You're wrong. I've grown the nightshade."

Aunt Helen squatted before me, bringing her eyes level with my own. Her head tilted like an inquisitive bird peering over a reflective piece of glass. Everyone knew the myth.

"You did it?" she asked. "You actually grew the nightshade?"

"Yeah. It took four years, but the markings are there."

"Have you…have you eaten the berries?"

The translucent skin on Aunt Helen's face stretched taut over her skull, pulling her mouth wide, displaying the roots of her back molars in a way I never thought possible. Her eyes bulged, greed for lost life swimming through the swollen orbs.

"No, but I will."

"How soon?"

"I don't know. This week."

"Could you bring the plant here? I'd make it worth your while. I buried money in the back yard of my old home. I could tell you where it is," Helen said, the strange smile creeping wider, tearing the skin at the edge of her lips.

"No. It's for Jessica. Why would I…" I began to say.

"Because I deserve it. Do you know how long I've been dead? Fifty-two years. I've looked at these exact headstones for fifty-two years. She's only been dead for what? A week? She hasn't earned it yet. If you can grow one, you can grow another. She can wait," Helen sputtered, a tone of anger underlying her words.

The surrounding ghosts drew nearer as her voice shifted, translucent bodies clumping together, wallowing in one another as their sluggish steps carried them up the incline. Helen's stone stood at the peak of the slight hill. Lower ground on all sides seethed with pale bodies, ants circling the mouth of their home.

"She doesn't need to earn it. I love her," I said.

"That's ridiculous. You're too young to even imagine what love is!"

I was on my feet.

She began to yell about how naive I was, about how no one truly deserved a second chance at life as much as she did. She was a saint all her life, that's why her heir would live so long. She, herself, hadn't actually lived. *Where was the fairness in that?* She was shackled to the land. They were all shackled to their stones, their caskets, the corpses lying beneath six feet of roots and soil.

A sea of transparent bodies swelled around me. Heads bobbed at varying heights, giving the appearance of a shifting landscape of mountains and hills capped by white-tufted trees. Their mouths began to join in the echo, pleading with me to give them the nightshade, lamenting the things they could no longer do. I lost Helen's voice amid the squall. I had disturbed their night and made an affront to their deaths. I had the days, the hours, the years they wanted, and wouldn't give in to their desires.

I made eye contact with a man much taller than myself. He swung at me, his fist sailing through my chest as I politely refused his request. Then came another and another. The crowd was a flurry of flying limbs, yet I didn't stumble. Some tried to tackle me, to bite at my throat. A young woman raked at my eyes with her acrylic nails, but only chilled the lashes. I moved onward, a supernatural calm stilling my heart.

Their voices yammered and howled. I picked out individuals momentarily before losing them to the overwhelming wall of sound.

A man on my left yearned to feel his wife's touch one more time. A woman at my elbow kept mentioning the ocean, the cool waves running over her legs, the salt drying on her bare skin. Sights of the homes they left behind, the taste of seasoned haddock, the smell of bread rising in the oven. The warmth of a lover beneath a comforter of down. The soft pads of a child's fingertips wrapping around their own. Everything they missed in life fell in torrents from their mouths. Someone was crying. Everyone was yelling. There were promises of rewards: a lifetime of servitude, riches, the deed to twenty acres of oceanfront property. Then there were threats not fit for recitation.

I parted their bodies like sheets hanging on a clothesline. Turning, I saw Helen above the rest, feet perched atop her stone. An arm waved angrily for me to come back, but I pushed the last of the ghostly linen from my path and stepped beneath the entrance gate.

When my feet reached the gravel parking lot, goosebumps steepled my arms and neck. The squall of voices dulled to a light breeze. A final call of *"Come back"* rose from several mouths, chanting in unison, but what good would it do? They couldn't hurt me, and I wasn't going to give them back what they sorely missed.

As I pulled out of the parking lot, rear wheels fishtailing, I told myself I would come back and visit Helen, Jessica at my side. We'd bring offerings. Those crooned desires from moments ago. The fried fish, the bread. I had a conch shell sitting on my bookcase. I couldn't coerce the oceans to spill over the cemetery, but I could bring the waves to the woman's ears.

I passed a police car on the narrow road leading up to the cemetery, their lights flashing, sirens up. Someone must have called in a second noise complaint. I waved as they passed, not stopping. They didn't turn. I still had one more cemetery to visit. There were only so many minutes in a lifetime and I felt like I could count each of them, my mind whirring through the past as my foot stepped on the gas. I could taste the nightshade berries at the back of my throat, sweeter than any fruit I'd ever swallowed.

CHAPTER 28

I stood at the foot of my father's grave, the rough wood of the shovel's handle scratching at my palms. I asked him to come out and talk. I knelt down, bringing my lips closer to his coffin, repeating my request. I tasted grass, bitter dandelions. The scent of wild chive seeped from purple flowers. He gave no reply. Neighboring ghosts twittered and stared in my direction, some rising from graves, others floating free from mausoleums. Their pale luminous bodies were the only light beyond the faint glow of stars. I worried another scene would erupt like it had with Helen, but no one approached; they perched over their headstones and watched as I scooped shovelfuls of dirt from my father's grave. They knew our story.

The sediment felt heavy, unfamiliar. I'd dug countless graves, shifted heaps of rocks and buried roots from marked plots. Nothing offered as much resistance. Silently, I repeated to myself that this was what I had to do, but my forearms ached, triceps growing tight with each movement, protesting the act.

I piled the dirt next to the road, tossing sections of grass to one side. Mark would hate me if we had to reseed the section after I finished. The murmurs at my back never rose. Clint had made his way to my side half an hour into the process and continued to ask me if I was sure I wanted to do this.

"A hundred percent," I replied. "What else can I do?"

Clint paused. "I don't know, wait a little longer? Focus on the plants. That's where you should be right now. This is sacrilegious. He's your dad. Did you think of that?"

"Yeah, I did, but two years is a long time. And the plants are ready. They're done."

"Then take that shovel and go plant one on top of Carla's grave."

"I'm sorry, Clint. That's not the plan anymore."

"What do you mean?" he began to ask, before the answer dawned on him. I saw the flash of insight move across his face like a cloud converging with the moon. The insistent madness that once spurred each of his movements was snuffed without deliberation. He shook for a moment as if suffering severe withdrawals. Then he lowered himself to the ground, sitting cross legged, his head in his hands. I knew the strength of his love, the feelings that pulsed through his dried veins.

He shut up after that, his head following the arc of the shovel as it rose and fell. I felt bad about letting him down, but there were no other options left.

My shirt was soaked with sweat. Streams of it flowed from my hair into my eyes. I wiped at the sting, but it wouldn't dissipate. The dirt from my hands crusted around my eyelashes. My arms jarred every time the blade met with a sunken rock. The hole was up to my chest. Only two feet left to go.

"Would you like some help?" Lenore's voice came from above me.

I dropped my shovel, tripping over the wooden handle in the process. I fell face first into the wall of dirt. I lay there, heart pounding in my ears. Lenore carried a flashlight, its iridescent beam illuminating the grave.

"No. This will only take me a few more minutes," I said, reaching for my discarded shovel.

"I'm glad you chose to do this at night. I would hate to see what the cops would do if they found you wading into your father's bones."

I let the shovel rest where it lay.

I never thought of it like that. I pictured the nervous grin on my father's pale, ghostly face looking up at me once I pried open the lid to his casket, not the decaying flesh and bones that were his only physical remnants.

"I can get him to come out," Lenore said. "We're on good terms."

"Why didn't you say something earlier?" I asked.

"I keep my word. He wasn't ready to talk. I still don't think he is, but it's better than seeing you dig up his body. I remember what happened at Doane's cave-in."

"I honestly don't know how you haven't attracted anyone else's attention with this noise," Clint said.

"I think all the neighbors are deaf. They never complain about my singing. I don't know why they would notice this instead," Lenore said, reaching an arm down into the hole. Her wrists were thin. Beneath my fingers, the raised lines of the dancing skeleton stood out against her skin. She tightened her grip around my forearm and aided my climb from the ditch, her strength surprising.

"I should just let you dig the rest of the hole," I said as she let go of my hand.

"Does that sound like the sort of thing I'd do?" she replied.

"Hopefully not," Clint mumbled.

"You know me better than that," Lenore said.

Clint nodded solemnly, his eyes fixed on his shoes.

"Good answer," Lenore said. "But, Dave, make sure you're not a jerk. You dad's not a bad guy. He's got reasons for not talking."

"I doubt that," I said.

"Promise me you'll be kind or I'm not calling him."

"Fine. I promise," I replied.

At that, she walked around the edge of my excavation site to where his gravestone stood. Bending down, she nearly put her lips to the stone and began to mumble a few sentences I couldn't make out. From within the depths of the hole, a faint sigh shifted through the last few inches of dirt. I leaned over, squinting into the glare of Lenore's flashlight. My father's face slowly materialized, nose and brow rising through the sediment, dragging lips and eyes behind until his full countenance was visible. Then his neck and shoulders hesitantly followed.

With a look from Lenore, he rose to his full height. I hadn't seen him up close in three years. The Armani suit he was buried in was impeccable, not a crease to disrupt the pinstripes. His eyes were more sunken than I remembered. His hair short and thinning. His glasses were lost somewhere, possibly tucked in the inner linings of the suit.

What was most shocking, though, were the scars. The pox had pocketed his face, leaving deep trenches across his cheeks and forehead. Some scars bulged; others dipped in slim trenches, faintly tracing his jawline.

"You're going to replace that, right?" he asked, looking over at the heap of dirt removed from his grave.

"Yeah, yeah, of course. Do you think I'd leave it like that?" I asked.

"Don't know. Can't say I ever thought you'd try to dig me up. Did you take care of the grass?"

"Yup. I cut it evenly. I'll just jam it back down once I bury you again."

"Good. That's the thickest grass in the place. All the organic fertilizer helps," my father said, his voice softening, losing the initial harsh tone. "How've you been?"

I looked at him in disbelief.

"How do you think I've been? I'm here digging up your bones," I said.

"Hey, it's just a formality. How would you prefer me to start this conversation? *Hey, Dave, I heard your girlfriend just died... How's the weather?*"

Lenore's sneakers kicked a spurt of soil into the open grave as she backed away from my side. Clint followed, tracing the steps he had just taken, nonchalantly fleeing to the Chases' mausoleum. Lenore's flashlight remained by the side of the grave, spilling its light over the headstone and the translucent shape of my father, allowing their receding forms to be engulfed by the surrounding darkness. I could hear Lenore whispering to Clint in the same way she had spoken to my father, this time nervously. I waved for them to come back, but they both shook their heads and picked up their pace.

"They told you more about me than I thought, didn't they?" I asked my father.

He nodded, smirking.

"Guys, hey, I don't care. Come back," I called.

"Nope," came their distant response as their shadows approached the gray mausoleum towering over the surrounding landscape. When I turned to face my father, he was no longer at my side. Instead he was crouching down behind his headstone, examining something resting on the marble base. Something I couldn't see.

"Come here," he said.

Bathed in the faint glow of the flashlight, the remains of a tattered envelope came into view.

"Jessica dropped it off. I think she wanted to be your ambassador to my unfriendly nation, if you get my drift. Probably a little over a month ago," he said. "She said some nice things about you."

"How'd you open it?" I asked, retrieving the flashlight from my feet so I could steady the beam on the folded words within.

"Lenore."

"Figures," I replied, opening the letter before reading it to myself.

Dear Mr. Gallagher,

I'm sorry to bother you like this, but we need to talk. I know Dave isn't the easiest person to deal with sometimes, and I don't know what would make me any different, but we both have questions. I love your son, love everything about him, but we can't keep living like we are. We've been talking about getting married for three years, but he has it in his head that we have to wait until he talks to you. I've told him that I don't care, that it doesn't bother me if we'll only be together a little while, but he's got his heart set on this. We can't move forward, not until he knows what's going to happen. He'll never be happy until this is behind us. It doesn't have to be now, but soon. Please, if you could just speak with him, I know...

"I'm sorry," my father said, reaching out a hand to comfort me, returning it to his side as a sudden shiver passed over my frame.

"Nothing you can do about it now," I replied.

"I didn't know what to tell her," my father said. I folded the letter and placed it in my pocket, letting the envelope fall to the ground. The wind picked it up and sent it tumbling across the grass, eventually spiraling beyond the tree line.

"Sounds familiar," I replied, leaning against his stone, clearing my eyes.

"Don't give me that," he said. "There was nothing to tell you. You think I should have lied?"

"Are you really going to dance around this?"

"No. I just told you, I had nothing to tell. And she was getting all worked up standing around here. I've never been good with crying women."

"What do you mean 'nothing'?"

"Exactly that. Nothing. The Spirits aren't coming. You're not immortal or anything. You'll die, but it's going to be from natural causes. No nooses. No bulls. No bone masks glaring at you while you bleed out."

"You're wrong. That doesn't happen."

"No, you mean that rarely happens. There is a difference."

I turned from him and picked up the shovel from where it stuck in the dirt. Hefting the dregs, I collapsed half the pile like an avalanche into the grave, swearing under my breath.

"What do you think you're doing? If you fill in the grave, it's not going to make me go away. It's not going to change anything I've mentioned," my father said.

"Why didn't you tell me? I could have made the last few years of Jessica's life happy, but instead..." I trailed off, throwing down the shovel, a surge of tears tracking my cheek. "I was expecting something terrible, an army of amputees coming for my limbs. Some needle shit, I don't know. This is the best news you could give. We could have gotten married. We could have had a kid. Now I'm alone, she's dead. All I have left is a greenhouse full of plants and an old wives' tale about resurrection."

"I don't know where you're getting this idea about it being good news."

"What?"

"Think about it. How many living friends do you have right now?"

"Does Lenore count?"

"Sure."

"Then one."

He started to nod. "Do you get what I'm saying? You're going to have to watch everyone you know, everyone you love, die, at least the ones that aren't already gone. Whenever you meet someone new, a girlfriend, let's say, what's the first thing you're going to ask yourself?"

I didn't want to say it. He could see it in me, the refusal, the knowledge that his gift may end up a curse.

"I'll tell you. When is she going to die? How? Is it even worth my time getting attached, falling in love? It would have worked out well if Jessica was still alive, but I'm sorry that's not the case. When you know the Spirits are coming, it creates this shared camaraderie. You bond over it. I didn't consider the full repercussions when I planned out my life. It's the sort of thing that comes to you only after you're buried. You're going to spend your whole life searching for someone else like yourself, and you know how rare they are."

He began to pace. My tears were making him uncomfortable.

"You honestly didn't do anything wrong? What about Mom?" I asked.

"You know I loved her. She was probably the only woman I ever cared about. She left me, not the other way around. I knew she loved Aunt Janey, knew it since the first time I saw the two together, but I wouldn't let myself believe it. And anyway, I wouldn't have done anything until you were grown and out of the house. Divorced parents can be terrible for a kid. She cared about me like a brother, maybe a cousin, but never a lover. In the end, she hurt me, not the other way around."

"I shouldn't have blamed you," I said, the sharp tang of surprise souring my throat.

"No, I wanted it that way. You were always closer with your mother, and Janey was the kindest woman I've ever met. I didn't want you to think poorly of her for leaving me if I could help it," he replied.

"I wouldn't have cared."

"I wanted to be on the safe side, you know, with the distance. I would have said something I would have regretted otherwise."

Then it clicked. My father's sacrifice. The years of hard work, the pro bono examinations and operations, volunteer work during Hurricane Katrina, Doctors Without Borders. He missed my soccer games, Aunt Janey filling his spot on the grass, for a reason. His absence from my life was actually a more focused and articulated love than I could comprehend at the time.

Our silence held for a few minutes. He quietly looked off into the distance, toward the blackened tree line. His eyes wandered over neighboring graves, pretending a calm ignorance to their eavesdropping.

"I've heard you and Clint talking about the nightshade," he said, refusing to look away from the edge of the golf course and the few ghosts huddling there.

"And?" I asked.

"It won't work."

"You don't know that."

"Yes I do. Do you know how many people I saw die poisoning themselves that way?"

I shrugged.

"Fifty seven. People try it every year. No one succeeds. I don't want to hear about you dying like that. You're smarter than them. I thought I taught you better with all our time spent in the woods. You don't mess around with poisonous plants."

"You haven't seen our plants, though," I replied.

"A myth is a myth. That's why it's not called science."

"And what if it is? I die. So what? Like you said, how many friends do I have left?"

"I didn't spend my whole life working to keep you safe for you to blow it on some stupid fantasy. Whatever happened to going to college? What happened to those trees you wanted to study?"

"They're nothing compared to Jessica."

"It's still something to live for."

"Thanks, Dad," I said, beginning to walk away. "Have a good night."

"Hey, no goodbyes yet. You've got to fill this hole," he said.

"I'll tell Mark to take care of it."

"Not if you eat those berries," he called over my shoulder, the wind carrying his voice, making it sound like he was right beside me.

***

As I walked to the Chases' mausoleum, standing black against the night sky, I thought about what I would say to those who were waiting for me. The unhindered years would seem an affront to the dead, salt in the wound. Lenore wouldn't show emotion, but that was her thing. They stood on the front step of the crypt. A single candle flickered behind the red and green window of the mausoleum, casting slim shadows across the wall.

I told them the news. Where I expected annoyance and disgust, I found sympathy. They had known for months. Not Clint, but the rest. They told Clint while I was conversing with my father. Lips pursed, eyes averted, a head shaking slowly side to side; no one wanted the news. You could see them calculating all the burials I would attend, the handfuls of sand I would throw on loved ones' caskets.

"Those twenty years were enough without my husband," Mrs. Chase said, putting an arm around the captain. "I wouldn't want any more."

"I could have used a few more," Clint said.

Lenore shrugged. "I'll let you know how bad mine's going to be when I find out. Maybe we can commiserate together or something. I'll be eighteen this year, so, welcome to all the fun, right?"

"Right," I replied. "I'm sure it won't be as bad as Jessica's, or mine."

My voice had grown shaky. I could see from the look on everyone's face they thought I was losing it. My lips had begun to bleed from dragging them between my teeth, the copper taste swilled on my tongue.

"Hey, you want to check this out real quick?" Lenore asked, grabbing my hand, gesturing to the unlatched door at her back. She slipped through, whisking me along in her wake. She took the candle from the windowsill and carried it over the coffins. "Look at this."

Lenore had repainted the wounded wood where the crowbars had left their marks. I couldn't tell they had ever been damaged at all. She must have sanded the whole surface or filled the gashes with something to make it even. I ran my hand over the varnish. It was smooth to the touch. My breathing grew steady, eyes focused on the restoration. She gestured to the second casket, which had been repaired in the same manner. She'd even replaced the brass handles that had been torn from their sides.

"Mark and I should have done that years ago. I don't think it ever crossed my mind," I said.

"I'm glad you didn't. I needed some way to repay them, especially after I spilled that can of beans in here."

I laughed. The noise reverberated around the stone walls, coming back to me as if uttered by a stranger.

"Are you going to be alright?" she asked.

"Who knows. Either I'll get the greatest reward of my life, or I'm going to die. How many people do you know that get that kind of chance?"

"Few. Clint's told me about the flowers. For what it's worth, I say go for it if she really means that much to you."

"She does."

"Then don't let your dad talk you out of it."

Outside, Clint and the Chases hovered around the front step, silent. The air was cool. The sweat along my back and chest dried against my skin in a frosted sheet. I needed to leave before I came down with something. A compromised immune system was the last thing I needed before testing the berries.

Clint moved to my side after I said my goodbyes. Wishes of good luck did nothing to staunch my welling anxiety. We walked toward my car, a faint black outline in the distance. He stuttered over syllables, attempting to push the words off his tongue. It sounded like he was gagging on them, a wad of phlegm adhered to his throat.

"I'd do the same thing," he said, passing out of earshot from other ghosts. "That's why I forgive you."

"I always intended on following through for you," I replied without looking at him.

"I know you did. It's better this way. We'd both be two halves of dead relationships otherwise."

CHAPTER 29

Nightshade vines lined the greenhouse table. Overhead, the dull hum of grow lights tittered, the voices of three dead sparrows mingling with the din. All the other plants with their purple flowers and off-colored skin were pushed to the side.

I moved between the offspring of Carla's flowers, manipulating petals with my fingertips. I turned them over, eyes desperate to observe the tooth-like markings. Some resembled flat-topped molars, others pointed canines. One flower was populated by incisors. It was a painful smile, a dentist's x-ray of foliage.

Jessica's voice played in my head, reminiscent of the night I promised I would forget the flowers. I saw her prophesied image of me, dead, flat on the dirt floor, blood trickling from the corner of my mouth. At least she wouldn't be the one finding my body. I recounted the symptoms in my mind: headache, sweats, shock, vomiting, trouble breathing, delirium, hallucination, death.

I reached for the closest plant, plucking a handful of berries from the vine. Sweat soaked my armpits. My mouth was dry, tongue stuck to its roof in refusal of my next meal. The note I left on the counter, seven hundred dollars paper-clipped beneath, requested a plot in Jessica's cemetery. Dying would bring us back together. If the plant pulled through, then life would end in the same fashion. I flung the berries into my mouth before I could reconsider, crushing them between my teeth, sucking down the sour pulp. My body reeled at the taste, knocking several of the plants to the floor. Their ceramic pots shattered, spraying jagged shards across the dirt. I reached for the stool to steady myself, but my hands were sweaty. I toppled onto the debris, feeling the sharp jag of the ceramic pot piercing my shoulder.

My sight flickered, receding into blindness, only to return in mocking clarity. Thousands of flowers swayed above me, grotesque in their contorted animation. Throat tightening, I gulped air, hammering my chest with my fist, forcing respiration with each thud. The overwhelming scent of rotting tomatoes choked my nostrils. The chunk of ceramic worked itself deeper between muscle and bone as I writhed across the ground. The pain was excruciating.

I lay on the damp dirt floor. The greenhouse ribs and plastic sheeting above me tore away into the night sky, unfamiliar constellations burning in the darkness. Where the tables of nightshade once stood, high walls sprung from the dirt, flecking my face with mud and grit as they rose. Yawning rooms and candle-lit halls diverged from where I lay, a cold stone floor surfacing beneath my prone figure. I couldn't remember getting to my feet, but I was running through the half-finished corridors, walls mere skeletons, bare boards protruding into passages. Labyrinthine tunnels cropped up and spread, as if endlessly breeding themselves across an infinite plane. I passed windows peering out into forests and glades lined with wildflowers, others into featureless deserts. Alien rooms blossomed into existence, libraries devoid of books, ballrooms without dancers, dungeons laced with fungus and the stench of rot.

I ran, peering through these windows, choosing doors at random. My hands shot through panes of glass, tearing my skin in sudden bursts of pain, in an attempt to reach what lay beyond. Outside, I saw trees only heard of in stories, phosphorescent will-o'-the-wisps glimmering in their boughs, the faces of long dead loved ones shifting through the foliage.

I moved on.

Steep lecture halls with gaudy Victorian decor and satin upholstery shifted before me. I couldn't hear what the professor was saying from her lectern, so I clambered over chair backs and descended to the podium.

The professor evaporated into steam, replaced by Jessica. She streaked out of the hall, plowing through an ornate doorway opening into thick forest. I followed as she dipped around swollen ferns, vaulting over moss-laden roots. I could taste pine on my tongue, the crunch of evergreen needles between my teeth. I lost sight of her around the bend in a narrow corridor of elm.

Pausing, I listened for footfalls, for the hint of breath. Nothing. My fingers found a doorknob on a tree trunk, gnarled and rough on my calloused hand. Twisting, I stumbled back into the half-finished rooms. The clack of hammer falls and the buzz of saw blades seemed everywhere, the walls constructed around me as I moved, following the sound of retreating voices.

They sounded familiar. Clint. Lenore. Lenny. All at once, their voices blended together, hints and notes of each breaking through, recommending doors to open, passages to follow. I did my best, but they outdistanced me. Only the sounds of construction remained. I wanted to rest, to let my bones sink down into the soil, but I couldn't stop.

At last, I came upon an open room where Jessica's body lay on the floor, a clear plastic sheet sucked tight against her features. The other Jessica, the version I glimpsed in the forest, stood at her feet, staring at herself, fingers reaching down, running along the edge of her cold calf. Forest scents were replaced with ancient decay, the over-ripe fruitiness of moldering bodies. I tried to say something, to scream, but the words came out as a grunt. Jessica turned. Where her face should have been rested the curved beak of the plague doctor's mask. A nauseous wave rose in my stomach, vertigo upending my world. I fell, face forward, colliding with something solid, and all went black.

***

Beneath my fingers, frayed red fibers blossomed. I tugged at the twine, curling the strings around my hand. My mouth was dry, lips cracked, an acidic taste on my tongue. A clear high note sang in my ear. I was in Jessica's father's chair, staring at my living room, one barren bookshelf, the other laden with scraps of novels, pages ripped from spines.

The television had been smashed. Blood covered my hands. Gutted furniture, toppled tables, and family portraits skewered on fork tines lay around me. Whole photo albums had been culled, the glossy images of Jessica's childhood strewn around the room like fallen snow. Sparks erupted from the neck of a lamp, bulb and shade forcefully removed. It was almost morning. Gray light filtered in through open windows. Curtains pulled from their hangers lay crumpled on the floor.

I was still alive.

The nightshade had worked.

Trudging through the debris-cluttered floor, I found the back door, no longer carved from the trunk of a tree.

I stumbled down the brick path to the greenhouse, praying I hadn't disemboweled the ceramic pots as I had done to everything else I owned. The door was torn from its hinges, lying on its side in the overgrown grass. The temperature had dropped inside, matching that outside. Most of the plants had been spared, besides the few that lay wilting on the floor. I almost expected them to turn their faces toward me in unison, frowning at my frenzy. Nothing stirred. With my good hand, I retrieved the nightshade, clutching it to my chest like a newborn child. I felt a warming sensation fill the hollow space in my chest.

For a moment, I considered going back inside my house, changing out of my bloodstained clothing, but I didn't. My clean jeans and t-shirts were probably smoldering in a pile of ash in the middle of my bedroom. What was the point?

Skirting the edge of the house, I found the keys still in the Volvo's ignition. I placed the potted plant on the seat beside me, strapping the safety belt around the base like any proud parent, and began to drive.

CHAPTER 30

I stopped by the Chases' mausoleum, the sun still resting its singular eye below the tree line. Only faint rays slipped between the branches. It was five-thirty in the morning. Climbing the stone steps, I rapped on the iron bars covering the stained glass. Lenore answered, her brown hair tossed in a million curling knots, eyes half closed. "I need to talk to you. We're going to the beach."

She coughed, clearing her throat. "Is it me specifically, or just anyone who will listen? Those are two very different things."

"No, it's you, I swear," I replied, not knowing if that was the truth.

"Give me a second," she said, dipping back into the mausoleum.

Mr. Chase leaned through the wall. His eyes drifted to my car parked on his lawn, to the flower belted into the front seat.

"Did it work?" he asked.

I nodded slowly, waiting for him to beg me to plant it at the base of his tomb. The request never came. He only smiled, lips curled back.

The door to the mausoleum swung open. Lenore stood there, black hair pulled into a loose ponytail. She wore a wrinkled Misfits t-shirt, a smiling skull on the front. She had neglected to change out of the plaid pajama bottoms she woke up in. Sandals completed the ensemble. Another yawn heralded her step into the blue glow of early morning. She kept one hand hidden behind her back.

"Make sure you have her home before sundown, young man." Mr. Chase laughed before withdrawing himself through the wall.

"Your car doesn't smell like vomit, does it?" Lenore asked, looking at my unwashed Volvo as it idled by the edge of the row of stones. "It took me three days to get the smell out of this place."

"I reserve that bodily function for your living quarters only," I replied. "Don't worry."

"Funny," she said. Then she opened the door and nearly screamed. "You did it?"

"Yup. That's what I want to talk about."

She stared at me in shock, then moved to unfasten the plant's tether. She lowered herself into the passenger seat, placing the pot in her lap, leaning the leaves away from her face. I sat in the driver's seat.

Reaching across the center console, Lenore dropped a plague doctor mask in my lap. The rough edges of papier-mâché left a thin white powder on my fingers as I picked it up. It was the same one I had seen sitting on her coffee table before our psychic reading. It seemed strangely harmless as I peered through the eye holes, the scent of glue and newspaper mixing in my sinuses. Lenore buckled her seatbelt.

"You're going to take that off while you're driving, right?" she asked.

"Of course. My peripheries are terrible in this thing. How'd you get it anyway? I thought you moved out of your mom's place?" I replied.

"She's a heavy sleeper, leaves the door unlocked. Not a good combination," Lenore said.

"Right. And why are you giving this to me now?" I asked, laying the mask beak-up on the back seat.

"It's a reminder of the past. Now you can just tuck the Spirits into some box in the basement. *Poof.* Gone. I thought it had some nice symbolic weight to it."

"What would you have done with it if I died?" I asked.

"Keep it as a memento. Some sort of reminder to never eat poisonous stuff."

"Well, thanks, I guess, and thanks for coming with me," I said.

"It was rough when I spoke to my ex the first time. When you can't touch them, it really nails it home they're gone. You won't have to deal with that for long though, but I get it," she replied.

Jessica's burial had been the day before. I couldn't bring myself to attend. I didn't want our first meeting to be nestled in the center of a mourning crowd layered in black. I didn't want her sister to be there, or the women from work, or the twins. Just the two of us. I knew I was going to lose it, fall to pieces, stammer unintelligently through a web of mucus and tears. We didn't need anyone there to augment the emotions. I fingered the wedding ring I kept in my pocket. The sapphire's smooth surface was cold beneath my touch. When Jessica peeled her way through the earth, I would bend my knee, right there, and ask her to marry me. It was part of the plan I assembled in my head, the plan I hoped Lenore could help me shape and mold until I knew exactly what I would do.

"That about sums it up," I said.

"I'll walk you through it. I bet she's been praying for this moment since her ghost appeared," she said as I shifted the Volvo into drive, slipping away from the Chases' mausoleum.

***

Off the coast of Nauset Beach, there was a stretch of shoals and sandbars only visible at low tide. When the water was in, the silt and sand was obscured beneath waves and tangled seaweed. Before innovations in ocean cartography, schooners ran aground on the hidden barriers, drowning crew and passenger alike. It always happened in sight of shore. That was the real kicker. If they could have swam a little farther, their ghosts would haunt family plots rather than sandbars.

At low tide, the wooden ribs of the *Orissa* or the *Montclair* were visible. On the bar, seals basked in the sun between remnants of wreckages. Sailors wandered amongst the seals, trying to sidestep bloated bodies to avoid their howls.

"I wonder why Mr. Chase isn't out there like that? I mean, maybe not right here, but on some other island farther out at sea," I asked Lenore, who sat beside me on the sand.

"Because they found his body," Lenore replied. "It washed up with a large chunk of the ship."

"He never told me that."

"You never asked. So what do you want to talk about? Are you worried she's going to be pissed you didn't visit earlier?"

"No. I'm worried what will happen when she comes back. If she'll be different in some way. The myth doesn't say anything after the kid's resurrected."

"Why worry about that now? Just do it. There's no other way to find out."

We fell silent and gazed into the surf, squinting at the white and blue sails of a schooner skimming across the horizon.

Before us was a bare stretch of beach littered with horseshoe crab carapaces and quahog shells. Seaweed lay heaped in stinking piles that smelled somewhere between rot and brine. A wall of dunes rose behind us. A seal bellowed from the sandbar. It sounded somewhere between a drowning elephant and a raucous fart. I laughed. Lenore gave me a look that asked if I was still five years old. My giddiness was starting to break through.

"Have you ever wondered why there aren't other types of Spirits? Ones that reward you for being a decent person," I asked.

"Well, why would they exist? You get rewarded, it's just not as in your face as a bunch of dudes in masks pushing a guillotine into the middle of your living room and decapitating your father."

"Is that what happened?"

"Maybe. I just think being good is reward enough, you get what I'm saying?"

"I guess," I replied.

"If people were decent, you wouldn't see Spirits in the first place. Ghosts would be able to sleep instead of wandering around on sandbars or cemeteries," she said.

"You're starting to sound a little preachy," I replied.

"Well, can you imagine what it would be like if we didn't have Spirits? People rape and murder every day even though they know someone will pay for it. We hunt species to extinction, poison the drinking water of poor communities, go to war over BS that no one wants to talk about. Things would be even crazier without them."

"Fair."

We fell into silence, looking out at the ghosts and the seals. Each had claimed their own corner of the sandbar, seals on the right, ghosts on the left. Occasionally one of the seals would waddle back into the water, propelling its bulk with flippers slapping against the sand. Other than that, they barely moved. That was their life, their afterlife. No movement. No change.

That sandbar terrified me.

That section of beach was always deserted. People didn't want to see those sailors, the passengers in their suits from the eighteen hundreds, the dresses that swept the sand. They didn't want to remember what could happen to them.

"So what are you getting out of this?" Lenore asked, casting a stone into the water. It skipped four times before sinking.

"That I still have no idea what the next step's going to be. I'm going to ask her to marry me, I know that much, but I destroyed the apartment. Can't go back there. I'm blanking on where to go next."

"You need to do something unstructured. Look at all those guys wandering around out there, staring off into the water like one of those ships is going to rescue them," Lenore said, pointing to the ghosts. "They would kill to be in your position. You guys can do anything. There's no invisible wall keeping you confined to your couch. There must be somewhere you two talked about going. Go there. Call it your honeymoon."

One of the ghosts on the sandbar, this time a woman wearing an evening gown fashionable in the twenties, began to wave at a sailboat in the distance. It looked like a postcard. *A young lover awaits the return of her sailor beau.* The rest of the ghosts shook their heads. One of them put a hand on her shoulder and murmured something into her ear. Her arm sank.

"We'd been talking about heading south, joining those protestors in the forests, at least for a little while anyway," I answered.

"Not the most romantic, but respectable," Lenore replied.

"It's messed up what those loggers are trying to do. We need more trees, not housing developments. I don't know how people blatantly disregard the Spirits like that."

"Hedonism, greed, stupidity. Take your pick."

"Greed sounds fitting."

"It always does."

CHAPTER 31

From a distance, it appeared as if Jessica's face floated in a shallow pool of water, the silver surface reflecting the sky above. Moving closer, I could see it was the vast circumference of her hair, strands mixing and mingling in a massive halo. Jessica's eyes were closed. Her tombstone stood at her feet, name and applicable dates etched in marble. Her chest didn't rise and fall, a sudden shock that stopped me in my tracks.

I wanted to preserve the moment, those unnoticed seconds of her beauty before she realized she was being observed. She had been buried in the floral-print dress her sister bought, large sunflowers blooming across her chest. Where the fabric had once been dyed yellow, now the blossoms surfaced as a pale, nearly gray blue. The hem hung just above her knee. The exposed stretch of skin sent a shiver through my body, desire flooding starved synapses.

Kate had picked out her plot in Seaside Cemetery on the corner of Crowell and Route Twenty-Eight in Chatham. The family graveyard in Falmouth was filled, too many uncles and aunts already interred. The early stones I passed dated from the late eighteen hundreds, simple spires and domed sepulchers eventually giving way to modern cuts of granite. The other ghosts seemed to sense who I was, parting as I stepped through their clusters, murmuring at my heels about the flower I carried.

"I brought you a gift," I said, my shadow clouding the pale waters of Jessica's ethereal form.

"And what's that..." she began, opening her eyes and turning her head until she saw the nightshade. "Dave, I told you not to do it."

Her anger surprised me. I was expecting joy, admiration, the unstoppable urge to swim to my side and blend our beings into one, my warmth and her chill body balanced in a moment of equilibrium. Instead, she sat there, hands clenching at her sides, disbelief coloring her eyes. With a sweep of her arm, she straightened stray hairs into a semblance of order and rose to her feet. Hovering, she circled around me, looking down at the plant I clutched to my chest.

"I know, but this warranted it. I need to bring you back. This isn't how we were supposed to end up," I said.

"You could have died."

"So? I would have paid for that empty plot over there," I said, pointing to an open stretch of grass at the end of her row. "We could have been together either way."

"That's not what I wanted. You still have life to live. There's no point rushing it."

"I talked to my dad," I cut in.

"He spoke to you?"

"Yeah. I'm not going to die, not because of the Spirits, anyway. It would have been too long. Do you understand now? I can't wait eighty years before joining you."

"That makes it worse," she said, frowning.

I leaned over and placed the potted nightshade at the foot of her grave. The purple petals stirred in the wind as a breeze ran over the cemetery grounds carrying the scent of sea salt. The shovel I brought from my car was the same I used to unearth my father's tomb. I began to dig a hole large enough to encase the plant's root ball. The myth said that was all there was to it. Plant the flower, then resurrection. The cool touch of Jessica's hand passed through my shoulder where the shard of ceramic had broken the skin. The red bloodstain still soaked the cloth. I hadn't changed since the night before. Ripped and ragged wasn't how I planned on showing up at Jessica's grave, but the thought slipped my mind.

After last night, I worried the hallucination hadn't let up, that I was still running through a dream only to find myself plucked from the ground a ghost, a small swarm of family members attending my burial.

"Wait. Please, wait. Tell me what happened," Jessica said.

"I ate the berries. Saw some weird stuff. Now I'm here. That sums it up. I don't want to wait. You have to know how I feel," I said.

I waited for her reply, but she just hovered there, eyes wide with a look of sadness. In the quiet, I began to dig, my patience unraveling beneath her gaze.

I loosened the soil, softening the bottom of the hole so the roots could navigate easily through the fresh loam. Then I dug my fingers into the pot, gently nudging the tendrils away from the ceramic walls. The soil was damp as my digits wandered about, residue from my watering earlier in the morning. When the plant dangled free, I bent low, placing the flower in its new home. I swept the dirt from the excavated pile over the exposed roots, leveling the ground around until it looked like the flower had always been there.

Jessica stood at my side, staring down at her hands, waiting to see if flesh would fill her hollow outline. Ghosts had gathered in the distance, close enough to observe Jessica's rebirth, far enough away to give us space.

"Any minute now," I said, looking at my watch.

"It's not working. I don't feel any different," Jessica replied.

"Just give it a minute, I promise. I followed all the steps, tested the plant every way I could."

"Dave," she whispered. "Can we please pretend none of this is happening, that you just showed up and we're seeing each other for the first time? This feels like a sick joke."

"It's going to work. We don't need to pretend."

Jessica fell silent as minutes dripped by. The gathering of ghosts swelled then began to recede as time expired. Jessica lay down the way I found her, feet just inches above the nightshade's stalk. Her eyes followed clouds and seagulls that coasted on gusts rising from the bay. Their calls cut through our silence, squawks mimicking the awkward unease that swam at the bottom of my stomach. A cruel joke. The promise of second life, of touch, the restoration of all senses, cut tethers and freedom. When I saw Jessica, I thought about all our plans, marriage, a house, a family. She must have seen the same when she looked into my eyes. Past promises. Dead futures.

"How long did the myth say?" Jessica asked without looking at me.

I didn't reply. The pages I read claimed it was instantaneous, that the boy had clawed through the earth, falling into his father's arms before the man could even breathe. I was beginning to feel the same tension building as the night before when I ate the berries. Doubt crept in and jabbed its cane into the soft organs beneath my ribcage.

The entire gathering of ghosts had drifted away, milling about their own stones, whispering to neighbors.

Half an hour died and nothing.

Lowering myself to the grass beside Jessica, I fought back the urge to vomit. Our shoulders brushed as they had in bed, but now the touch of cold frosted my deltoid. I lay there, scanning the sky, searching for the correct step, the next move to prevent a total breakdown. I wanted the earth to open up and seize me. I wanted it to gnaw on my flesh with teeth made of stone. I wanted to be obliterated, yet there I was, the smell of autumn leaves and brine swirling in my sinuses. The taste of my stomach in my mouth. Every sense was a reminder that I possessed what Jessica lacked, that we belonged to different worlds. She was tethered to the cemetery, and I inhabited the physical realm, no matter how much I wished to fade away.

"I missed you," Jessica said, as thoughts of suicide bloomed in my head. "But I think this is a good thing."

"No. This is the worst thing," I replied after clearing my throat, the sound of a half-stifled sob welling within.

"You're focusing too much on what was. We all end up here eventually; I was kidding myself thinking our lives could play out happily forever. Even those eighty years I might have had would have been brief."

"What about our plans?" I asked, watching years of memories evaporate like steam.

"Now they're yours. Think about all the stuff you wanted to do. College. National Park Ranger. Paleo-botany. Discovering a flower in the rain forest to name after me? Don't think I forgot about that last one."

"But you were supposed to be there with me."

The excitement and joy that had welled inside me had turned to rot. Now the life I had dreamed about in youth was being presented to me, but all I wanted was my life with Jessica: dinners on the couch, jogs on the bike trail, sleeping on the beach.

"Maybe in some other reality, but not this one. You can't stick around here waiting for death to creep up on you. You need to leave. Get off Cape, do something you would have wanted to do if we weren't together."

Jessica rose on one elbow, looking down into my face. Her long hair fell around me, curtaining my body like a waterfall. Where the strands caressed my cheeks it felt like a fine drizzle. For the first time since I arrived, she was smiling, eyes wide, holding my gaze. I reached up. My hand passed through her chest. I attempted to pull her down like I would have in bed, but my hand slipped right through. I wanted her, wanted her more than I ever had in life. The tears that had been forming in my eyes slipped down my cheeks, following the riverways of her hair.

"So where are you going to start?" Jessica asked once she rolled to the side, parting the sheets of translucent water that surrounded me.

"I'm going to join those protestors down south," I said without thinking through my response.

"That's probably the best answer you can give me," Jessica said, leaning over and kissing me on the lips. Her face passed through mine until I was looking out the other side of her neck, at the ghosts that had gathered once again to view something very different than they had the first time. Jessica regained her balance and straightened up. "Sorry about that. I'm still getting used to all this."

"Me too," I replied.

From inside my pocket, I fished out the wedding ring. I held it up, the blue stone catching a brief glint of sun through the clouds. Jessica bit her quivering lip. We had talked about marriage for years. Planned so many iterations of the ceremony and reception. I could practically recite the vows we drafted for one another off the top of my head. But she'd never be able to wear it. We both knew that.

"I was going to ask you..." I began to say.

"Oh, Dave," she said, a stifled sob climbing out of her. "I really appreciate that. Really, I do, but let's not talk about it. I can't bear the idea of saying it out loud. Please?"

"I'm sorry, I didn't mean to..."

"No, no. It's fine. There's just so much of everything going on inside me right now. Ghosts lose their senses, not their emotions. Can we just stick to happier things?"

"Yeah, of course," I replied. I propped myself up on my elbow and placed the sapphire ring on the polished base of her headstone. I couldn't carry it with me anymore.

We spent the next two hours lying on the grass, recalling memories: Senior Prom, skinny dipping in Long Pond, the redwoods along with the rest of our cross country trip, the days when she and Lenny actually got along, Clint's twenty-first birthday where he got drunk and dove off the fish pier to catch bioluminescent squid.

After our failed attempt at physical contact, we stayed away from sexual recollections, letting the nostalgia for late nights drift away, replaced by sun and shade, miles and hours. We had spent seven years together. Seven years of early mornings, of sleeping in. Seven years of embraces, closeness, days spent transfixed to one another's side. So many days where we would only speak to one another, the rest of the world forgotten.

It was better to stick to the past, because that was the only place we could be together.

Traffic began to build outside the cemetery gates. Fishermen and realtors were finding their way home after the day shift. Several people slipped in and out of the graveyard, some stopping to talk to the deceased, others doing drugs behind the overgrown hedges. We watched it all go by, shoulders less than an inch apart, never touching. The sky darkened, growing swollen with rain clouds. An occasional burst would plop down in thick drops only to dissipate a moment later. Each time I remained, letting the precipitation collect on my skin. After the fourth spritz, I stood up, knowing we couldn't lay there forever.

"Are you going to come by tomorrow?" Jessica asked as I stretched, my fingers wandering over the bloody patch on my shoulder.

"If everything goes as planned, yeah," I replied.

"Wrong answer. If you're going to the forest, you can't wait. Who knows how much time is left?"

"But I didn't expect to leave so soon."

"Remember what I said about time? Think about how quick it passes. The sooner you go, the sooner you can come back and tell me stories."

"True," I replied, lifting the shovel from the ground. I dug the tip of the blade into the soft dirt around the nightshade, prying it under the roots.

"Could you leave that?" Jessica asked, hand passing through my shoulder. "It looks nice. A little bit of your landscaping to remind me. The guys don't cut the grass around here as well as you do. They really leave something to be desired."

Her smile was immense.

That wasn't how I pictured walking out of the cemetery, on the heels of a work-related joke. I expected to hold Jessica's hand as we passed through the front gate, not wave to her from the other side. A drop of rain hit me clear in the eye. Then the sky opened up, the rain refusing to pass as it had before.

"I love you," I said, standing in front of her, rain drenching my clothes.

"I love you too," she replied. "Don't come back until you have a new story to tell me. I mean that in the nicest way possible."

"I know," I replied, taking my first step on the cemetery road leading away from Jessica and the life we spent together. At the gate, I stopped and waved, finding her stone amidst the sea of monuments, the dull white bodies drifting in the rain. She was the most beautiful ghost I had ever seen, standing there in her floral dress, her hair swimming in thick turning tresses. I dropped my hand and moved off to find my car, knowing her eyes would follow me as long as they could.

CHAPTER 32

Mark drove the dump truck. I sat in the bed, leaning on the edge of the casket, feeling the damp mahogany beneath my palm. Clint stood with one arm draped over the tailgate watching Route 137 slide by, restored colonials and white clapboard churches rising on either side. He looked like a dog with its head out the window, ears back, absorbing the sights of his last trip. The casket smelled of freshly turned earth. I tried to ignore the stench of decay lingering within the aroma. Every bump and pothole jostled the casket, causing the muscle and bone within to clunk against the inner lining, heavy and hollow. We both tried to ignore the reminders of what Clint once was.

Car horns honked. Joggers called out to us as they paused in their strides. A ghost on the move was a rarity. Mark and I had lifted Clint's metaphoric anchor and taken to the waves, carting it all of a few miles down the road. Permits were required for such transactions. Town plates on the rear fender diverted suspicion. If anyone asked, we agreed to say his corpse was polluting the groundwater, a response Clint didn't particularly care for. *You show me one corpse that doesn't decay after it's buried. Basic biology, guys.*

At the three-way stop in Harwich Center, the casket slid with the sudden application of brakes. Clint whirled around, panic lining his face. He had been worrying the coffin might spring open at any moment, the wood and nails giving out, showcasing his rotten corpse. Sitting on the coffin was the only way I could calm his nerves. I rapped my knuckles on the cover.

"Still solid," I said. "Just chill out. We're almost there."

***

The gate to Island Pond Cemetery stood between two stone pillars. It was nestled back in the woods across two lanes of bike paths and power lines. Part of the graveyard consisted of neatly trimmed grass and manicured trees. The other was a mess of moss and roots only discernible from the surrounding forest by the headstones that cropped up around the bases of elm and oak. Paved hills dropped off to dirt roads, all circling a murky pond in the center. The only color breaching the black water were the spines of goldfish long ago abandoned in the pool. They had grown every year since I started working in the cemeteries. I paid Lenny a few bucks to paint signs to post around the water's edge: *Five Hundred Dollar Fine for Fishing.*

We turned right after passing through the gate, dipping down the aforementioned hill. Clint quaked at my side, anxious anticipation tremoring through his body.

"You two ready back there?" Mark called through the open window, gently easing on the brakes after the earlier skidding casket fiasco.

"Totally," I said. Clint's lips moved in affirmation, but the words didn't come out. Nerves weren't strictly left to the living.

The newer section of Island Pond bordered the muddy waterhole, grass giving way to wetlands within ten feet of the nearest stone. The lawn was thickest there, naturally irrigated by high groundwater levels. All the stones lay flat; only their faces peered up from underfoot. To the left was a stretch of forest deemed unfit for burials, not for health reasons or anything, just there were too many roots and rocks in the way. That was where we dug the new grave.

The subtle grind of brakes dissipated. Mark killed the engine and walked around the side of the truck, struggling with the rusted latch holding the tailgate in place. Pulling out the cotter pin, the heavy steel swung down, caught by chains before it collided with the bumper. He gestured to me, offering his hand in mock concern. I swatted it away. Mark laughed. It was the first time he let me bend the rules. I credited his sudden softness to the fact he could finally put his old shirts on, discarding the XLs with most of the gluten and sugars in his life. I told him I'd buy him a kale smoothie or something once we were done.

Our recently excavated hole dropped off by the side of the truck. The heap of removed dirt stood at the head of the ditch.

I hopped out of the bed, landing hard on my heels. Clint remained seated on his casket, unable to take the first step until we lowered it to the ground. His fingers ran in repetitive patterns over the surface of the cover, his eyes fixed on a point over my shoulder. I turned. Carla stood with her back to us, looking over the pond. I had told her we were doing a routine burial that afternoon, some fishermen dragged overboard by Spirit tentacles as penance for pirate relations. She hadn't noticed our approach.

Short hair, thin frame, Carla hadn't aged more than a month past eighteen. A fitted thrift store suit coat clung tight to her shoulders and waist. A pair of skinny jeans stretched beneath the tails. She had always prided herself on eccentric outfits. Her parents knew she wouldn't be pleased to be buried any other way.

Two ratchet straps ran the length of the casket. The synthetic material was rough beneath my hands as Mark and I grabbed hold and heaved, slowly dragging the casket out of the bed.

"Careful, careful," Clint whispered.

The wooden box must have weighed four hundred pounds. Once again, the Bobcat would have helped, but Mark and I managed to lower the casket to the ground without any damage. The mahogany underside echoed off the pavement with the impact, enough to cause Carla to dart around, spinning one-eighty until she was staring straight at us. A question hung over her features, mouth parted, forehead lined as eyebrows furrowed.

Clint still sat on the casket, unsure if he could step off.

The question faded from her features and she began to run at us. Clint rose, jumping off the coffin and diving at her full sprint. They collided in a mass of translucent legs and arms. I couldn't tell them apart: her head jutted through his shoulder, his leg dropped from her thigh. Two bodies became one, only to divide back into their original states. In another light, it might have seemed grotesque, like some Hindu deity composed of dead limbs, until their lips met.

Clint ran a hand through her hair. Carla rested her chin on his shoulder, eyes closed.

Mark tapped me on the shoulder, my end of the strap slack in my hand.

"Give them a moment. We've got to get this in the ground before anyone shows up," Mark said.

"Right," I replied, tightening my hold on the lashing.

We pulled the casket across the pavement, then plowed shallow trenches across the grass until we jostled the casket over the edge of the hole. It teetered there for a moment as I ran around the opposite side, stretching the straps with me so we could lower the coffin evenly, avoiding the accident Clint dreaded. I leaned into proper squatting form, a position Jessica hammered into my brain when she tried to entice me to go to the gym again. The weight caught me off balance, pulling me forward. I caught myself before plunging head over heels. Mark grunted as the straps sped through his hands, halting as the wood hit the bottom. Neither of us bothered to untie the straps, not wanting to sink six feet under to retrieve them. Instead, we threw them on top and began to shovel dirt over the mahogany planks as fast as we could. It was the quickest burial we ever did.

Mark and I leaned on our shovels, letting sweat dry in the cool shade. Clint and Carla hadn't separated since we arrived. The two spun in waltzing circles, untrained dance steps guiding them around the edge of the pond. We followed their looping movements as they circled back to her grave. For a brief second they parted, staring down at her flat headstone, before clasping hands and walking in our direction.

"I'm just going to say a quick goodbye and hit the road," Mark said under his breath. "I've never been good at this emotional stuff."

"No worries. I'll walk back to my car. It won't take more than half an hour," I replied.

"Good. I didn't want to cut into your time with them."

"Naw. I'm not going to stay much longer anyway. I've got places to go."

"You sure you want to quit?"

"I am, can't spend my life living in cemeteries. There are things I've got to see. I appreciate everything you've done for me though. Really."

"I know. It's just going to be a pain mowing all that grass by myself."

Mark jabbed me in the arm, a substitution for his usual clunky embrace. I felt the sentiment as the brief numbing shot through my shoulder. Carla and Clint were feet away. They were both tall, thin specters, a snapshot of youth that wouldn't dim with years. For a moment, I wanted Jessica and I to be like that, but knew it wasn't what she wanted. Their movements were silent, feet skipping inches above the lawn. Death didn't seem so bad looking at them.

"Thank you so much," Carla said, drawing up short. "I didn't think I'd ever see him again."

"What? I thought you believed in my nightshade?" Clint said.

"No, but it kept you going, so that was enough," she said. "I'm just glad Dave didn't die."

"Me too," Mark cut in. "Terrible way to go, but yes, I need to get heading. Kids to feed and all that. I'm glad you two are happy now. It was always such a downer seeing him mope around the cemetery like that."

"I owe you one," Clint said to Mark.

"Eh, I'm just glad I could be part of this," Mark replied, a sudden sniffle choking his words. He turned, speed-walking to the dump truck before the waterworks could flow. The engine revved and he was off, retracing our path out of the cemetery.

I was going to miss working with him.

"So, does everything look alright to you?" I asked, gesturing to the covered grave. We had to leave his headstone back in Mount Pleasant. An unauthorized grave didn't need a marker to point it out. Clint's parents would just think he no longer wanted to talk to them, but that's what his father deserved for purposely keeping Clint and Carla apart.

"I'd never notice the difference," Carla said.

"Good. I don't think anyone would do anything about it even if they did," I said.

"Who'd want to break this up?" Clint asked, bending forward and kissing Carla.

"Doesn't bother me," I replied. "Enjoy yourselves. Seven years apart is a long time. I'd probably be suffocating Jessica with my tongue if I was in the same position."

"Nice visual." Clint chuckled.

"I try. Seriously though, is there anything I can get you guys before I head off? I won't be around for a while."

"Where are you going?" Carla asked.

"Down south for a bit, then I don't know where. I told Jessica I'd name a flower after her, and I doubt I can do that around here," I said.

"Remember, UMass has a pretty excellent botany program if you find yourself lost," Clint said.

"I'll keep that in mind. So, anything you need?" I asked.

"I've got everything right here," she replied, gazing at Clint.

"Same," Clint replied, beaming.

"Then I guess I'm going to head out," I said. "You guys have fun without me."

"We will," Carla said, embracing me in her translucent arms. Clint followed suit, drenching me in a flurry of frost. We separated. I stared up at Clint. For the first time in a while he stood at his full height, the slouch of death thrown off.

"If you end up in the forest, make sure you don't eat any berries you can't identify," Clint said as I began to walk away.

"Got it," I replied over my shoulder. The two coalesced into the tangled limbs and torsos as they had when we first arrived. When I reached the top of the hill, I looked down over the pond to where their bodies reclined on the grass, a pool of crystal water occasionally resembling human silhouettes. Feeling a bit of a voyeur, I turned and followed the road out between the two stone pillars. I had a thirty-minute walk back to my car at the other cemetery, glad I had packed my things beforehand.

***

In the back seat of my Volvo, I had gathered the few possessions I hadn't destroyed the night before. One cardboard box of novels. Three weeks' worth of clean clothes, folded in an orderly heap. The sleeping bag, recently laundered at an outrageous price. Glass jugs of water. Cans of tuna. The entirety of our shared bank account folded into my wallet. Different odds and ends. My Japanese maple was tethered with the rear seat belt, the Packypodium beside it. I managed to plant the remainder of my seedlings before leaving.

A handful of photographs I gathered from the torn albums now peered over the edge of a cardboard box. My favorite was the one of Jessica, age sixteen, her mother braiding her hair into a long twisted strand. I had printed out college applications to several schools, job applications for national parks around the country. Atop all of this lay the papier-mache plague doctor mask Lenore had given me. Whatever was left and salvageable from our apartment went to Jerry's junk heap.

I looked over my shoulder into the back seat, scanning the physical remnants of my life with Jessica. It wasn't much, but seven years of memories were enough to fill those lonely moments on the road, the sleepless nights to come. I'd imagine her there, in the passenger seat, unfolding road maps, long hair twisting as wind slipped through open windows.

But she wasn't there. She never would be. I knew what she wanted, the life she spoke of as we lay atop her grave. I'd do it for her. The flowers, the forests, new growth on distant shores. I'd make the most of my long life because she never would.

Beyond the empty passenger seat, I was greeted by my angled reflection in the door's mirror. No one was going to read me the map.

I charted a course south and began to drive, passing sunken cranberry bogs and salt water inlets, lily-choked ponds and stretches of scrub pine. Turning onto the highway, I focused on the road ahead as lanes merged then branched around cement barriers and curving exit ramps.

ACKNOWLEDGMENTS

This being my first book, I need to thank a lot of people throughout the history of my life...and I think I need to start with my parents, Kent and Kelly. Dad, thank you for instilling a solid work ethic in me. I will always appreciate those long hours you put in at the fire station to support us. Thank you for that promise you made me when I was in middle school to always buy whatever book I wanted as long as I read it (it was a lot of books). Mom, thank you for always believing in me, for encouraging my imagination, and for always reading to me. You made my life of books possible with every story. Thank you for all the proofreading...you definitely know how you use punctuation better than I do. I love you both very much.

A special thanks to my Uncle Larry and Aunt Fran, who have always been there when I needed them and have done everything in their power to make sure I've lived a good life.

Huge thanks to the entire Dresser family for always being there to read and share my stories, especially my Aunt Eileen!

I've had a number of teachers over the years who I owe a great debt of gratitude. Particularly, Lisa Doyle, my high school English teacher. You were always about creativity...pure creativity...and letting whatever inspire you inspire you, and I've always loved that. Thanks for being a true champion of young writers and readers. Thanks to John Hennessy, my Capstone creative writing professor at UMASS Amherst. I wasn't in the honors college but you let me into the class anyway, which was where I learned I could actually write a novel. It might have been a rough novel, but a novel nonetheless. Thanks for all of your kind critiques and reading recommendation and just general kindness. I still think back to your concrete writing exercises all the time. And a big thanks to Adam Zucker, my college Shakespeare professor, for 1. Being absolutely hilarious, and 2. for being the guiding light I needed when I was really unsure of who I wanted to be after college. Also, for the amazing stack of reading recommendations. I'll always owe you for that.

I want to say a special thanks to everyone who's given me work at odd times of my life when I really needed it, but an especially huge thank you to Lucy Loomis, the director of Sturgis Library. You opened the door to the library world for me and I'll never forget that…I really hated my previous job before you took me on as an adult services librarian. I can't express how much misery you saved me from and how much opportunity you provided.

Thanks to everyone I worked in cemeteries with for the Harwich DPW, but special thanks to Marvin and Jim. You guys always had a great sense of humor and made some dreary days not so dreary.

Enormous thanks to my editor, Scarlett R. Algee, at JournalStone Publishing for the enthusiastic love you've given to my book and for giving it such a wonderful home. And a big thanks to everyone else on the JournalStone team, especially Chris Payne!

I can't thank my agent, Marie Lamba, enough for the tireless years of work she's put into this novel and for always believing in it. Such a weird book, but you always loved it, and that's what I've always needed. Thank you for your amazing editorial eye and the guidance you've given me over the years. I'll always remember the day we had our first phone call and how surreal and life changing it was. I'll always be glad you pulled my query from the slush pile.

There are so many writers I need to thank for their friendship over the years, and I'm sure I will miss a bunch of you, and I hope you forgive me for that, but I need to say particular thanks to Paul Tremblay, John Langan, Laird Barron, Sam J Miller, Andy and Crystal Davidson, Gordon B. White, K.C. Mead-Brewer, Eric Raglin, John Crostek, A.C. Wise, Gabino Iglesias, Thomas Ha, and Evan Fleischer. Thank you for your mentorship, or your story swaps, or just your endless kindness, it's always meant a lot to me.

I have so many friends who have supported me over the years and believed in my writing, and for that I will be forever grateful. Huge thanks to Diane, Taraneh, Daria, Sam, Austin, Brent, Calvin, Stephen, Natalia, Katie, Tori, Law, Annisha, Jules, Cowan, Kirby, Mike, Emily, Justine, Cesi, and Dave.

To my Saturday morning Generative Writing Library group, you are the best.

To my therapist, Walter—you are a godsend. I can never thank you enough for everything you've helped me work through and the future you've helped me envision.

To Faith and James for being wonderful human beings and always being down to talk books with me.

Big thanks to Mia for being the perfect writing group partner and for always being a ray of sunshine. Thanks for always being up to read my stories and for always being there when I've needed you.

Big thanks to Ben Parson for giving me the freedom to feel good about writing whatever I want to write and for guiding me towards genre fiction when my heart wasn't in the other camp.

Rusty, thanks for being the best hype man a friend could ever ask for.

Cori-Rose, you've probably read everything I've ever published and I can't tell you how much that means to me. I always appreciate your Corey Farrenkopf story rankings and the belief you've always had in me. Thanks pal.

Mark, it's really hard for me to put into words how much I love you. Thanks for introducing me to so much I love about the world and for all the humor. My life would have been a much grayer place without you...and a lot less weirder, which would be a drag :)

Cashel, I wouldn't be the person I am without you. Thanks for all the years of friendship and creative mentorship, and music, and skateboarding, and just generally trying to get me out of my anxious worrying so I can enjoy my life. I've drawn so much inspiration from your art over the years and I hope you can see a little of yourself reflected back in this book. Love you buddy.

Ooli, the best dog a man could ever ask for. You'll never read this, given your lack of English comprehension, but you are wonderful.

And finally, Gabrielle. There aren't enough pages in this book for me to accurately thank you enough. You are the best writing teacher, editor, first reader, reviewer, and muse a writer could ever ask for. This book would be a shadow of itself if it wasn't for your help. But beyond all that, I love you. I love you more than anything else in this world. You've been the biggest supporter of my dreams, and I don't think I would have made it without you. Seriously, you've pulled me out of some dark times. Hopefully we both get to share Dave's fate together. This book's for you.

ABOUT THE AUTHOR

Corey Farrenkopf lives on Cape Cod with his wife, Gabrielle, and their tiny dog, Ooli. For a number of years, he worked as a landscaper in the historic cemeteries of Harwich, MA, but now he's a librarian. Books > Graves. His writing has been published in *The Deadlands, Nightmare, Vastarien, SmokeLong Quarterly, The Southwest Review, Bourbon Penn*, and elsewhere. He has a mini collection of stories in *Seasons of Severance* alongside Sara Tantlinger, Red Lagoe, and Jessi Ann York. To learn more, follow him on twitter @CoreyFarrenkopf or on TikTok at @CoreyFarrenkopf or on Instagram at @Farrenkopf451 or, if all that isn't enough, on the web at CoreyFarrenkopf.com . He really appreciates you picking up this book...like really appreciates it.

Printed in the USA
CPSIA information can be obtained
at www.ICGtesting.com
CBHW022043240424
7440CB00004BA/20

9 781685 101190